Heart of a Warrior

Angela K. Couch

This is a work of fiction. Names, characters, places, and incidents either are the product of the author's imagination or are used fictitiously, and any resemblance to actual persons living or dead, business establishments, events, or locales, is entirely coincidental.

Heart of a Warrior
COPYRIGHT 2020 by Angela K. Couch

Cover Art by *Nicola Martinez*
Prism is a division of Pelican Ventures, LLC
www.pelicanbookgroup.com PO Box 1738 *Aztec, NM * 87410
The Triangle Prism logo is a trademark of Pelican Ventures, LLC

Publishing History
Prism Edition, 2020
Paperback ISBN 978-1-5223-9873-8 Electronic ISBN 978-1-5223-9860-8

Published in the United States of America

Dedication

To my sister...Christine
Thank you for the inspiration.

1

Autumn 1859

Eyes clamped shut against the subsiding ache in her abdomen, Christina Astle sucked in cool mountain air. Pine saturated the breath and constricted her lungs like the corsets she'd happily given up only months earlier. Her hand stole across her extended stomach. What had she been thinking, agreeing to follow Anthony away from society, safety, and a house with four walls? What if they didn't make it to Oregon in time? She refused to give birth with nothing but canvas overhead.

The wagon wheel dropped into another rut, and a gasp escaped her, drawing her husband's gaze. "I'm sorry. I wish I could go slower, but we're at least a mile behind them." He glanced at the sun hovering above, then slipped the gold watch from his breast pocket and flipped it open. "It's after three already."

"I know…and I am fine." Christina raised her chin a degree but refused to look at him and his perpetually concern-laden eyes. Anthony did everything within his power to keep her comfortable, stopping often, even when it meant trailing behind the rest of the wagon train. As long as they caught up by nightfall. Still, heat rose in her chest. They should have waited another year, or—better yet—never left Cincinnati in the first place.

The crack of a discharging rifle pierced the valley and deepened into echo. Then a scream, soft and haunting. More gun fire followed, ricocheting off the high mountain ridges.

The wagon lurched to a halt, and Christina grabbed for the seat. She stared ahead at the empty trail scarred with evidence of those who led the way. Horses. Cattle. Families with children. *God, no!*

The wagon jerked and rocked off the trail, reins slapping the backs of the mules.

Christina dug her fingertips into the raw wood. "What are you doing?"

"I'm taking it away from the trail. I'm not leaving you sitting in plain sight."

"Leaving me? You can't. We don't know what's going on." Her head spun. "No, Anthony. Not with these mountains full of savages. Don't you dare leave me here."

The wagon tipped slightly then righted, dropped over the slope, and rolled into an aspen grove. White bark glimmered in the bright sun, and young saplings sprang back into place as the wheels passed over.

"There's only one way to find out what's happening. If they're being attacked, they'll need help." Anthony lunged to the ground and unharnessed the mules, fastening them farther out of the way. All except the one trained to ride. Anthony left him near the wagon, heaving a saddle over his withers and forcing a heavy bit into his mouth.

Christina remained paralyzed on the seat.

"Anthony…no. Don't go."

He said nothing as he loaded his revolver and strapped it to his thigh. With the Winchester tucked under his arm, he swung onto the back of the animal and twisted the reins through his fingers. "You'll be safe here. Most likely it's nothing." He looked away, giving the mule an angry kick. The animal balked but lurched to a trot toward the trail.

"Anthony!"

He rotated in the saddle enough to meet her gaze and yanked back on the bit. His brown eyes studied her face, and his chest released a sigh. "Chris, I have to go. You know where the other rifle is, and the shells are under the seat if you have any need of them. I'll be back soon."

Christina sagged against the back of the wagon seat. The edge bit her spine. Hooves scraped the loose rock of mountain trail and faded with the distant gun fire.

~*~

William T. O'Connell.

The sharp point of the flint scored the flat surface of the boulder, deepening each letter, faded by time. Eight years. One would think the memories, the pain, and the anger would have faded as well, but those wounds had been etched deep.

Towan stood and chucked the flint against the broad base of an overgrown pine. He dusted the forest debris from his buckskin leggings. Enough hiding. He was no longer the hate-filled boy. Eight years in these mountains had made him a man. A warrior. Sucking breath into his lungs, he stepped away from the headstone, the resting place of everything he had been—everything his father had made him. William O'Connell Junior was dead. A fate that should be shared by the man who gave him that name.

Resting his palm over the hilt of his knife, Towan turned to his horse and mounted. A few more days would see him in Fort Bridger. If rumors held any truth, his father would be there.

The horse jerked its head as the cliffs behind him echoed thunder. Yet not a cloud in sight. He encouraged his sorrel mare down the slope into the thicker foliage and toward the Oregon Trail. He'd planned on staying away from the wagon trains and settlers that frequented it, but curiosity nagged.

With the sound of gunfire reverberating off every mountain ridge, it could not be trusted to pinpoint the source. Keeping to the shadows, he followed the trail east until the first team of horses came into view. Angry and frightened shouts had already replaced the booming discharge of rifles, and Towan slipped to the ground to secure his mare out of sight. He didn't want to draw the fire of a nervous teamster.

Keeping his head down, Towan crept through the underbrush lining the trail, the silent placement of each step foremost on his mind. With little more than a dozen wagons, and this late in the season, it was improbable they delayed their journey for anything trivial. Something had armed every man and put them on alert. Most perched on their high seats, scanning the forests, rifles ready, while others hurried along the line, also carrying weapons. The only sign of women or children were the round eyes peeking from behind canvas.

"What do you see, Cal?" a large man hollered as

he made his way from the front.

A lanky one slapped his wide brimmed hat against his thigh. "Not a thing. Do you reckon they've gone?"

"One can hope." The first swore. "I thought the folks at Fort Bridger said we shouldn't have any problems with Indians through here. Anyone hurt?"

"Just Wilson. He dislocated his shoulder. Still hasn't learned to hold that Winchester right." He pulled the hat back over his greying head, his gaze wandering over where Towan crouched behind a low juniper. "Makes you wonder if they were even trying. What if they're scouts for a larger war party?"

"Let's pray that's not the case. With all that paint on their faces..." His head shook. "They obviously have something on their minds. I think its best we move again, find a safer place to set camp."

Cal sent a worried glance to the back of the train. "What about the Astles? We can't abandon that young couple out there with Injuns set on trouble. I don't want that woman and her baby on my conscience."

The large man spewed a string of curses. "Do you propose we wait here, or send someone back for them?"

A cry rang out and both men spun. A rider appeared around the last bend. "That might not be necessary after all. There's Anthony now."

Towan sank deeper into the woods and started back to his horse. Enough wasting his time. The first snows would soon settle into these passes. The fate of these people was none of his concern, and if he left now, he could travel another mile or so before nightfall.

Besides, as far as he knew, none of the people of the valleys were on the war path. Only vigilantes...like him.

~*~

Christina pressed her eyes closed, her breath jagged. The sounds of approaching night closed in around her. She'd waited for hours, and still Anthony had not returned. Why? Between pacing back and forth in the confines of the small grove and huddling in the back of the wagon, she listened with the hopes of hearing beyond the pounding of her pulse.

Nothing.

The first few hours she had cursed her husband, cursed leaving civilization, and cursed her stupidity for letting Anthony talk her into anything. Now her cursing faded, becoming silent pleading, sometimes vocal, to the God she hardly knew.

With hands clasped and knuckles white, Christina tried to remember everything Anthony had taught her about prayer. She'd joined her husband enough times to understand what was required. Pray to the Father in the name of the Son. Ask in faith. Have faith.

If only it were as easy as it sounded.

From a nearby branch a small bird sang its lonesome farewell to the sun. Christina shivered, whether from the growing chill in the evening air or the fear gripping her heart so tightly. Still no sign of Anthony.

Oh, please hurry back.

The darkness would be more than she could bear alone, but what could she do? Christina crawled into the small space at the back of the wagon and curled into a ball. With the rifle loaded and tucked close, she closed her eyes and tried to sleep.

Impossible.

The animals of the night began the many rituals they carried for the torture of innocent women abandoned by their husbands. Owls passed along hidden messages to the coyotes or wolves, who answered back in their mournful, yet oft times disturbingly gleeful calls. Deer wandered close, acting as spies. All would soon know she was a helpless woman.

A sharp crack, like a large tree being felled, or the discharge of a gun, jerked her head up and tightened her grip on the rifle.

All this work of espionage against Christina's poor nerves was soon put to shame by a high pitched, soul rending cry. The scream tore through any resolve she had to stay relatively sane. Though Anthony had told her only last night it was nothing more than a lonely mountain lion, Christina pictured the evil face of a painted Indian. He crept through the woods toward her, aided on by the animals who betrayed any form of trust she'd once had in them.

After the longest night ever endured by humankind, the early light of a dearly coveted dawn glowed through the thick canvas. How could nature feign such peace and serenity while a nightmare continued? Anthony still hadn't returned.

Eyes burning from both lack of sleep and all the tears she'd cried in the dark, Christina yanked Anthony's satchel from a hook at the back of the wagon and stuffed two-day-old flatbread on top of the book already nestled in the bottom. She didn't bother to change from the blue calico dress she'd put on yesterday morning but hung the satchel over her shoulders with a canteen and tucked the rifle under her arm. One of the mules brayed, and Christina released a sigh. She could probably figure out the harness if she had to, having watched Anthony enough times, but to back the wagon through the grove and up over that incline? Forcing her lungs to expand, she turned and took the first step toward the trail.

On foot, the way proved only slightly less rough than on the wagon. The trail wound in the easiest course through the Rocky Mountains, around boulders, up and down slopes, and through valleys. With sharp and jagged rocks raking the worn bottoms of her boots, her feet and ankles soon ached. How much farther could the wagon train be? At least in the daylight the nightmares weren't quite as pungent, though they remained vivid.

Coming around a sharp bend, a dark form appeared on the edge of the meandering trail. As she drew near, what at first looked to be large stone, or perhaps a tree trunk, transformed into a man. A corpse. Two feathered arrow's marked the deed. One protruded from his shoulder, the other from his chest. A wide brimmed hat lay near, no longer covering the familiar, peppery head of Cal Stewart.

Not Cal. He'd been one of their closest friends for the last thousand miles, his encouragement and sense of humor making their journey so much more bearable. And now he was dead? She lifted her gaze upward, but froze at the sight of two brown boots protruding from the brush only ten feet away. As she staggered forward, her jaw sagged, and her free hand rose to cover her open mouth. The tan pants. The moss green shirt. Crimson stains.

Anthony.

The revolver lay at his fingertips. His eyes stared

blankly toward the heavens.

"No." The cry scratched Christina's throat. She stumbled forward and pulled his head onto her lap. A sob strangled her, and she buried her face in his tousled locks. She screamed, her eyes stinging. How could this have happened? Surely it was still a dream—and not real...it couldn't be real. He wouldn't leave her like this.

No, God, no!

How could she possibly keep breathing, keep existing, when the very foundation of her life lay dead? Nothing else mattered. Not the numbing of her legs from how she sat, the sharp pains spiking up and down her back, or the persistent kicks of the child within her womb. She couldn't let Anthony go. Not until she woke from this insanity.

A throaty cry from the thick foliage directly behind her jolted her to her feet. Not a loud cry, but it sent lightning through her. Christina whirled to the shadowed man, the high jaw, the narrowed eyes, and the dark, evil face.

Anthony's murderer had not left.

Forfeiting the rifle not three feet away, she scrambled into the thick branches of the nearby aspen and down a slope which steepened with each step. Horses' hooves against stone and shale drove her on. The yells of the Indians behind her chilled her blood. Did they follow? How long before the cold tip of an arrow pierced her own back? Hopefully it would kill her instantly. She'd heard enough gruesome stories about what they did to captives. Better to die quickly.

In the depth of the valley, a stream meandered as much as the trail. The sight of it did not slow her as she raced forward, sending a fury of spray into the air. She grabbed at her hem, trying to keep it from getting soaked. The water deepened past her calves. Her foot slipped on a slime-coated stone, and she fell sideways, arms flailing. The cold mountain water pulled her down, the current twisting over and around her, drowning out her scream.

The force of the stream towed her deeper, rolling her over, the weight of the baby making it all the harder to claw her way from the water's grasp. Then warmth clasped her upper arms, and strong hands pried her upward. As her legs gained possession of the ground, she rotated to her rescuer. Charcoal hair hung wildly past his shoulders, feathers braided into the thick locks. Buckskin leggings with loincloth and shirt were stained with soil and sweat. And the face she had seen in the shadows.

Christina scampered backwards about three feet before her heel slid between two rocks, catching. She shrieked as her body sank. The man lunged at her, again snatching her from the water's cold embrace. Mouth agape, she stared at him and his icy glare. Icy blue. A color at odds with the bronze of his skin and everything else about him.

She jerked away, this time backing up slowly, the placement of each step meticulous. "Stay away from me."

He remained in place.

As her feet touched dry land, Christina dared a stray glance, looking for anything that would fend him off. She stooped and wrapped her fingers around a knobby branch. The coarse bark pricked her palms. Hardly a weapon compared with the bow that hung across his shoulders or the long bladed knife at his side, but she wouldn't go down without a fight.

2

Towan raised a brow but stood his ground—if it could be called that. The stream swirled around his feet, saturating his moccasins and leggings. He tightened his lips against a smile at the sight of the half-drowned woman threatening him with a spindly stick, her red hair plastered to pale cheeks. What a spunky one she was. Scared out of her wits, but spunky.

She continued to inch away from him, her chest heaving. "Just go back to wherever you came from." Her teeth gritted together and fire lit her eyes, what appeared to be hate covering the terror he'd recognized moments before.

The semblance of a chuckle rose in his throat, and he choked it back. Twice he had saved her, but of course, she hated him…hadn't they all? He'd gone to their schools and lived in their world, but they'd never seen him as one of them. Not once they learned of his mother.

Towan reversed his steps. Why should he waste any more time on this woman? She obviously wanted nothing to do with him.

He blew out his breath as he reached the bank opposite her, forcing past the resentment that burned in his chest. How could he abandon her in the middle of the mountains, soaked to the bone and obviously pregnant? Was that her husband's body she'd held? Likely.

So no one would come looking for her.

Still, she needed time to burn off some of that hate, and the sun was warm enough to dry her clothes. He'd be back.

Towan kept track of her direction while he hiked up the slope to where he'd tied his horse. A curse formed on his tongue as he reached the spot. The rope hung limp, severed at the knot. He fingered the smooth cut. Why had he been foolish enough to leave his mare so close to the trail? No wonder she'd been found.

Dropping the end of the rope, Towan set his jaw and turned east. The marauders couldn't have gone too far. Keeping to the trees, he followed the trail. Less than a mile brought him to a halt where hooves had scarred the earth down a shallow slope and through an aspen grove. A wagon had passed through, as well.

With movements low to the ground, Towan stole toward the makeshift campsite. A mule's throaty bray greeted a higher pitched whinny. He crouched behind a partially uprooted pine leaning against its neighbors and peered past the white bark of a dozen saplings. Two…three…four men. All with their own mounts and one to spare—Towan's mare. Stained buckskin clothes and painted faces. Too painted. These weren't men from any of the valley's tribes. They were white.

Towan rocked on his heels, his fingers clenching the hilt of his knife. What crimes had they committed, only to turn the blame on his people? Terrorizing a wagon train. At least two murders. Theft. And there was nothing he could do about it. Not today. He settled back to wait as glass shattered, fabric ripped, and men laughed. Soon they had scavenged what they wanted and led the mules from the grove, again heading east on the trail.

Crawling from his hiding spot, Towan surveyed the damage. Women's gowns strewn across the thin grass, a busted sack of flour spilling its powdery contents near the back of the wagon, and books scattered by a broken wooden crate. He stooped and brushed his fingers over the words engraved in a black spine—*The Pickwick Papers* by Charles Dickens. The pile was a treasure of novels. *The Three Musketeers. The Hunchback of Notre Dame. Persuasion. The Count of Monte Cristo.* Towan picked up *North and South* and thumbed through the pages. He hadn't read this one, but no wonder. It had been published only four years ago. His chest expanded with air saturated with pine and weathered pages. Strange how much it ached. How tempting to sit under the shade of the aspen's golden leaves and lose himself in fiction. Isn't that how he'd survived his youth?

He straightened and dropped the book back in its pile. That had been another life—one he'd put behind him. And what of the pregnant woman? He couldn't risk losing her trail, as unlikely as that was. What was he supposed to do with her? With no horse or wagon? How long would it take them to reach Fort Bridger now? Fort Hall was no closer.

Towan made his way over the littered ground and into the back of the wagon. He tossed a shovel out. He'd need that for burying the two men alongside the trail. The wagon train wouldn't come back for them, and it seemed wrong to leave their bodies over winter to rot or be eaten. Besides, since most of his supplies had been taken with his horse, a burial would only be fair recompense for what he'd scavenge from the wagon.

He rummaged through the crates and sacks remaining. What would he need for their journey? What would *she* need? How greatly would this detour slow his revenge?

~*~

The shale shifted under Christina's shoes, and she slid backward. Sharp rocks bit her knees. She yelped, her petticoat and skirt providing little shield. Pressure built behind her eyes and spilled as droplets of moisture. She rotated into a sitting position to look out over the valley. The mountains loomed over her. How would she ever survive with Anthony dead and unfriendly savages lurking near? What had even become of the wagon train?

Setting her hand over her contracting abdomen, Christina forced a breath. "Somehow…somehow I'll survive this. We'll survive this." She stared at her rounded middle and blinked back more moisture. "I'll be all right, darling. All we have to do is find the trail. We can make it back to Fort Bridger." *Somehow.*

And then?

Pulling her torn skirts higher, Christina hauled herself to her feet. She couldn't think about that right now. She had to reach the top of this ridge. The wagon had to be close. A few more steps.

Christina ignored the burning ache of her muscles as she picked her way over the bald slope and into the thicker foliage. When the terrain levelled, she quickened her pace. A branch snapped to her left, jerking her head in that direction. Nothing…except the feeling that someone watched.

She pushed past the tightening in her center and ignored the growing ache that accompanied the contraction. The trees thinned ahead. Surely she was close. But instead of the trail, the forest opened for another stream, winding its way downward. Two sharp cliffs v-shaped to the trickle of a waterfall. A dead end.

Where was she?

A misty breeze touched her face, sending a shiver through her. She hugged herself. Little good it did since her clothes refused to dry on the inside, and the sun had already sunk halfway behind one of the peaks. Another shiver. The sun was in the wrong place. If its setting could be trusted, she was headed directly west, not south-east as she had planned. Could her sense of direction be that faulty?

Two stones ground together and she spun again, her breath hitched in her throat. A shadowed form passed out of sight. The Indian. He had followed her. Backing away, she tracked his course until he reappeared, closer now. Christina gathered her dress to her knees and waded across the narrow stream. Then glanced back. He leaned against a large tree that had died years earlier. The last rays of the sun played against the contours of his face. She stared at the feathered arrows peeking from behind his shoulder. *Like the ones that killed Anthony.*

Willing strength into her legs, Christina bolted from her pursuer, racing to the forest. When she looked back, he had not moved. She needed to lose him this time.

Christina tried to run, stumbling over logs and brushing against branches. A deep guttural moan sounded from somewhere ahead, followed by the thundering of steps and the crashing of a path being cleared, perpendicular to her course. A scratchy throated raven seemed to laugh. Or did it screech at her to stop, informing her that escape was futile? Christina's breath pinched in her chest. Her abdomen shot with pain. She grabbed onto the narrow trunk of an aspen and listened for following footsteps.

None.

She struggled to catch her breath, the lack of oxygen strangling her as she slumped against the nearest tree. "Why did you leave me, Anthony? Why did you have to leave?" The narrow trunk dug into her back and the weight of her load pulled at her neck. What made the satchel so heavy? She pulled it in front of her and flipped open the top. Anthony's Bible lay among the remains of soggy bread. She'd forgotten it was even there. Her stomach turned, forcing the taste of bile to the back of her throat.

"Where is your hand in all of this, God?"

~*~

He shouldn't have been concerned about losing her trail. Towan picked up the waterlogged book, his motions slowing. The Holy Bible. Had it been lost by accident, or discarded? Like before, the black marks on the pages drew him in. But this wasn't just any book. He couldn't so easily set it aside. Cleaning its cover on his leggings, he forced it into the already full saddlebags slung over his shoulder, and followed the perfect shoe-shaped indentions on the forest floor.

Long shadows stretched themselves across the valley by the time the woman stopped from exhaustion near a small lake encircled by high cliffs and dense forest. No doubt she was truly lost now and would be more welcoming of his help. He crouched down to watch a while longer. Reds, greens, and golds quilted the valley as the light dimmed.

The woman sank onto a boulder and dug into the sack she carried. After a moment or so she yanked it from her shoulder and tossed it aside. Her gaze rose to scan the meadow and its low bushes. Spiny, arrowhead-shaped leaves only partly concealed a bounty of purplish-blue berries, now shriveled with age.

Towan frowned as she pushed off her perch and kneeled in the thick of them. Those were not what she should be eating in her condition unless she wanted to have that baby in the next few days. Like it or not, he could no longer postpone an introduction.

He hung the packs he had brought from the wagon in the low branch of a pine and leaned his bow against the trunk. Moving slowly, he made it within ten yards of her before she clambered to her feet, her deep brown eyes widening. She stumbled back a step, and he held out his hands so she could see that he intended her no harm. He'd planned to tell her she had nothing to fear from him, but years of anger kept his mouth clamped. Why should he speak her language? He'd already given that world seventeen years of his life. If he spoke Shoshone, she'd understand what it felt like to be alone and afraid among a people who weren't her own—as his mother had been.

And he'd be guilty of everything he hated them

for.

She continued her retreat, and he ground his teeth. No use terrifying her any more than she already was. The goal was to keep her from going into labor, not put her there. She'd already suffered enough for one day.

"I...food have." He stumbled on the words, having to translate in his mind from Shoshone to English. It had been so long since he'd forced his tongue to speak it. Years. By the way she looked at him, he couldn't tell whether she even understood him. "I not hurt you."

She froze in place, her eyebrows pressing together.

Towan glanced at his knife. Maybe if he gave it to her as a sign of trust, she would understand his intentions. Of course, she was frightened enough to use it against him. That would do neither of them any good. He waved to the slope where he left the supplies. "Come..." Shoshone words again bombarded his brain. He tried his best to push them aside. "I feed."

Wiping the perspiration from his brow, Towan shook his head. What was wrong with him? He could understand English well enough, and could even read it as easily as he ever had, but getting those same words past his tongue seemed another matter altogether.

~*~

Christina didn't dare remove her gaze from the Indian. He inched toward her. The few English words he apparently knew were interspersed amongst those of his own language. Although it appeared as though he wanted to help her—as far as she could understand him—perhaps he only wanted to take her captive without a struggle. A trap.

His mouth twitched, and he mumbled something that sounded like, "I show you." Without any further warning, he lunged forward and grabbed her arm.

Christina tried to jerk away, swinging her free fist into his solid shoulder. Pain spiked down her wrist, yet his vise-like grip kept her locked in place. A shallow crease formed between his eyebrows. Frustration? She slapped her palm across his face, but he didn't so much as flinch. Instead he turned and dragged her in the direction of the forest.

She struggled against his unrelenting hold. "Let me go!" Christina slammed her hand against his back, but still no reaction. He no longer wore his bow, only the buckskin quiver angled over his spine with a dozen or so straight shafts dressed with feathers.

What if this was the Indian who had murdered Anthony and Cal? If so, what would keep her from the same fate, or worse?

Christina sprang at the arrows and yanked two free.

The Indian spun back to her.

She slashed the razor-like tips toward his arm.

He flinched upon contact, his grip on her releasing, and then fell back another step.

She waved her newfound weapon at him.

He showed surprise, then quirked a smile. A trickle of blood ran down his right forearm as he raised his hands.

Christina sliced the air with the arrows, but he side-stepped them and again claimed her wrist. With a jerk, he swung her around, pulling her into him and snatching the shafts from her hand in one swift motion. Both of his arms held her firmly against his chest, rigid against her struggles. Involuntary tremors shook her body. Shivers. From cold, from fear, or from the pain of another contraction.

The man gradually released her, and then stepped away completely.

Christina didn't look at him but sank to the ground and hid her face in her hands. What hope did she have? Anthony was already dead, and she was utterly lost in this labyrinth of mountain valleys and cliffs. Even if there was a way to overpower the Indian, would she find her way out of the Rocky Mountains alive? She'd probably starve or freeze to death first.

A hand cupped her shoulder then slid down her arm to her elbow, bracing it. His cobalt eyes were now shadowed by dusk. Crouched beside her, he seemed to wait. The ice in his gaze had melted some. He looked almost apologetic. "I do not want to hurt you."

His words were surprisingly clear, and Christina blinked to clear her vision. Then allowed him to help her stand and lead her to the edge of the meadow where he had left his bow and several packs. Indicating a place to sit, the Indian slipped his hand into a small leather pouch and passed her a thin slice of dried meat. She shifted her gazed from it to him. Did he expect her to eat this? The smell wrinkled her nose, but hunger won and she nibbled the end. Not awful.

As soon as she began to eat, the Indian appeared to relax and moved to collect sticks and twigs from the immediate area. Within minutes he had a fire lapping at a carefully constructed pile of tree debris. Christina inched closer to the welcome warmth, never fully taking her gaze from the Indian.

He dug through the larger packs that hung several feet above the ground.

She stared, familiarity seizing her chest. The monogram *AMA* was etched into the thick leather. *Anthony Mark Astle.* They'd been the ones fastened to his saddle when he'd ridden off to find the wagon train. Her stomach threatened to expel the jerky she'd just swallowed. This *was* her husband's killer. What did he want with her?

Christina peered over the flames at the man, trying to remain calm. She had to think clearly. He had more strength, more skill, and he knew the area. Who could guess what he wanted, but the knowledge of what he was capable of smothered her. He glanced at her over his shoulder then followed her gaze to the knife fastened to his thigh. His mouth flattened. A moment later he dropped it, sheath and all, beside his bow. Next, he pulled a shawl from the pack—one of her shawls. He stepped away from the tree and made his way toward her, but Christina didn't shift her gaze from the knife at the base of the pine.

She wet her lips as he passed her the shawl, and then seated himself across from her, blocking the knife from view. Her fingers ran over the knitted wool as she pulled it over her shoulders. So he had found the wagon, as well. What else had he brought with him?

Obviously not food. He dusted off a large flat stone with his hand and emptied a small sack of seeds or nuts onto it. With a smaller rock, he began to grind them.

"That looks less appetizing than this meat."

He made no indication of hearing her.

"Where did you learn your English?"

Still no response. He didn't even look at her.

Christina snipped off another tiny bite of jerky with her front teeth and chewed. Maybe he only knew how to say certain words and didn't actually understand them. "Have you heard of Cincinnati…or even Ohio?"

She may as well be talking to herself.

"I should have stayed there." Christina sighed. "I should have convinced Anthony to wait." Her eyes watered. "But he was so stubborn." He would have left her behind for an extra year or two and then sent for her rather than postpone his dream. Hadn't that been his suggestion when she'd told him of her pregnancy?

The orange and red flame glowed in the Indian's eyes as he raised them to meet hers. The jerky fought against her attempt to swallow. "I hate you." Her words seemed to dissipate with the thin veil of smoke that separated them, leaving him as unaffected as the stone in his hand. His hair fell forward around his face as he began to mix the powder he had ground with a small amount of water. He added a handful of shredded meat to the heavy paste, and then handed it across to her.

"*Dicaromaric…* Eat."

"I'm not eating this. It looks worse than gruel."

His eyes hardened, his face becoming as flint. "Eat."

The edge of his voice made her shoulders ache from the tension between them. Now was not the time to infuriate her host. Christina took some of the brownish paste with several fingers and pressed it past her teeth. Surprisingly, it was not a horrid taste. Still, she couldn't let him have the last word.

"I can see why you're not eating it. Is this how you torture your enemies?"

He settled back and cocked an eyebrow.

"Why are you alone? Don't Indians usually have

tribes? That's what I heard." Christina took another mouthful of the substance, warming to the nutty flavor despite its crude presentation. "Were you exiled from your tribe? You were probably forced out for making all the women eat this mush." She looked at him, her heart quickening as he held her gaze. How cold-blooded was this savage?

Christina inhaled and glanced away. When she looked back, his gaze remained steady on her, interest glinting in his eyes. She fought the urge to squirm. "Isn't there something else you need to do besides sit here and make me nervous? I'm sure there are cute, furry animals to hunt or other wagon trains to terrorize." The last comment hung between them. She might never know the fate of the families they had traveled with for the last five months.

He continued to study her as she finished the last of the food and set the stone aside. *Maybe if I ignore you, you'll go away.* Christina looked to the meadow and the gathering darkness, and then glanced back. What was buried in his expression? Annoyance or revulsion? Perhaps both. Gathering her shawl around her, Christina scooted closer to the fire and lay down on her side, arm raised as a pillow. Though the fire now obscured his face, she had a perfect view of his knife. Surely he was human enough to need sleep.

3

Towan linked his fingers behind his head as he stretched out on the ground and hooked his ankles. Definitely not where he'd pictured himself when he'd awakened this morning. But what other choice had there been? Though he bore no responsibility for the woman, walking away from her conjured images of his father. He refused to be that sort of man.

Peering past the extended branches of the pine to the specks of light plastering the night sky, he let the air seep from his lungs. A chill had stolen into the breeze. With the season as late as it was, there would likely be no more wagon trains headed east or west along the trail. Was Fort Bridger the answer?

Of course. What was *he* supposed to do with a weak, spoiled white woman about to give birth? He'd take her to the fort and be done with her. Tomorrow. For now, he needed sleep. They had a long walk ahead of them, and forcing himself to think in English after this long was exhausting. He wanted to be prepared the next time she required it of him. No more fumbling for the right word, tongue-tied, and feeling like a fool.

Closing his eyes, Towan willed himself to relax, to

deepen his breath. The woman already slept, he'd just replenished the kindling on the fire, and nothing else would bother them tonight. Tomorrow would take care of itself.

Sufficient unto the day is the evil thereof.

The corner of his mouth pulled. He could hardly remember the last time he'd thought of the Bible, never mind read from it. He should have taken the book out of the saddlebag to finish drying. Sitting wet all night wouldn't improve its condition, but already his mind drifted, his conscious thoughts fading into sleep…as footsteps brushed across the cushion of pine needles and steel slid against heavy leather.

Towan's eyes flickered open to the glint of flame on a blade. Instinctively he rolled, distancing himself from the weapon and the woman who wielded it. His heart jammed against his ribs, and he shouted at her in a jumbled mess of two languages.

The woman lurched back a step to the edge of the fire. Then screeched, leaping out of reach of the flame. Too late. Already it clung to her skirt, feeding on the dry cotton. Towan propelled to his feet and threw himself at her. Tackling her to the padded ground, he grabbed at the earth, anything that met his hands, to smother the blaze. Finally only smoke and a charred hem remained.

His gaze moved to her flushed face. He forced himself to pause and rehearse the words in his mind before speaking. "Were you trying to kill me?"

Her mouth opened…and then closed again. She swallowed hard. "I don't know."

Towan raised his brows, his teeth hurting from the pressure applied. He pushed himself off of her. "You don't know?"

She managed a sitting position, her feet tucked awkwardly to the side, her singed hem hiding her shoes. Her stomach probably made most other positions impossible. "Did you kill my husband?"

A sigh collapsed his lungs. He rehearsed the sentence in his mind. "The man you knelt beside? On the trail?"

She nodded, blinking rapidly.

"No. None of my people did." Towan gathered the knife and its sheath from where she'd dropped them.

She motioned to the saddlebags dangling near, her teeth barred. "Then where did you find those?"

"On ground near you wagon." He winced and tried again. "The ground near *your* wagon."

She hesitated then shook her head. "That's impossible. He had them with him. Besides, it was Indians who attacked the wagon train. And the arrows in Anthony's..." Her hand pressed over her mouth as her eyes clamped shut. Her shoulders trembled.

Towan sneered at her easy verdict. Like all white people, she was confident in her belief—despite her faulty memory. The older man had been killed by arrows, but not her husband. He'd been shot.

Things are not always as they seem.

The sound of her sobs stole his anger, notwithstanding his desire to hold it close. He wanted to hate her—not an easy thing with her hair flowing past her shoulders, a halo of flame in the glow of the fire. He dropped the knife and sat cross-legged. Why bother telling her the truth? It wasn't as though she'd believe him anyway. He rubbed his palms together to dust them off.

As her tears dried, her brown gaze rose to his. "What will you do with me?"

He flexed the muscles in his jaw and all resolve slipped away. "I don't know."

She wrapped her arms around her stomach, rocking. He should ask if she felt all right, make sure she hadn't been hurt by the fall, but the words lodged in his throat and he swallowed them back with any reassurances he should also give. Of course she was fine. And he didn't owe her any insights into his plans. He pressed the heels of his palms into his eyes. Why couldn't she have let him sleep?

A groan pulled his attention back to her. "What's wrong?"

The flames flashed in her eyes. She squeezed them closed and breathed deeply as her back arched and a hand clasped her abdomen. After a long moment she relaxed and again glared at him. "Why should it matter to you?"

Exactly. Why did it matter to him? Other than the fact that her having a baby before they reached Fort Bridger was far more than he'd bargained for.

Fort Bridger. Was that still the best option?

~*~

The hard surface of the wagon floor pinched Christina's spine as she rolled onto her back. What she wouldn't give to reach Oregon so they could have a real home—a real bed. She reached out for Anthony. His shoulder would make a better pillow than...Christina's eyes fluttered open to the dim blue of breaking dawn and the extended branches of a massive pine.

Anthony.

She tried to breathe but it came as a pained gasp.

Her chest refused to expand.

Anthony.

Her sore eyes remained dry as the ache expanded through her numb body and soul. If only she could wake up in that miserable wagon next to her husband, to feel his warmth, to breathe him in…what would it matter if she never slept in a real bed again? If only she could have him back. If only he were alive.

Christina hugged herself, clasping her shawl. She stared across the dead coals at the man. He appeared to be sleeping, his face no longer rigid with severity. But still dark like everything about him. Could she really believe he had not been involved in Anthony's or Cal's deaths? Knowing he understood what she said made him slightly less terrifying. Surely he had worked as a guide, or a translator, and was at least a little civilized. Either way, he now slept with the knife and would easily find her if she tried to leave without his knowledge. She'd probably get lost again anyway. Or worse. What choice did she have but to trust him? For now.

As Christina pushed herself to a sitting position, her abdomen contracted. Pressure expanded in a ring around her pelvis, and she paused until it passed. The growing intensity of these tightenings did not bode well. "Not yet, little one." She set a hand over her stomach. "I need you to wait until we find a safe place." She did not want an Indian brave to play midwife. She peeked up to find him watching her again and winced. The muscles in his cheeks danced with…irritation?

He stood and dug through his pouch then handed her another strip of dried, raw meat. Wonderful. Even the thought of it destroyed her appetite. Unfortunately, what else was there to eat? Other than those berries in the valley. They'd been tart, but not horrible. All right, slightly horrible and a little aged, as well. Her Indian had seemed quite adamant that she not eat them. Perhaps they were poisonous. Christina bit off a piece of the jerky and chewed.

Before she finished eating, the man had everything slung over his shoulders and motioned for her to stand.

"Where are you taking me?"

He simply waved at her to follow.

"I think not." She folded her arms and steeled her courage. "You can't pretend you don't understand what I'm saying anymore."

Mumbling in his own language, he gripped her arms and hauled her to her feet.

As soon as she gained her balance, Christina braced her hands against his solid chest and shoved. He raised a brow but didn't budge.

"Let me go!" She jerked her hand up and across his face.

His blue irises were replaced by dark slits. "Walk or be carried."

Carried? Was he serious? Christina pressed a smile. She should let him try, see how long he could heft the extra weight this pregnancy had produced, but even the thought of his touch twisted her stomach. "I will walk, thank you very much. Though I don't understand why you can't simply tell me where we are going? Are you taking me back to my wagon?"

He turned away with a shake of his head. "It's useless to you now."

She followed him two steps. "But the mules…"

"Stolen."

No doubt by the same Indians who had raided. "Then can you help me catch up with the wagon train?"

"Too far." He kept walking down the slope into the meadow.

Christina hurried to catch up. "Are we going to Fort Hall?"

He paused long enough to indicate the highest slopes and peaks just north of them, white with a light powdering of fresh snow. "No time."

No wonder the morning held such a chill. She rubbed her palms up and down the thin sleeves of her dress. She had nothing but the woolen shawl to ward off the approach of winter. "Back to Fort Bridger, then?" What other option remained?

Again his footsteps hesitated, but he didn't look at her. "No."

Christina stumbled to a stop, almost turning her ankle on the uneven ground. If not Fort Bridger or Fort Hall… "Then where?"

"Somewhere safe." He started walking.

Safe? There was no place safe out here. Her breath came in short gasps, and her head grew light. Safe was Anthony at her side. Safe was back in Cincinnati with her family. Not here. Not in this forsaken wilderness where everything sought a person's life. Her vision hazed. "I want to go home. I just want to go home." She clamped her eyes closed, yet hot moisture still squeezed from the corners. Her abdomen began to tighten, and then deepen with pain, stealing the last of her breath away. She gasped. *Dear Lord, not now. Not yet. I can't do this.*

As the pain ebbed, Christina opened her eyes and sucked in more air. The Indian still stood with his back to her, his body rigid. What did he want with her? Obviously he detested her. And that was fine. The feeling was mutual.

The hard edge of his voice cut the silence hanging over the valley. "We must go."

Go where?

No other option given, she trailed after him past the lake and up along the stream that fed it. They hadn't traveled far before Christina slowed her steps, the now familiar tightening spreading through her middle. Her chest compressed as well, but with pure dread.

The pattern continued as they followed the soft gargling of clear water winding its way in the course of least resistance. Teeth gritted, she continued to walk, one foot placed in front of the other. She did her best to ignore the increasing strength behind each contraction. After a while, it was no use. She leaned into the face of a cliff and attempted to breathe through the spasm while her mute guide glared, obviously impatient. He reached out for her arm.

"Don't touch me," she snapped. "Get away from me."

His mouth formed a taut line, and his brows lowered. His jaw worked as though he would say something. He remained silent.

"Ahhhhhhrrr!" How was she supposed to keep on like this? How long could she ignore what was happening within her? Christina gripped the rocks, several small ones coming lose in her hands. "I'm not going any farther. Not another foot."

"You must."

"No!" She flung the stones at him.

Her target ducked as his hand shot up to block his

face. A rock ricocheted off his head, making him wince and leaving a bloodied gash above his temple. Christina grabbed for more, but he caught her wrists and held them fast.

"Let me go!"

"So you kill me—so you can *try* to kill me again?"

She glared at him, meeting his steady gaze. Then pain embraced her center and dragged her to her knees. He followed, keeping hold on her wrists. With a moan Christina rocked forward to brace her forehead against his shoulder. Why did it have to hurt so badly? And why now? They were supposed to make it to Oregon. She couldn't have a baby here, in the middle of nowhere. Not now.

As the contraction ended, she followed his gaze upward to the blue sky…and the dark clouds building over the western ridges. When he looked back at her, their faces were only inches apart. He looked into her eyes and searched her face, his lips parting slightly as his expression melted. He shoved to his feet, releasing her.

"Wait here." He darted away.

Christina stared after him. "What?"

No answer. She looked back to the heavens and the approaching storm, wanting to scream. She leaned sideways into the cliff and wiped a hand across her brow. "Oh, God, I don't want to do this on my own. Don't leave me here."

An eagle cried as it soared overhead. Petite birds danced in a nearby bush, chirping a carefree song. A breeze sighed with the aroma of pine mingled with moss. A twig snapped and a squirrel scampered up the lone juniper stretching itself over the stream. A whole world at peace with itself.

Christina spread her fingers over her cramping abdomen as a tremor traveled the length of her body, reality settling into the ache that pressed against her heart. Her and Anthony's baby would be born in this wilderness and the only help she had was that bronze-skinned man with the blue eyes.

~*~

Towan sprinted along the side of the mountain. His eyes searched the slope rising from the opposite bank of the stream. It had been years since he'd hunted in this valley, but if memory served, there was a cave…somewhere. His chest burned, reminding him to breathe, his mind too consumed with the woman about to give birth and the sky darkening with moisture-laden clouds.

A large fawn, its speckles mostly faded, and two does bolted from his path. He watched their ascent, fighting the urge to arm his bow. If they were delayed in this valley, they would need more food, but now was not the time. He needed shelter, like the overhang the deer had just passed by. Towan scaled the gradual slope, a smile spreading. The hollow in the cliff deepened into a cavern. The cavity in the rock was not large, the ceiling less than five feet high, but it would house them comfortably enough.

After unloading his bow and the saddlebags, Towan started back the way he'd come. The first cool droplets of rain struck his head and shoulders as he reached the woman, still collapsed exactly where he'd left her.

Her flushed face tilted to him, relief widening her eyes.

He extended his hand. "Come."

She barely made it to her feet when a moan doubled her over. "I can't," she panted as she sank back to the rocks.

Strands of red hair clung to her moist cheeks, a steady drizzle already soaking though their clothes. Staying was not an option.

He crouched, slipped his hand around her back, and then scooped her legs. She gasped as he swept her up but quickly settled, her arms encircling his neck. Her eyes closed. For a moment Towan forgot to move, the warmth of her slow breaths and the sweet scent of her wet tresses, drawing him in. He swallowed hard. *She's not a part of your world.* And she never would be.

With his focus redirected ahead, Towan began to walk, but only made it ten paces before her body tensed and her fingernails dug into the tender skin of his neck and upper arm. Clenching his teeth, he struggled not to drop her. His steps faltered, but he kept his hold. The quicker they got to the cave the better.

"Where are we going?"

"Somewhere dry."

"How…far?" Her face pinched in pain and again her grip strengthened, making him wince.

"Almost there."

His arms were ready to give out by the time he lowered her to ground untouched by the torrents spilling down on the rest of the earth. He shook the tingling sensation from his fingers as he plunged back into the shower. Thankfully it was still easy enough to find dry kindling under the thickets of pine along the neighboring slope. He needed to get a fire started before she chilled—and before her baby arrived.

Dropping the wood to the floor of the cave as he entered, he drew his knife and stooped to dig flint out of his pouch. A deep groan pulled his gaze to the young woman.

Her teeth clamped down on her bottom lip, drawing blood. "Help…me."

4

Tiny arms stretched, hands searching. Towan brushed his finger over the infant's smooth, damp skin, and then tucked the child's arms into the folds of a cotton blanket. Thank goodness he had found the stash of baby items in the wagon and thought to bring them. What would they have done otherwise, with their own clothes soaked through? He still needed to start a fire.

Towan tucked the bundle to his chest and assisted the new mother to lie down, propping her head up with the saddlebag. He pushed a wet strand of copper from her ashen cheek. Her hand trembled as she reached for the child, her eyes glistening like pine bark after rain. "Why hasn't he cried? Is he all right?"

With a nod, Towan lowered the babe onto her chest. She pressed her lips to the silky hair dark against his scalp. A tremor passed through her…then another. She clutched the child as her shivers became more violent. "What's wrong with me?"

"We need to get you warm." Towan's movements held a tremor of their own as he gathered the kindling and his flint near the door. He mumbled a prayer heavenward as he encouraged the sparks to flame.

Hallelujah. By the time the fire began to heat the immediate area, her teeth chattered and she could barely hold onto her baby.

"Let's get you closer." With no room to stand, his back pinched from the strain of hauling her even those few feet. Maneuvering under her upper body, he let her head lean into his chest as he braced her shoulders. He rubbed her sleeves the length of her arms, but moved his focus to the flames and the curtain of rain just beyond—anything to distract him from the feel of her against him, or the tug in his gut. Concern? Surely that was all. Concern was understandable. The woman was alone in the world with a new son.

His gaze dropped to the infant, wide eyed staring into his mother's face. Another boy who would grow up without a real father—someone to teach him to be a man, to help him navigate in the world, to love his mother…to never hurt her.

Towan let his eyelids close as he struggled against the hard lump swelling in his throat. With both the past and present filling him with poison, he focused his thoughts on the future. Someday he would find a woman to build a life with, to create a family, a moment like this—her in his arms and their new son in hers. Except her hair would be black…not the deep, coppery tones of the sun setting behind the mountains. This woman was like these mountains—unpredictable. Both strong and weak. One minute crumbling from the strain of existence, the next making an attempt on his life. He needed to get far away from her.

Her shivers subsided a bit, and Towan extracted himself from under her, lowering her to the ground. "He will want to eat." After setting the saddlebags beside her, he moved around the fire. "We need more wood."

He stepped from the cave, and cool water rushed down on him. He kept walking. This was exactly what he needed—to distance himself from her long enough to clear his mind. The birth of the boy muddled his thoughts and feelings. Like a shadow from the past. Even now the images grew stronger. The cabin, always perfectly clean. The early morning light filtering through small windows draped with threadbare cloth, casting a yellowy glow. A cry pulling him from his sleep. The beginning of a new life... If only it had lasted.

Towan wiped his hand over his face, a futile action against the moisture that continued to pour from the heavens. Wood. He needed wood. Enough to last them a while. Quickening his pace, he compelled his brain into the here and now. They wouldn't be able to travel for several days. He would stock up enough logs to keep the fire strong and then track the deer he'd seen earlier. Already the rain let up a little. That was good. Towan crouched, extending his hand to a large branch. His fingers spread, hovering over it. Small white flecks vanished as they met his skin. He swallowed hard and glanced to the sky.

Snow.

~*~

Shifting against the wall closest to the fire, Christina cuddled the child to her bosom. She cupped his head in her palm and smoothed his silky hair with her thumb. So small. So perfect. From his button nose to his tiniest finger. Midnight-blue eyes played peek-a-boo behind tired lids. She brushed his brow and they closed. "Sleep, my precious boy." Her lips pressed against his head and lingered as she breathed in his honey-sweet fragrance. Her chest squeezed. What would she do if he were ever taken from her? Now that she held him in her arms, she would never be able to let him go. Love had never been mingled with such exquisite fear—a fear only deepened by the large icy flakes building on the ground just beyond the cave.

Christina peered past the white veil. Her Indian left ages ago. When would he return? The uneven surface of the rock wall bore into her back, but the discomfort was nothing compared with that man's presence. She should feel more gratitude for his help, for his warm hands, for the fire he'd built, but she couldn't summon it through the anxiety that prickled her spine whenever he came near.

Trying to put him from her mind, Christina reached for the saddlebags and dragged them to her. What else had he brought from the wagon? Another small blanket for the baby. A handful of napkins, an undershirt, gown, cap…almost a complete layette. How was this possible? How could such a man be so thorough? Surely he'd simply grabbed a handful of items, and sheer luck had performed this deed.

From the pack, Christina next withdrew a pair of woolen stockings. Dry stockings. How glorious. She bundled the baby with the clean blanket and then dragged the long, damp socks from her feet. With only one hand free, pulling on the clean one proved an awkward exercise, though not completely futile.

A masculine chuckle caught her mid-motion, the second stocking halfway to her knee.

Christina yanked it the rest of the way and pushed her skirt back in place. "Couldn't you come up with a less original way of announcing your presence?"

Sticks clattered to the ground as he unloaded his arms. Then he set some thick moss near the fire. "Let it dry a little before you use it."

"Use it? For what?" As soon as the words were out of her mouth, heat swept across her face. "Never mind." As much as her life, and the life of her child, depended on him not abandoning them out here, couldn't he collect more wood, or find some other occupation elsewhere. Instead, he dusted the snow from his shoulders and tossed more kindling on the fire. Sitting cross-legged, he extended his hands toward the warmth but thankfully said nothing more.

Awkward silence settled between them.

"That's a lot of snow."

He nodded, absently brushing his fingers through his thick locks as though to sweep away the evidence—or at least the water that remained. He flicked his fingers over the fire which hissed as it devoured the spray of droplets. His gaze remained steadfast on the entrance of the cave and the white horizon.

Christina studied him. All she knew of the Indians west of Ohio were from news articles her father had shown her in an attempt to change her mind about leaving, and stories told around campfires. As of yesterday, she could not doubt the truth of those horrific tales, but truth generally held as many layers as an onion. Where did this Indian fit? She cleared the apprehension from her voice. "What is your name… I mean, what do they call you?"

He glanced at her. "They?"

"Other…Indians." Christina squirmed. "You have a name, don't you?"

"What do you think?" His tone carried

chastisement.

Redirecting her attention to the babe in her arms seemed the best strategy. "Then what is it?"

"Towan."

"Towan," she mouthed, not wanting to forget it should she have to spend much time in his company and at his mercy. "My name is Christina Astle."

"That's what *they* call you?"

She raised her chin. "Yes. Yes it is."

His attention returned to the gathering snow outside the cave.

"Is there food?"

With a grunt, he tossed her his pouch.

Christina grabbed it up and shot him a glare. "Is there anything besides this jaw-breaking meat?" she mumbled under her breath.

"Don't worry. Won't last much longer."

"And then what?" She hadn't considered the diminishing supply. "You can hunt, can't you?"

A muscle in his jaw tightened. "Of course. I am sure there are plenty of cute and furry animals out there…or perhaps I should track down that wagon train again."

Her mouth fell open at the mockery of her words then pressed closed. "How was I to know you understood half of what I said?" But he did understand her, and his speech improved every time he spoke. He seemed to think about what he wanted to say, his words halting, yet correct in most every other way. "I thought you were one of those savage Indians I'd heard so much about."

Towan's spine straightened, and his hands balled into fists. His knuckles showed white. "Because I speak as you, this changes your opinion so great?" He looked at her sharply, his azure gaze penetrating. "I do not ask you to think differently. I would rather be 'savage Indian', as you put it, than haughty white man who thinks anyone who doesn't look or talk like him is nothing. I speak like you, but because I look differently you feared me." He pushed to his feet and snatched his quiver and bow, slinging the first over his shoulder. "You were wise to fear me."

Christina stared after him as he vanished into the haze of snow. Towan was right. She had feared him, and she still did. His temper, the anger burning behind those unusual eyes, but especially his appearance. All the same, she hoped he wouldn't go far. Not until they reached a fort or some settlers…anyone normal.

The baby squirmed in her arms and Christina sighed. "It would probably be wiser for us not to make him mad. Towan. I wish we weren't so dependent on him."

Pushing past the uncertainty the future presented, she tightened the blankets around her newborn and placed the cap on his head. Her finger traced down his forehead to the tip of his nose causing him to crinkle his brow. "You already look so much like your father." Christina pinched the inside of her cheek between her teeth but the pain did little to distract from the overwhelming ache within her chest as though someone had a hold on her heart, wringing it like wet laundry. "He would have been so pleased…so proud. His own son." She brushed a finger across her wet cheeks but didn't attempt to dam the tears. What was the point of trying? She pulled the baby higher and tucked the crown of the tiny head under her chin. "Oh, Anthony…"

Anthony. That was it. The name. The only one this

child could possibly be called. After his father. But could she bear to know him by it so soon after losing the man she loved? Like salt to an open wound. What of *her* father, now a grandfather though he didn't know it? She would name the babe William Anthony Astle after the only two men who had ever owned her heart.

5

Sweat beaded on Towan's forehead, joining the flakes of snow that continued to melt upon contact. He wiped his wrist across to clear the moisture away—for all the good it did. Cupping his hands to his mouth, he breathed warmth into them. The one part of his body that truly felt the cold. Them and his feet. Soaked through for most of the day, his moccasins had ceased to provide much insulation. All the more reason to hurry back to the cave. Still, he loitered with the deer, taking his time to decide which cut to take with him and which tree to hoist the remainder out of the reach of bears and other possible scavengers. Then he set the meat aside to gather more firewood. Finally, bereft of any more excuses, he made his way back.

Christina lay on her side, saddlebag under her head, woolen shawl stretched across her body and the newborn cradled into her chest. Her wide eyes searched his. "It's already dark."

Hardly. The full moon peeked through the clouds in the northeast and every last ice crystal reflected its light. But Towan said nothing. Why should he? He'd stoke the fire and cook her something substantial to eat, but he didn't owe her words.

"Is there more water?"

Towan finished with the fire before snatching the canteen and ducking out into the storm. Thankfully the stream wasn't far. The cold water nipped at his fingertips as he dipped the container deep, then he jogged back up the slope. She took it without a word and he turned his attention to preparing the venison, cutting thin slices and extending one over the fire at the tip of his blade. Soon the aroma filled the cave, reminding his stomach how long he'd gone without food.

A thud against the soft ground made him look up. Christina's hand hovered over the Bible, its pages rippled from moisture. "You should have left it there. I don't want it anymore." Her gaze moved from him, back to the book, and then to the dancing flames. She wrapped her hand around the thick spine and leather cover. "Though I suppose it would make good enough kindling."

No! Towan grabbed the book from her and placed it behind him as he sat back down. Her eyes bore into him, but he refused to give them any heed until the first strip of venison was cooked through. He extended it to her. Pulling herself up against the wall and maneuvering the infant onto her, she accepted the offering. The flat side of the tin canteen served as a plate. Gratitude showed in her eyes but never touched her mouth. That would have to do for now.

He began cooking the next piece of meat while she chewed. She paused between bites. "I wouldn't have burned it. But either way, why does it matter to you? It's not as though you can read—" Her eyes narrowed at him.

Towan pressed his lips together against the urge to tell her what he thought about her easy assumptions. All she saw—all anyone ever saw—was the outside appearance. Preconceived judgments.

"You know how to read, don't you?"

The corner of his mouth tweaked a smile. What would she say, and think of him, if she knew the full truth?

Christina finished the last of her venison before speaking again. "How? Your English is surprisingly good. But to read…where did you learn?"

Towan had to remind himself that her *surprise* was not out of place or an insult. He passed her more meat. Hopefully that would keep her mouth busy a while longer, keep her from opening Pandora's Box.

Any success was short lived.

"You don't want to answer me, do you?" She chewed down another bite then cleared her throat. "That's fine. Sit there pretending you don't hear me. Or glare at me. I can make my own conclusions." With a subtle smile and raised chin, Christina studied him. Her gaze froze on his eyes. He looked away though it was too late. "Wait. That's it, isn't it? The color of your eyes. You—you're a…"

Half-breed. His jaw hardened as the word echoed in his head along with every derogatory name or remark that had preceded or followed that term. He challenged her gaze, daring her to say it.

Instead, her expression relaxed, and she slipped the last bite of her food past her lips.

Towan released a stale breath. Then looked down at the charring venison. He yanked the knife back from the flames but with too much speed. The strip flew over his shoulder, slapped against the rock wall, and dropped into the dirt. A chuckle flittered to him before being subdued. Ignoring her, Towan speared a fresh slice of meat with his blade.

"Oh, William."

The name rang like a bolt of lightning through him. His head shot up. How could she know that name? *How…*

Christina jostled the bundle in her arms, raising the infant to look into his face. "Hush, my little boy."

Towan forced air into his lungs. "You named him William?" Of all names, why that one?

"Yes. William Anthony. After my father and his." Her lips curved, but her eyes remained sad. "I think I might shorten it to Will, though."

Towan kept his breath regulated, though his lungs burned. *Will…Will O'Connell.* He was supposed to be dead, yet his memories continued to wreak havoc, unearthing emotions that had been buried long ago.

At least they should have been. Somehow they lived on. Wasn't that why he was out here in the first place, on his way to Fort Bridger to confront a man he hadn't seen in almost fifteen years?

"Are you all right?"

"Fine." But was he? He'd been ready to kill his own father. Towan glanced down at the Bible laying on the ground beside him. Then to the woman and babe. Was it possible that she and her child had been brought into his life for a purpose? He looked to the steady fall of snow. *Is all this Your doing, Lord?*

~*~

A soft mewing pulled Christina awake, and she forced her eyes open to the orange and blue flame dancing against the backdrop of night. Within the fire's glow sat Towan. Her Indian. Though not quite that. His hands held Anthony's Bible so the light reflected on the pages. His head tipped forward, what appeared to be sorrow etched into his usual intense expression. So he *could* read. Half-caste. Isn't that what they called the child of mixed races?

The baby squirmed, and Christina pulled the shawl over his head as a shield. He was probably hungry again. When she looked back to Towan, he seemed oblivious to her. No doubt he had an Indian mother and white father, most likely a trapper or explorer. A common enough occurrence, or so she'd heard. He seemed at home in this wilderness, so wild—at least as far as appearances went—when had he learned to read, and to speak so well? And why was he so intent on the Bible? If judged from most of the mountain men Christina had met, his father hadn't been responsible for his introduction to God.

Towan's eyelids lowered and he pressed his thumb and forefinger over them. His eyes probably burned from trying to read that small print in such dim lighting. And it was late…or early. What sort of man was he?

The answer remained elusive.

Covering a yawn with the back of his wrist, Towan looked directly at her, meeting her stare. Something flickered in his eyes. Surprise? Vulnerability? He closed the book, averting his gaze, and then stretched out on the floor of the cave. "You don't plan to try killing me in my sleep again, do you?"

Had that been last night? It felt as though a week had passed. "I wasn't trying to kill you."

"That only answers the 'again'."

Should she even acknowledge that with a reply? She shook her head. "Not tonight."

He grunted, crossing his arms over his chest, his face toward the ceiling. "Then I should sleep while I can."

Christina pulled the shawl so she could see William snuggled beneath, again content and asleep. She should do the same. She allowed her eyes to close, but instead of drifting into happy rest, she pictured Anthony coming back to her, telling her that the wagon train was fine, the gunfire was nothing. They hitched the mules and hurried to catch up. She may have had the baby in the back of the wagon, but what would it have mattered? Anthony would have been with her. They would continue past Fort Hall and on to Oregon and some semblance of civilization. But everything had gone wrong. Anthony was dead, and she was in the middle of the mountains with a half-caste Indian and a new babe.

The fire warmed her face, but even the red embers in the heart of it couldn't burn as hot as the tears leaking from the corners of her eyes.

When Christina awoke again to the baby's cries, the sun's earliest rays announced its approach, the fire appeared to be freshly stoked and Towan…already gone. Her body ached from the uneven ground, and the rigors of the past two days. She pushed herself into a sitting position, reclining against the wall and massaged her temples with her free hand, but it did little to alleviate the pressure building in her head. As soon as she fed William, she needed more sleep. Much more sleep. If only she had a softer place to lay and air temperature that didn't fluctuate between freezing and scorching.

Snuggling the baby to her under the shawl, Christina gazed out the opening of the cave. The sun crept into the sky, broaching the opposite peaks. Morning. After his stomach was appeased, as much as Christina longed to close her eyes again, William refused to quiet. He whimpered, then cried, then whimpered again, then wailed. "Hush, little boy. Go back to sleep." He refused to nurse for more than a few minutes before he pulled away, bawling, his tiny voice cracking.

"What's wrong with him?"

Christina looked up at Towan as he ducked into the cave, her eyes brimming. All she wanted was to lie back down. And for her baby to be all right. "I don't know."

Towan reached out for him.

She clutched tighter. "No."

"Let me see him."

She shook her head. This was her child. She had to protect him. "I don't want you to touch him."

Eyes hardening, Towan crouched. His lip twitched, but not with a smile. "Do you believe I would harm him?"

Christina opened her mouth, but no words came. Looking at the man, yes, she still feared, and yet everything he'd done for her should have been enough to wipe away some of that distrust. The baby continued to cry, tearing her insides. She extended her priceless bundle toward him.

Mumbling in his own language, Towan took the child and propped him against his shoulder. The man's attention focused solely on William as he stroked his back, bouncing him slightly. The bawling only increased.

"He doesn't like that. Give him back to me."

Towan ignored her, continuing his motions.

"Please, give him to me n—"

A loud noise erupted from the infant's throat. The crying ceased, and Towan slowed his caresses. "He had air trapped in his stomach. He is too little to get it out himself." He narrowed his eyes at her. "Do you know anything of babies?"

Christina jerked upright. "I know plenty." She held her breath to keep it from exploding from her as reality seeped past her pride. *Plenty of nothing.* Her mother hadn't taught her, and with no younger siblings, all she knew was gleaned from other women on the wagon train. Obviously insufficient. How was she supposed to take care of a child when she didn't even know about air bubbles in their tummies? What sort of mother was she?

Christina leaned back into the wall, unable to remove her gaze from the wild man whispering soft Indian words into her son's ear while the little boy stared at the man's tanned face. "How did you know what to do?"

The blue in his eyes clouded, and his mouth thinned. Then his shoulder rose just a little. "There are many babies in my village."

She blinked. "Your village? Is that where you were taking me?"

He answered with a single nod and moved to hand William back to her. "Today you will rest, and the next. Then we must leave this place."

"How far is your village?"

"It will take us several days."

Christina cuddled William to her. His eyelids fluttered as he again contemplated sleep. Her chest tightened at leaving the warmth and protection of the cave. Strange, considering how much she didn't want to stay here. "What will happen when we get there? To your village, I mean. What will happen to me and my baby?"

"You still fear my people." He pushed himself up. "You will be safe there, treated kinder than in any white man village." He slipped from the cave and stretched his back.

"Where are you going?"

He retreated a couple of steps. "Not far."

Now that Christina had him talking, she needed more answers. "If your people are so kind, who attacked the wagon train?"

Indignation lit his gaze as he crouched down to meet hers. "The people of my village had nothing to do with that."

"Then who?" Someone was responsible for Anthony's and Cal's deaths.

Towan half laughed. "You would not believe me."

"Tell me."

His lip curled. "It was your own people. White men with painted faces. That's who frightened the wagon train and killed your husband and the older man." He straightened and stalked away.

"You're right," Christina murmured as he disappeared down the slope. "I don't believe you." Mostly because it made no sense. What did *white* men have to gain from such a deadly game?

6

Towan's spine tightened. He didn't have to look up to know those pretty brown eyes were locked on him. Instead of giving in to temptation, he focused on sliding the blade in a straight line. He only had one small deer hide to work with, and though he'd seen these made, he'd never actually crafted one himself.

Christina's voice broke his attempt at concentration. "I give up."

He glanced at her from the skin draped across his knees, the knife pausing as he cocked an eyebrow.

"What are you doing with that?" She feigned a grimace, her nose wrinkling. "You won't make me eat it, will you?"

Not letting himself be drawn in by the glimmer in her eyes or the hint of a smirk adding form to her lips, Towan returned to cutting thin strips of partly tanned leather. Still stiffer than he liked, but not so much that he couldn't work with it. "This is for a *kona*. It's for carrying your boy."

With a handful of the makeshift ropes now cut, he weaved them through the small punctures he'd already made in a larger piece of deer hide, fastening it around a flat slab of wood he'd carved for the back of the cradleboard. The coals in front of him glowed, but already the sun eliminated the need of keeping a fire stoked. The last two days' temperatures left only traces of snow in the valley, though the higher mountain ridges remained cloaked in white.

"With the weather warming again, I don't see why there isn't time to go back to Fort Bridger." Christina's gaze stared past him.

He shook his head. Returning her to the fort was out of the question. Especially since the baby's arrival. His village was half the distance and full of women who could help the new mother adjust to her role. Christina seemed to have little difficulty feeding her child, but most likely that was the doing of the boy, not the mother. Otherwise, she fumbled through each day. She needed a family to support her, care for her—something a fort full of coarse men could not provide.

"Then show me the way to Fort Hall." Tension sharpened the pitch of her voice. "Please." The last word squeaked out as if she'd rather not say it to him at all.

"No."

"Why?" Her glare singed him.

He retained his answer. Let her fume.

"I don't want to spend all winter—months—with a bunch of..." The bite in her tone faded with her words as she sagged against the rock wall. "In your village."

If he'd felt at all sorry for her predicament, that particular sentiment went out the window...or would have if there were any windows handy. Strange how being around her summoned so much from his youth. Not a lot of it pleasant.

"There has to be another way." Her pleading turned genuine, desperate. "Some place I can go besides there."

"There isn't." He tried for finality. Hopefully she'd quit asking before she talked him into delivering her to one of the forts. She wasn't far off, but he had more than just the woman to think about—in fact, he was trying hard not to think of her at all. The boy. He deserved a chance despite his mother's ability to offend and infuriate.

Several minutes of silence relaxed the taut muscles in his neck.

Then Christina made a little cough. "I would only need you to show me how to get back to the main trail. I'm sure from there—"

"No." Towan's voice echoed within the cave's walls. He finished weaving the first strand of hide then reached for a second, stealing a glance at her.

Christina stared at her baby though she had him propped up on her shoulder, her lips pressed against his head. Her fingers rapped gently but briskly against his back.

The boy merely cooed.

"We'll leave at dawn." He wouldn't bother explaining all his reasons for not heeding her wishes as she'd no doubt argue every point. After all, what could be more horrific than spending any amount of time with a bunch of 'savage Indians'?

Christina didn't look at him as she lay down, and then rolled to face away from him. Good. Maybe she'd stop pestering him. Only, now guilt pricked his insides. Of course she was scared. Who knew what stories she'd heard? She had no idea what to expect. Even he had been apprehensive when first returning with his mother to her band eight years ago.

Tying off the end of the strand of leather, Towan set the kona aside. He braced his elbows on his knees and wiped his hands across his face, swallowing his pride. It clung to the back of his throat making it hard to speak. "I will not let anything happen to you and your boy. I swear it to you."

Pushing himself off the ground, Towan took the knife, laying it across his thumb as he moved to her. He drew blood.

Christina jerked up. "What are you doing?"

He knelt at her feet and smeared the trickle of scarlet across her hem. "You have nothing to fear as long as I have breath and you are in my care." He met her gaze and held it. "I will protect you with my life."

Wide eyes stared as he withdrew from the cave. He should have sat back down and finished the kona for their journey, but he needed a moment to compose himself. He'd meant every word of his promise but hadn't expected the passion that accompanied them. So much for distancing himself from her.

~*~

A hand on Christina's shoulder pulled her awake to the dim glow of approaching dawn. Her eyes closed again. William had been up much of the night and the remainder she'd been awake dreading the morning. She wanted to sleep. Her head ached and felt disconnected from the rest of her body, and her eyes simply refused to stay open.

The hand returned with more vigor. "It's time."

Christina blinked against the grit, willing her vision to clear. Towan knelt near with a strip of freshly roasted venison and held it out as his hand, still at her shoulder, guided her into a sitting position. Strange she hadn't heard him at all this morning. Had she slept that soundly?

"Eat quickly."

Doing as ordered to the best of her weary ability, Christina rocked William, nibbling at the offering. The strong taste and scent turned her stomach, but she forced it down.

The baby stirred, a pout forming, transforming his whole face. He seemed much more eager for breakfast, though not so content a few minutes later when Towan bundled him in the fur bound onto the cradleboard.

"Turn around."

Smoothing her skirt as she stepped from the cave, Christina turned so he could strap the baby to her back. William whimpered. "Is he all right?" Not being able to see him was unnerving.

"Just settling. He'll probably fall asleep as soon as we start walking." Towan moved around her and glanced toward the sun. It made a radiant appearance between two peaks, but still his breath formed white clouds in the crisp morning air. He collected his weapons and the saddle packs and set out across the sloped terrain.

Falling in step behind him, Christina took one last glance at what had been her home for the last four days. As awful and uncomfortable as that time had been, walking away tugged at her heart.

Towan set the pace and the path over the rise and through denser forest. Sometimes he wandered ahead and her slow steps forced him to pause for her. Christina's burning muscles cried with relief when William began to wail, announcing the need to stop. As

Towan lifted the cradleboard from her back, she slipped to the ground, not even bothering to find a log or something to sit on. The little patch of moss was good enough. How would she ever continue?

After Towan handed her the infant, he paced, impatience deepening the creases at the corners of his eyes. Trying to ignore him, Christina slipped William under her shawl. She had no plans to hurry.

"I'll be back." Towan started away.

"Where are you going?"

"To scout the best route."

Good. Hopefully that will take some time. But not too long. The idea of sitting alone and defenseless in this wilderness with her baby... She cuddled the child tighter, all her senses coming alive.

Unfortunately, Towan didn't take nearly long enough before returning and collecting the contraption from where he'd propped it against a tree. He stood over her with the cradleboard, obviously with hopes of speeding their departure.

I think not. Even though William finished nursing, she kept him hidden. What Towan didn't know couldn't hurt. Her whole body begged for just a few more minutes of not moving.

If only the man's glare was easier to ignore.

Finally Christina relented and handed him the babe so he could again hurry them on their journey.

The way remained mostly level for the rest of the morning and through the early part of the afternoon, with William supplying regular opportunities to rest. And then they started to climb again.

Towan led her along a thin path scratched along the steep incline, probably by some animal. Half eaten shrubs and droppings marked the trail. Only part way up and already her legs trembled from the excursion. Her whole body ached, chilled sweat soaked her clothes. How could she feel overheated and cold at the same time?

"I can't do it." Christina slipped to her knees and then rocked back. "I'm not going any farther. I can't."

Towan rotated. "We can't stop here."

She folded her arms across her chest. "I cannot take another step."

"We've hardly traveled any distance at all today. Did you ride your wagon the last thousand miles? Surely you can't be so weak."

Christina's jaw slackened. *So weak?* Try as she might to hold her emotions at bay, tears sprang to her eyes. She blinked them back, willing them not to fall to her cheeks. He didn't need any more evidence of her *weakness*. She wasn't as frail as he believed. Yes, she had ridden some of the way, but she'd walked plenty, as well. Did this man have no sympathy? She'd given birth not four days ago. He acted as though that were plenty of time to recover, but it wasn't. She wasn't ready to scale a mountain with a baby on her back.

She closed her eyes to block the moisture, but it breached the dam all the same.

"Where is your pride now? The women of my people are strong. They never complain when the journey is far."

Hot indignation rose in her chest. "I'm not one of your women. The most uncomfortable thing I ever endured before I married Anthony was a corset. That's my life. That's who I am." She groaned, glancing heavenward. "I hate this place."

"Then stay here and hate it." Towan crossed the distance between them and dragged the cradleboard from her back, then spun and started away.

Christina shot to her feet, grabbing at him and the cradleboard. "Give me my baby. Let me have him."

He seized her arm and held her at bay. "We have a long journey and little time in which to make it. If you stay here, you and your child will die."

His words ringing in her ears, she sank back to the rocks, breaking from his grasp. "I'm so tired." More than just physically. The weariness seemed to stretch itself deep inside her, draining her emotions and thoughts.

"All right." He released a long breath. "We'll rest."

With no warning or explanation, the dam crumbled completely and tears spilled down Christina's face. She sobbed, burying them behind her hands. "What's wrong with me?" Why couldn't she stop crying?

Towan said nothing, but silently looked on until all tears were spent and her face dried. Then he stepped to her side. Warm fingers wrapped around hers and drew her to her feet. "Only a little farther, *Moqone*. Then you can rest more." Without releasing his hold, Towan again led the way.

Christina followed, somehow finding strength… perhaps drawing it from him.

~*~

The sun lowered behind a high, jagged ridge which stood in majestic brilliance. Rays of light danced across the snow-covered peaks then faded and fled. Christina let her body lean against Towan's. He came to a stop and released her hand. Without thought she sank to the ground at his feet. He pulled the cradleboard from his shoulders and propped it upright against a large rock beside her. Other than several straggly junipers, there was little shelter from the frigid wind whistling over the rise. Christina hurried to unbind William and slip him under the protection of the thick woolen shawl. The child screamed until he found her breast. Only then did she look to where Towan cleared the stones and residue of snow from a small nook between the large boulder and three junipers.

"This is where we're spending the night?"

He nodded, intent on his work.

"Isn't there anywhere better?"

"No."

She shivered "Can we at least build a fire?"

"Maybe, maybe not."

"Why not?"

Towan glanced at her. "The wood might be too damp."

Damp? That was exactly why they needed a fire. They had climbed high enough and it was cold enough that patches of ice still clung to the cold ground. Christina closed her eyes, unable to stop the prayer that spilled from her heart. *Please, Lord, help him build a fire.*

She agonized as Towan gathered branches, and then shaved slivers from one. In the center of the shavings, he buried a handful of cattail fluff. The saddlebag carried a dozen or so of the brown heads because evidently they provided absorbency when stuffed between the layers of William's diapers. Towan's purpose for bringing them now seemed doublefold as the sparks from his blade against the flint burst to flame.

"Please light the wood. Please light the wood." Hardly conscious of her mantra, her gaze never left the tiny blaze lapping at the kindling.

Finally Towan sat back and set larger sticks on the growing fire.

"Hallelujah," she breathed.

After dividing some of the meat he had cooked that morning, along with some pine nuts, Towan went in hunt of more branches. The sky had blackened by the time he returned with a full load. He stoked the flames and then found a place perpendicular to the fire. He stretched out, crossed his arms over his chest and closed his eyes.

As she chewed her last bite of cold meat, Christina glanced around for the best place to lie down. There was little room cleared and little more protected from the elements. With no other alternative, she moved to Towan and lowered herself beside him, but with as much distance between them as she could manage—about two inches. She peeked under the shawl at William, fast asleep and tucked against her chest.

Ignoring Towan's presence at her side, Christina willed weariness to dull all her senses. Though she forced her eyes closed, her ears could not block out the howl of the wind, a small rodent digging nearby, the crackling flames, or Towan's deepening breath. Not completely conscious of the motion, Christina slid closer until their arms touched—the security she needed to let sleep take her.

~*~

Towan remained motionless as Christina's arm pressed against his. He took a long, slow breath of chilly air combined with traces of smoke…and her. In moments her body relaxed into sleep. He hadn't told her, and didn't plan to, but she had done well today. She'd needed more rest than he'd anticipated, but he should have expected as much. New mothers were generally encouraged to rest for a full month after birth, not just days. Of course, now he suspected it was more to keep them in their *wickiups* while their emotions surged. Christina's tears—the thought of them still grated his soul. He had been cold toward her, cruel even, trying too hard to remain detached.

As if that were possible.

Christina stirred beside him and he turned his head, finding her face there, hair piled as a pillow. With how rough and frozen the ground was, she would have trouble sleeping well. And she needed rest for the next leg of their journey. Exhaling, Towan reached his opposite hand over her to slide under her head and gently raise it. He extended his arm until her head came to rest on his shoulder. With a sigh humming from the back of her throat, Christina rolled onto her side, letting the boy settle over their arms. Towan rearranged the shawl so it didn't lie against the baby's face, but covered the full length of her arm. Her eyes remained closed.

Expanding his lungs to their full capacity, Towan dropped his head back. The starless sky spread itself over him. What if he pushed her too hard? What if she wasn't recovered enough? She'd looked so pale in the evening light. But then, she always looked pale.

Stifling the desire to groan, Towan held still. His mind, however, ran rampant with images of his mother crying in the night when she'd thought he slept. But things had been different with her births…the babies had not survived. Not until the last one. She'd been so happy. A healthy boy—a brother for him. Matthew O'Connell. Even Father had seemed pleased with another son. He'd stayed close to home and spent much less time in the taverns. For a couple years everything had been perfect. Only to fall apart so completely.

Towan gritted his teeth against the pain pulsating from his center. And the anger. He would always blame his father for sending him away when his mother needed him the most—when all Towan had wanted was to be with his family.

For most of the night, Towan lay awake, unable to put out the fire in his chest. He braced himself when the babe began to whimper then cry. Christina moaned as her eyes opened. One of her hands smoothed across his chest then froze with her breath. She looked to his face. With a gasp, she pushed away, sliding back until she reached the boulder. She pulled the shawl around her and the boy, sending one last glance at Towan. "I'm sorry."

Sorry? When he was the one responsible for her position? He drew himself up as well and moved to encourage the fire back to life. Silence extended the short distance between them. Was she as anxious for dawn as he? It wasn't as though he were getting any sleep tonight. Giving up on even the thought of rest, Towan opened the Bible, his back to Christina, his focus on the tiny black marks strewn across the page as words and sentences. He tipped the page toward the growing light and tried to read while shaking feeling back into his arm. His mind refused to grasp any meaning, too aware of the woman behind him.

7

Christina didn't look at Towan or the hand that braced her elbow. "Just over this rise. Soon you can rest."

After four days of walking, reaching their destination seemed too good to be true. She almost didn't care anymore who she'd live amongst. Nothing could be as miserable as that cold night on the ridge. Still, her steps slowed as they mounted the ridge and gained a view of a valley embracing a dozen or more dome huts.

"*Yngani.*" An expression of relief pulled the corners of Towan's mouth in an upward direction.

"What?"

He looked at her, an actual smile forming. "My home." He released her and started down the slope.

Instead of following, Christina glanced around for a place to sit. She settled for a bare spot of earth crowned with dead grass.

Towan made it five or six paces before he looked back. "*Moqone*?"

She hugged herself, steeling against the usual impatience in his voice. *Stall for time.* "You've called me that before. What does it mean?"

He moved to her and reached for both of her arms. "It means hurry."

Doubtful. Christina motioned to the cradleboard on his back. "Why don't I feed him first?"

"He's sleeping. He'll be fine until we reach the village."

Of course Towan was right, but Christina still refused to move as she looked over the valley. The huts did look inviting after living in the cave, and days and nights winding through these mountains—they would probably prove more comfortable than the wagon, as well—but what of Towan's people…his family, his tribe? She could see them down there among the huts.

"You have nothing to fear."

Christina glanced at Towan's hard gaze. Warmth rose to her face, and she looked away. How could he read her thoughts so well? Thankfully he didn't say anything more but stood there, waiting. She sighed. "You're right about me. I am weak." Images from home drifted through her mind, and pain radiated from behind her eyes and across the bridge of her nose. "I was always sheltered by my parents. Youngest of four." A laugh escaped her throat. "My brother is an over-achiever. The oldest of us. He's in politics. Probably the governor of Ohio by now."

A tear trickled down, tickling her cheek. "My oldest sister married young to a southern gentleman. He owns a huge plantation down in Tennessee, if you even know where that is. I've never been there." She tried to swallow. "I never went anywhere." Her gaze moved to her tiny babe. Was she really a mother? Had she created this precious boy? "They have six children. And Lillian will probably follow a similar path when she finds a suitable man. She was touring Europe with my aunt when I left. Europe. Can you imagine?"

Towan remained silent.

"Maybe that's why I was taken with Anthony in the beginning. He was practically fresh off the boat from England when I first met him, a taste of Europe and full of dreams. He was going to bring to life all those novels I'd read. Adventure. But I was miserable by the time we got to Missouri. My parents were right." She raised her gaze to Towan, though he remained obscured by the moisture filling them. "You were right. Poor Anthony spent the last five months listening to me complain." She couldn't blink fast enough. "Now I just want some place to lay down, some place warm." Another glance to the huts and the copper-skinned people of the valley, "...and alone."

Towan crouched beside her. "Nothing else would be expected. When the women of my people give birth, they move into a hut away from the village for a full month, with only their mother and grandmother coming to care for their needs."

But how did that apply to her? In a hut by herself? Away from anyone else? She didn't mean *that* alone. As improper as it was to share such close quarters with a man who wasn't her husband, the thought of staying in this valley, or anywhere in this wilderness, without Towan near constricted her chest. He had promised to keep her safe.

Christina dried her cheeks with her soiled hands and sleeve. What she wouldn't give for a proper handkerchief. "Unfortunately my grandmother has already passed, and my mother is far from here." The image of her mother, always so elegant and poised, in this setting, bubbled up as a chuckle. What a different world this was from the one she had been raised in. Why had she been so stubborn about following Anthony away from all that?

Towan raised a brow, probably at her mirth. "My mother will take you in. She will treat you well. I know you need rest, but this is not the place." He extended his hand.

Sitting here only delayed the inevitable. Ignoring his offer of assistance, Christina hauled herself to her feet. No turning back now.

They made it half way down the slope when an excited shout rang out. The whole village seemed to move to meet them. Children flocked around, pointing and talking excitedly. A small boy jumped onto Towan, dangling from his neck. The adults came slower and with less exuberance. All but one.

The small woman pushed her way past the rest; surprise mixed with concern marked her beautiful face and large dark eyes. "Towan."

He pulled the child from his neck. "Moqone." His voice held both affection and apology as he kissed her temple.

Christina studied the woman. Towan had spoken of a mother, but not of a wife…if that's what she was. She could be a sister, perhaps. She seemed older than him. Her thin black eyebrows rose, questioning. Towan shook his head and the tension drained from her face. She turned her attention to Christina. The woman asked something and Towan answered with motions toward the cradleboard. He pulled it from his shoulders. Other women gathered in, blocking Christina's view of her baby.

Pulse thundering, she shoved her way past buckskin-clad bodies. "Pardon me." Though clothed similarly to the men, their *dresses* hung about to their knees and beadwork adorned necklines and hems. Not bothering with the cradleboard, Christina fumbled to loosen the straps. She pulled William into her protective arms. The chatter of the women persisted and she looked to Towan for help. "What are they saying?"

A chuckle rose from his chest. "They've never seen such a peculiar child before. But then, we don't have many women here with hair like fire."

The first woman moved to Christina and set a hand on her arm. "My name Quaritz. You welcome our village. My son tell of you trouble."

Christina stared at her for a moment, not immediately understanding. This was Towan's mother? But she seemed so young. Not knowing what to say, Christina managed a nod.

"Come. You must rest." Quaritz led her through the maze of huts, past fire pits, racks of drying meat, and a woman kneeling behind a large stone on which she ground nuts similar to the ones Towan had fed her. Quaritz paused in front of a hut constructed of grass and bark and draped with animal skins. She held a large hide up and motioned Christina inside.

Red coals burned within a ring of stones. A pile of furs lay on one side of the hut and baskets—some empty, some filled with what looked like small potatoes—lined the other. Towan ducked in after her, dropped his bow and the saddlebags near the door, and then disappeared the way he'd come. This left Christina alone with his mother and two other women, one an adolescent, and the other with mostly white hair.

"She is Hivezotsie." Quaritz waved her hand

toward the elderly woman. "The girl is Sheherbit."

"Nice to meet you," Christina managed, not sure what was expected.

At her words, Sheherbit giggled, apparently entertained. She laughed even harder after a comment aimed at the other women. The older one smiled, but Quaritz did not look amused. A word silenced the girl.

"What did she say?" Christina could only imagine.

"It is nothing." Quaritz took William from her arms and handed him to Sheherbit. The girl seated herself on the thick furs, jostling the infant to pacify him. Christina eyed her until Quaritz pulled the shawl away. The grandmother stepped in as well, and together they helped Christina from her dress. Down to nothing but her drawers and chemise, she screamed as the hide over the door was swept up. Another middle-aged woman ducked in with a large clay pot of water. Christina could only hope Towan had no plans to return anytime soon.

With the extra hands available, the grandmother took the baby, washed him, and swaddled him in a soft pelt. Christina endured a similar treatment, but oh, to be clean again. They helped her into a jumper made of skins. Much like the ones they wore, it hung to her knees, but had no sleeves, almost like a heavy chemise.

As the other women left, Towan's mother led Christina to the pile of pelts. "You rest." Quaritz tucked her between layers of fur, William at her side. "I bring food."

Christina managed a nod as she drew her babe into her. "Thank you." After feeding him, she closed her eyes and the busy sounds of the Indian village faded.

~*~

Towan pulled the hide back over the door and stepped to the fire, sending a furtive glance toward Christina's still form and peaceful face. The corners of his mouth pulled slightly. Her and the boy were safe and would be cared for by someone more adept than him. He could rest easy.

"Did you see him?" His mother's words flowed easily in her native tongue as she scooped a large stone from the fire and dropped it into a pot. The water hissed and spit, then settled to a gentle boil.

She looked to him, and he shook his head.

No reply. He doubted her thoughts were so simple. Though she rarely spoke of William O'Connell anymore, she had once loved him, had married him, and had followed him thousands of miles, leaving her family and everything she knew behind. Only to have him betray both that love and trust.

Towan crouched and set another log on the fire. "I never made it that far."

"I thought as much. I know you are still angry, but..." She sighed. "What are your plans with the woman?"

He glanced toward the bed of furs. "I will take her to Fort Bridger with me in the spring."

His mother's head jerked up and a shadow darkened her gaze. "You still plan to seek him out, then?"

"I do not know. I try, but I cannot seem to let it go."

"You cannot kill your own father, Towan. It would not be right."

"I know." He stared into the flames, not able to

return her steady gaze. Had he not considered taking William O'Connell's life? The shame of it weighed heavy.

"Then why find him now? You have been happy here."

Happy? Did he even know what that meant? Hardly. He nodded toward Christina. "I will need to speak with the elders about her, though I foresee no problem with her wintering with us."

"Do you not?"

Towan twisted back to his mother. She stirred the camas roots with a long wooden spoon, her mouth a tight line.

"She's lost her husband and has a child, a son. She will need a provider and protector." He crossed his arms. "That is why I brought her here."

"Yes, but you are not the only man aware of her position and needs. Nor that she is beautiful."

Was she implying…? "But surely the others will agree she needs to be returned to her own people. She does not belong here." *Just as you did not belong in their world.*

His mother raised an eyebrow, driving the uncertainty into the pit of his stomach where it soured. "Sheherbit said her brother appeared quite affected when he saw her. You know Tucwatse well enough." She pointed the spoon at him. "As the son of one of the elders…"

Towan wiped his hand across his mouth. "He would not. She just gave birth. A period of time must pass before—" He swallowed hard. Winter was on the verge of settling into the valley, the feel of snow hung on the air. There would be plenty of time for Tucwatse to convince his father and the elders that Christina should be his. "I swore my life to her, that I would protect her."

A funny little cough deepened into an airy grunt, and he turned to where Christina slept. Her boy flailed his arms, his mouth agape as though searching for his fist to suck on. Towan moved to the child, his gaze brushing Christina's face, white against the honey-brown fur upon which she lay. Perhaps he would be able to give her more time to rest. Careful not to disturb her, he scooped the boy into his arms and returned to the fire.

"Does the child have a name?"

Towan looked from the wide blue eyes of the boy, to his mother. "William."

Her mouth opened slightly as sorrow brimmed in her eyes. "William?"

"Yes."

Her eyes darted to Christina. "Did she—?"

"No. It is the name of her father."

A smile touched his mother's lips, and then faded. "You've done what you can for her, Towan. You have preserved her life and the life of her child. If Tucwatse takes her, she will be treated well and provided for. Your promise will still be kept."

Towan shook his head, cuddling William to his chest. "She would not see it that way…and neither would I."

8

Somewhere beyond her dreamless sleep an infant cried. The resonance of deep baritone hummed, attempting to sooth the babe. The desired effect lasted only a moment or so. Christina pushed past the craving to remain in blissful oblivion. She opened her eyes to the dim glow filling the hut and shadows that danced on the curved walls. Towan's mother knelt across from the circle of stones, her hands busy. The aroma of food enhanced the ache in Christina's stomach. William's cry suggested he shared the same thought.

Towan stood near the door, the babe tucked in one arm. His swaying motions came to a quick halt as their gazes met.

Christina sat up and extended her arms. "I'll take him."

Towan moved across the hut and knelt at her side. "How are you feeling?"

"I forgot what it felt like to be warm and comfortable." Taking the child, Christina pulled the fur blanket up over her shoulders for privacy. At home she'd understood nursing was something you simply did not do in the presence of a man, other than perhaps your husband, but her upbringing also spoke against spending days in a tiny cave in the middle of the wilderness with a man. It no longer seemed strange to have Towan there. He simply was.

Getting the child situated, Christina glanced at Towan who had stepped away. His gaze remained locked on her face, his expression drawn.

"What's wrong?"

Towan shook his head and moved to his mother. He arched over her shoulder and snatched a thin strip of the cooked meat she cut. Quaritz slapped at her son's hand, exclaiming something in their language. A smile contrasted her tone, no doubt glad to have her son home.

Christina cuddled her own son closer as they exchanged words—words she had no hope of understanding. The language flowed from their tongues and was actually quite beautiful—even if being excluded grated her nerves.

Towan glanced at Christina with a feigned wince. *"Nia ma ma an deg aro."*

"Sov ve gesh."

Christina narrowed her eyes at him as she fixed her small dress and brought William out to see the world. Large eyes stared from a content face. "Now you're happy, aren't you? You were just hungry." She propped him against her shoulder and patted his back. How quickly the action became second nature. Christina's gaze wandered to Towan who still watched her. Again his face grew solemn. While a common expression for him, it seemed to extend deeper. She nestled her chin against the baby and murmured in his ear. "Or maybe you were upset because you can't understand what's going on—everyone speaking and you unable to figure out what they want."

Towan glanced at Quaritz who sat silent but nodded.

He shook his head, looking at Christina one last time before slipping from the hut.

"What's wrong?" Christina's hand came to a rest on her son's back. "It has something to do with me, doesn't it?" Alarm plowed through all the security she'd enjoyed moments before. "Do your people not want me here? Will they make me leave?" As much as she had dreaded this place, the thought of going anywhere, facing those mountains again, twisted her gut.

"No, you welcome here." Quaritz set the wooden tray of meat aside and dipped a spoon into a clay pot, stirring once before filling a bowl full of creamy paste flecked with herbs of some kind. She took the infant from Christina and handed her the dish. "Eat." She made a scooping motion with two fingers.

With the consistency of mashed potatoes, it held similar flavor but sweeter. Christina had eaten more than half of the offering when Towan plunged back into the hut with a cold gust and several flakes of snow. He didn't appear any happier than when he'd left and rewarded his mother's raised brows with another shake of his head. Without a word, or looking at Christina, he sat and picked at the tray of meat. What a heavenly smell, much milder than the venison they'd been eating, and it would probably round out the flavor of the potato-like paste nicely.

"No. No, good."

Christina jerked to Quaritz and her stern expression. "Excuse me?"

"Meat no good for you. No good for baby."

A deep chuckle brought Towan into focus. His mouth hinted a smile. "I already got a full lecture for feeding you as much as I did. New mothers are discouraged from eating meat until…" His gaze dropped momentarily. "For a few weeks."

"Oh." What an awful rule. Hopefully their vegetables consisted of more than these tubers. She was already tired of pine nuts. Christina stuck her finger, coated with the last of the paste, into her mouth, then set the bowl aside and sank back into the comfort of the furs. Oh, to never have to move again.

Quaritz waved her back up, saying something she couldn't understand. Christina looked to Towan.

"She wants to brush your hair."

"My hair?" Christina didn't even want to think of what a tangled mess it had become. She tried to force a smile as she took William, and Quaritz fetched a misshapen wooden comb. The long claws intimidating, Christina moistened her lips. She could get through this.

Working from the ends, Quaritz picked away at the long tresses. Christina attempted not to wince when it pulled, but found herself eyeing the blade tied to Towan's leg. She'd watched him sharpen it. Surely a quick cut would be preferable to this torture. Her mother wouldn't be here to say anything.

"Ouch!" She clapped a hand over her mouth. "Eee." Having someone else comb her hair had never been enjoyable, but after so long without the use of a brush, the long locks had tangled beyond anything Christina ever imagined—never mind, experienced. She twisted, grabbing at the comb. "I'm sorry. I appreciate that you want to help, but I think maybe I should do it on my own."

Towan's mother stood.

"Can you take Will again?" Christina's face burned and she kept her eyes lowered as the exchange was made. Very carefully, she worked the thick teeth of the comb through her hair, a fraction of an inch at a time, bracing the roots.

Towan's laughter lit a fire in her. She scowled. "Yes, my scalp is weak, too."

He merely smirked.

She hated when he looked at her that way.

What a relief when the task was finished and she could pass the comb back. Quaritz handed her William, and then made a crossing motion with her hands. "I will *narangushek*."

"Braid?" Christina repeated the motion and received a nod. She steeled herself, knowing Towan watched. He obviously hadn't endured two older sisters.

~*~

Towan clenched his teeth as he made a beeline out of the village. He was in no mood for conversation—no mood for people in general. He needed to get away and think this through. What did the elders mean when they said they wouldn't acknowledge Christina as his unless he took her as his wife? He'd brought her here, he'd promised her protection—they had no right to decide her fate.

Slowing his pace once he reached an aspen grove, Towan blew out his breath. What was he supposed to do? Leave things as they stood and hope the rumors were wrong and Tucwatse had no design on her? The man would probably try to take Christina just to infuriate him. They'd never liked each other. Could he take her someplace else? The last two weeks had piled several inches of snow into the valley and more on the ridges. There was no safe travel through the mountains until spring. What option did that leave? Marry her himself?

With his thumb and a finger pressed into his aching temples, Towan leaned his shoulder against a thick, white trunk of an aged aspen. Marry her? The image of red waves, the stubborn pout of her lips, and the flash of brown eyes tormented his mind. She represented everything he had taught himself to hate.

Why then did the thought of her as his wife swell within his chest such longing? To protect her…to love her.

He wiped his palm across his mouth, pain spiking through his center. Didn't this fit the irony of his life perfectly? His father's world had constantly taken everything from him and given nothing. As a youth he had tried to fit in with his peers, only to be railed upon because of the heritage his mother had given him. He'd tried everything to please his father, yet it had never been acceptable—*he* had never been acceptable. Now his heart was attempting to bind itself to a proper 'white' woman—one who would never see him differently than any of them had.

Most of them, anyway. But the kindness of one teacher did little to offset the scale.

One way or another, he had to not feel anything for Christina. He nudged the snow with the toe of his moccasin. Maybe it would be better for everyone if Tucwatse took her off his hands. It's not as though Towan could marry her—be her husband.

If only he hadn't made her any promises.

Towan shoved the thought aside. He had no time for this. He pushed away from the tree and headed back to the wickiup. *Sufficient unto the day*... He'd cross other bridges when he reached them.

Ducking past the hide covering the doorway, Towan glanced to where Christina sat rocking, babe in arms, a lullaby on her lips. He diverted his gaze, but the melodic hum of her voice followed him to where his bow lay against the wall. *Distance.* He knelt and began gathering enough supplies to last him a few days. He'd almost finished when his mother entered the wickiup with water. Her eyes narrowed as she lowered the clay pot. His words came quick and sharper than intended.

"Excuse me." Frustration edged Christina's tone, breaking his explanation. "Unless it truly is none of my business, why can't you speak so everyone can understand you?"

Towan shouldered his quiver with the new arrows he'd formed the last few days. He refused to look in her direction but switched to English—no longer an arduous task. "I'm going hunting. I'll be back in a week or so."

"A week or so?" A tremor touched her words. "That's a long time. And with you gone..."

"Who will protect you?" He fought down his impatience. Most of it was directed at himself and his own concerns about leaving for any length of time. All irrational. She was safe here and nothing would change for a couple more weeks. He'd return well before Tucwatse advanced. "My protection will do you little good if you starve."

He looked to where the saddle bags sat, the Bible

still tucked out of sight. One more tie to his father's world that proved difficult to sever. Though, it never had truly been a part of William O'Connell's world, had it? Otherwise life might have been much different.

With his mother's attention turned away, and his body blocking Christina's view, Towan slipped the book in with his food. *You do have a Father who cares.* Isn't that what Mrs. Anderson had told him so many times? *He's there when you need Him, and will extend His hand when you ask.* Towan almost smiled at the thought of the old teacher and her passion for written works…and her kindness to him. He glanced heavenward as he stepped out of the wickiup. Maybe it was time to test her words.

~*~

Christina stared across the hut…at nothing. Absolutely nothing. William slept, Quaritz had left hours ago to do who knows what, and Towan, though he'd returned again yesterday after nine days of hunting, she'd seen little of him. The relief of being warm and having a place to rest had worn thin after the first two or three weeks of lying around with no other thoughts than caring for her newborn. Now loneliness laid itself across her, smothering her with thoughts of Anthony. She wearied of crying herself to sleep and the brokenness inside. She needed something to distract her, something to help her heal.

Leaving William snuggled in the furs, Christina crawled to where Anthony's saddlebags sat. She ran her fingers over the heavy leather, tracing his monogram. Maybe she'd been avoiding God and His words long enough. She flipped open the top and peered in at…nothing. The other side still held some cattail heads but no Bible. She slumped back, dropping the saddlebags. So much for that idea.

Returning to the bed, she released a sigh. Now what?

As the hide door opened, a ray of sun broke into her small prison. Quaritz hooked it up out of the way, allowing a refreshing breeze to air out the stuffy hut. "Go out now. You need air—need sun."

Freedom from this confined space, a chance to stretch and work the aches from her hips and back. She stared into the blinding reflection of the sun against the snow covered ground. Children squealed. Two women walked, chattering together. Christina's confidence fled. "I'd rather stay here."

Quaritz shook her head and set an armful of clothing on the bed. "You go. I sit here with child."

Christina relented, but flipped the door covering back into place before slipping the buckskin leggings on under her dress and a rabbit pelt wrap over her shoulders. She looked to Quaritz who merely waved her toward the exit.

Fine. She could do this. Surely it would be safe enough. Towan was out there somewhere. Maybe she could find him. Better than wandering around with no guide or translator. She squinted against the radiance of the sun and every ice crystal it touched. Deep breath. Arms folded tightly across her abdomen. Nothing to worry about.

The two women Christina had seen stood outside the neighboring hut. Their gazes locked on her as she walked past, their voices low as they murmured in each other's ears. She sucked frigid air into her constricted lungs. No wonder the sun had little effect on the snow. She forced her chin up as she tried to figure the best route away from the village. With eyes averted, she ambled past the huts toward the river. Clear water washed over and around patches of ice along the banks. Laugher drowned out the gentle rush.

Curiosity led Christina through the thickets lining the bank. A group of boys, a few young girls, and three men gathered around two deer hanging upside-down from a large willow. Towan stood near one, knife in hand, but he wasn't working on the deer. He watched the boys. One who looked to be around ten shouted something and then took off running. Dropping the knife, Towan raced after him, grabbed him, and swung him over his shoulder. A slightly smaller boy came to his friend's rescue, latching onto Towan's leg. Towan staggered, but remained upright, keeping his hold on the first. As he twisted, his eyes lighted on Christina and he paused—as an adolescent plowed into him with his whole body. Against the sudden force, they all tumbled to the cushioning of the snow.

Towan's laughter joined the children's as he pushed himself up and dusted the white powder from his clothes. He extended his hand to the adolescent, his voice light as he pulled him to his feet. Though the young man and most of the group's focus had been drawn to where Christina stood, Towan's gaze seemed to purposefully avoid her. She began to turn away and one of the men gestured to her, calling for Towan's attention.

The man said something more, and Towan glanced at Christina. He shook his head as he answered. Everyone chuckled except the Indian, whose lips tightened to suggest a sneer as he slipped a knife from its sheath. The long steel blade glinted in the sun.

Towan raised his hands and motioned to where his knife stuck from the snow under the deer. One of the boys immediately grabbed it, racing to him. The corner of Towan's mouth twitched, and he wrapped his fingers around the hilt.

With a shout, the first Indian lunged.

9

Towan lurched to the side as the knife stabbed toward his stomach. Raising one arm to block the other man from redirecting his attack, he slashed his blade through the air, missing his opponent's torso by less than an inch. Breaking from each other, they circled, gazes locked. Towan tweaked a smile. Again the other man lunged. Towan stepped aside, deflecting the blow as cool steel grazed his arm. Too close. With the side of the man's torso open, he slid in. With his free hand, Towan grabbed the other weapon as he rotated behind. His knife slipped to the other man's neck. Then froze.

His opponent gave a nod.

Regulating his breath, Towan stepped away and clapped his friend on the back. Havne was getting better.

As Towan sheathed his knife, he couldn't resist a glance at Christina. Despite the cool air's success in adding rosiness to her cheeks, the rest of her face matched the snow. Not a healthy shade of white. Her hand resided over her mouth as she spun and staggered away. He fought a grin but only for a moment. She wasn't headed back to the village. With her luck she'd probably get lost…if she wasn't already.

Lengthening his stride, Towan easily caught up. "Where are you going?"

"Back to the hut. Will probably needs me."

He grabbed her shoulders to stop and then redirect her. "You'll want to head in that direction."

She flashed a glare. Two steps later she pivoted back. "Why were you fighting? He could have killed you."

Ah, concern for his safety. No doubt because it remained tied to her own. Still, a laugh refused to be withheld. "We were only practicing. It is vital in these mountains to be able to protect your family and village, to be both a hunter and warrior."

Instead of being appeased, Christina narrowed her eyes at him. "Why did he point at me? What did he say?"

Of course she had to ask that. But what answer to give her? "He was offering to fight me for you."

Her mouth dropped open, but her eyes remained thin slits. "He what?"

Towan held his voice even. "I told him the white woman is weak and poor medicine. She could not even carry her own child over the mountains." He suppressed a smile. "He would be happier with the wife he has."

"He's already married?" Christina's face turned the color to almost match her hair.

"Actually, no. He isn't." But Towan wasn't about to tell her their real conversation. She didn't need to know that Havne teased him for only practicing with children when his older brother had already begun speaking with the elders about Christina's position in the village.

With a toss of her head, she spun and hurried to the village.

Towan followed slower. Not far into the gathering of wickiups she paused and glanced around as though analyzing each dwelling. Being the first time she'd ventured into the outdoors on her own, she was probably trying to figure out which one was theirs. Towan stood back, crossing his arms over his chest. Hopefully the form of his lips didn't look too smug, because he couldn't help it.

She spun to him, and he raised a brow. Her mouth opened as though about to say something, but quickly clamped shut, her arms taking a position similar to his. She spun and again started away. He followed.

Weaving past wickiups and people set about their own tasks, she garnered many curious glances. One woman repairing a fishnet questioned where they were headed

He shrugged. Who could be certain?

As they neared the border of the village Christina pulled to a halt, a hand coming to her mouth. Towan followed her gaze to two riders on horseback leading pack mules. White men, probably trappers by the looks of them. He stepped beside Christina so he could see her expression. Relief. Excitement. Hope. Something heavy settled in the pit of his stomach.

~*~

Maybe a kind God existed after all. What other explanation could there be for two men, one appearing half-way civilized, to appear out of nowhere in the middle of the mountains? Christina started forward only to be hindered by a strong hand.

"You should go back to your son."

She jerked away from Towan's grasp. "I'm sure he'll be fine a little while longer."

"Those men could be dangerous."

"Or they could help me return to civilization."

He blew out his breath. "If it were safe for you to travel, I would take you there myself. Maybe—*maybe* you could get as far as Fort Hall or Bridger, but I assure you that is further from civilization than here."

Christina gave her head a shake. "You think I can believe that after watching you and your friend try to stab each other to death?" She rotated back toward the riders and the several men going out to meet them. The older of the riders had already dismounted and was talking to the Indians while the other remained atop his horse, scanning the village. His straight-cut trousers and heavy tweed coat did some to recommend him—especially when compared to his companion's stained buckskin attire. Even the older man's teeth and heavy grey beard wore stains. She cringed, looking back to the younger man and meeting his gaze. His eyes widened, and she flashed a smile. Time to see who these men were and if they could do anything to help her.

Towan remained at her side, stepping halfway in front of her as the man swung from his horse and moved to them. Christina nudged past. Though the man wore a full beard, it had obviously been trimmed recently. He swept his hat from his head, revealing dark brown hair to contrast his creamy skin and greenish-blue eyes.

"Hello."

"Ma'am?" An uncertain smile created dimples in his cheeks. "What on earth is a woman like you doing in the middle of these mountains?"

She hugged the fur cape tighter about her shoulders. He had little clue how out of place she truly was. "Our wagon train was attacked and my husband killed."

His brows shot up. "What? Tuttle told me these Indians were peaceful," he growled, sending a glare at Towan who stood at her side with arms folded. The man sized him up and lowered his voice. "How long have they been holding you here?"

Towan glowered.

After seeing him wield the knife over which his palm rested, Christina could only hope he could contain his temper. "Oh, no. They weren't the ones who attacked us. I was separated from the main wagon train and these Indians saved my life. But tell me, who are you? What are you doing here?"

His shoulder lifted in a shrug. He motioned to the old mountain man. "Trading. Keeping up relations. I'm new to all this. The name's Edwin Ryder. And that's John Tuttle."

She extended her hand. "Christina Astle."

A grin stretched across his face as he tipped his head forward. He brought her knuckles to his lips before releasing her. "It is a very unexpected, but extreme pleasure to make your acquaintance, Christina Astle. May I call you Christina?"

The answer clogged her throat. How presumptuous to even ask at their first meeting? Had he no breeding or sense of propriety? She'd expected better after hearing the refined southern lilt to his speech. In Ohio, at least, it would be inconceivable to give such permission to a complete stranger...but in this wilderness a body needed friends. She swallowed her distaste. "I—I suppose. Though I should probably know more about you than just your name."

"Of course. I hail from a small town just north of Nashville and am the oldest of four boys. My father was your typical farmer, but I'm afraid my aspirations have been too high to settle for that life. I'm thirty-one years of age, and I believe your hair to be most stunning shade of red I have yet seen." He gave a slight bow as though finishing an applauded oration.

"Most interesting." Christina forced her lips in an upward direction, though his flattery did little to encourage it. "And thank you. Tell me; are there only the two of you?"

"Just us."

His partner stepped to join them, nodding. His gaze floating between her and Towan. "A lonely existence, but worth every minute when we take our load of furs down in the spring."

Christina raised a brow. "You're trappers?"

Edwin clapped the other man on the back. "John is. I give him a hand, but my hope and fortune lies in a claim I've staked in those mountains. I've been seeing good color. I know there's gold."

A treasure hunter. Not an employment she'd ever respected, but if he could help her… "Surely you don't hide up in these mountains all winter. Is Fort Hall or Bridger really that far?"

Tuttle opened his mouth to speak, but Edwin waved him off. "I take it you want to leave here? I can't blame you at all, and I'm sure I can assist you in your endeavor." He grinned but his eyes remained unaffected. "Fort Hall is less than a week's ride as the crow flies."

Christina's heart thudded in her chest. Hope

battled uncertainty. Could she trust this man? Something about him seemed detached from who he portrayed. What if Towan was right? They could be dangerous. She pushed the thoughts and doubts aside. No. This was her miracle. She had to get out of these mountains, this village. She didn't belong here. "And you could take me there?"

"Of course." He planted a hand on the trapper's shoulder and forced him to make eye contact. "Can't we, John?"

"Fort Hall?"

"Of course, John. You heard the lady. She can't very well spend the winter stuck out here with these savages."

John Tuttle glanced at Towan then away. He scratched his fingers through his thick grey beard. "So long as it's her choice." He stalked away. "We leave in 'bout an hour."

"See?" Edwin again pasted a smile on his face as he turned back to Christina. "It won't be a problem. Why don't you go get your things together?"

For some reason, she couldn't even force a smile. Her stomach churned. What if this was the wrong choice? What if it was safer to stay here? "All right." She turned and walked to the cluster of grass and hide huts, Towan again on her heels. She didn't want to know what he thought, but she did need his help finding her way back to her baby…whom she had completely forgotten to mention to Edwin and his friend. Would they change their minds after they found out about the infant?

Christina halted in the middle of the village. "Can you please tell me where I am going?"

Towan turned her to face him. "First, tell me you

don't intend to ride off with those men. That would be extremely foolhardy."

She shoved his hands away. She did not need him voicing her own fears. "Foolhardy? How do you even know that word? You're not supposed to speak as though you walked out of a novel."

"And how exactly should I talk?"

"I don't know." She waved a hand at him—his long black hair, his buckskin leggings and loincloth. "But look at you. You are..."

Anger flashed in his blue eyes and her words fled. In truth, she had no idea who or what he was. He didn't seem to fit in any category or preconceived notion. A mystery she would never solve. She didn't have the time. She needed to feed William and get him ready for a long journey. She had to focus on reaching Fort Hall, and not let her doubts keep her here.

"Can you please show me which hut is yours?"

He mumbled something she couldn't understand and pointed. Yes. That one did look familiar.

"Thank you." Christina crossed to the hut and laid her hand on the flap over the doorway. Then glanced back at her blue-eyed Indian. He'd saved her life. He'd fed and protected her, and all she'd given him in return? A pain in his side for well over a month. "Thank you, Towan." Words far overdue.

His countenance softened, but his frown deepened. "Don't go with those men, Moqone."

That word again. But she wasn't about to ask its meaning. Not this time. "I have to." She ducked into the hut and let the thick hide fall back over the door. A soothing melody met her.

Towan's mother sat cross-legged on her bed of furs, William cradled in her arms while she sang.

The babe stared up at the kind face.

Christina hugged herself. *I have to go.*

10

Towan spun on his heels, but only made it a couple of paces before rotating back to the wickiup. He couldn't let Christina leave with those men. What of his promise to protect her?

He turned away again. If she wanted to go, it was her choice. He couldn't force her to stay. Besides, if she removed herself from his protection, it would solve more than one problem. He could continue on with his simple existence here, and Tucwatse could find some other maiden for his wife.

Releasing the air from his lungs, Towan glanced heavenward. *If she leaves, she's no longer my concern.* He'd done everything to help her. It wasn't his fault if she was so shallow minded and prejudiced that all she wanted was to be back with her people, even if it meant risking her life. And William's.

By the time Christina climbed out of the wickiup, every inch of snow in the immediate area had been packed by his moccasins. She pulled his makeshift cradleboard over her shoulders as she straightened. Her gaze met his briefly before dropping to the ground where it stayed. "Again, thank you for everything you have done for me and my son." Her mouth formed a pathetic smile.

Stepping around her, Towan looked to the cradleboard. William's small round face peeked from the fur wraps. His stomach ached as though someone had punched him, and he ran the tip of his finger down the infant's smooth cheek. How could he let this child from his sight? Or the mother? He had to protect them. But what choice did he have?

"Where are Ryder and his partner?" Christina turned, removing William from his sight.

Towan straightened. He let his chest expand with a full breath, but it did nothing to alleviate the sensation of suffocation. The whinny of a horse answered her question, sparing him from the task. Christina met his gaze briefly before she tucked her husband's saddlebags over her arm and hurried away. Towan trailed her to where the two men loaded one of the mules. Several very nice hides. Beadwork. Who knew what else they had stolen from these people for only a fraction of what they could be sold or traded for at a fort or back east?

Edwin looked up and smiled as Christina approached. His expression froze…then faded. He motioned to the cradleboard. "What's that?"

Tuttle raised his head. His heavy whiskers twitched with the suggestion of a smile. "My guess would be a baby."

"A baby?" Edwin's frown became more pronounced. "What are we supposed to do with a baby?"

"Take it safely to Fort Hall." The old trapper appeared almost smug as he stepped past his younger counterpart. "Maybe it's best you stay here, Ma'am.

I'm sure you'll be comfortable enough and well taken care of. No use hauling that youngster through the mountains in this weather."

Christina shook her head. "Please, he won't be any trouble."

Edwin seemed to reclaim some of his senses and took her free arm. "Come on, John, the lady knows her mind. She doesn't want to be stranded in this place for months. I'm sure we can manage."

Tuttle threw up a hand and turned back to finish preparing the mules.

A smooth smile slid across Edwin's face as he reached for the saddlebags. "I'll tie these someplace safe for you." As he took them, his eyes widened. He glanced from the monogram to Christina, his lips tightening. Still his smile remained in place.

Towan stood back, helpless to do anything but watch, his intestines knotting as Edwin returned for her, helping her onto the back of his horse. As he slipped into the saddle, Christina's gaze remained on her hands, gripping the back.

With the mules tied behind his mount, Tuttle thanked the villagers. His gaze darted one last time to Towan before he led the way out of the valley.

Towan wiped his hands down his face, then turned and walked in the opposite direction.

~*~

Christina stared past Edwin's shoulder at the long trails each hoof had made in the snow. The drifts grew deeper the higher into the mountains they rode. How long had they been traveling now? Hours—each taking her farther away from any form of security since

Anthony had left her. But closer to Fort Hall. A few days from now they would arrive. With the lateness of the season, perhaps her wagon train had decided to winter there. The option had been discussed in case the weather turned too quickly.

A soft grunt announced that William had awakened. Gradually the cooing became a whimper and then a cry.

Edwin stiffened.

Tuttle glanced back. "Whoa, fellows. Whoa now." He pulled his mount and the mules to a halt, leaving Edwin no choice but to do the same.

"We don't have time to stop. It'll be nightfall soon."

Tuttle gave his head a shake. "This was your idea, so give the lady a hand down so she can see what that young'un needs."

Edwin didn't say anything more, but his frown seemed well etched in place as he helped her off the horse.

"I'll only take a few minutes." Christina glanced around, seeking anyplace that would give her privacy. A juniper shielded a fallen log about twenty paces from where they stood. Perfect. Hauling William from her back, she trudged through the ankle-deep snow.

"Where are you going?" Edwin called after her.

"I need someplace to sit down."

"There's a boulder right here."

Yes, but you're right there as well. She kept walking.

Concealed behind the evergreen, Christina fed William and changed his diaper. Only wet, thankfully. After wrapping him in the clean napkin she'd packed, she slipped him into the cradleboard and returned to the waiting men. She held the wet napkin out to

Edwin. "Can you put this into the empty side of my saddlebag?"

He stared. "Is that a...?"

Heat surged to her face. "Never mind." She hurried to the mule he'd tied the bags to and fumbled with the straps. So much for not being a hindrance to them. At least the bay mule seemed to enjoy the break. He stretched his head between his front legs and rubbed his nose along his snow-encrusted cannon. Christina patted his neck. Her hand paused on his thick winter coat. Three dark socks and one light. The shading around his eyes. The streak of white in his mane. Impossible. It had to be a coincidence. Just a similar looking mule.

A hand gripped her arm and she jumped, twisting to Edwin. His eyes narrowed. "We can't stand here all day. Come, I'll help you back on the horse."

She managed a nod, but it felt as though someone had a hold on her windpipe. What if that was Anthony's mule? The other one looked familiar, as well.

It was your own people. White men with painted faces. That's who frightened the wagon train and killed your husband and the older man.

Towan's words thundered in her head. How could she have so easily discounted them at the time? He had no reason to lie. Her body stiffened, but she allowed Edwin to heft her onto the back of his horse. Had he been involved in Anthony's murder?

His cold eyes met hers, and he flashed a smile before mounting in front of her. Did he suspect she knew?

Small flecks of white floated from the darkening sky. They came into view of a tiny log shack. Tuttle and Edwin reined the animals toward it, stopping out front.

Christina eyed the cabin. "Where are we?"

"Home sweet home," Edwin said with a hint of mirth.

Her pulse accelerated. "Are we stopping here until morning?"

"More like until spring." He reached for her.

He pulled her from the horse, and panic fought to take over. What could she do, run into the woods and hope to not freeze to death with her baby? Hope for a miracle? God had already given her one…and she'd walked away from him. *Towan.* Why hadn't she listened?

"No need to worry, Ma'am." Tuttle swung from his mount. "Ryder is as much a gentleman as you'll find west of the Missouri."

And yet Towan had already proven himself more of one. She pulled away from Edwin and darted to the door of the cabin. "Gentlemen keep their word. I give you warning. If either of you come near me or my child, I'll find some way to make your lives truly miserable or end them altogether."

Edwin moved around to face her. He leered, the look in his eyes raising the hair on the back of her neck. "I don't see why you're all worked up. You should be thanking us for saving you from those savages down there. You would have been someone's squaw before spring. Maybe you would have liked that…" He stepped to her, his fingers catching a loose strand of her hair. "Living in one of those bark huts for the rest of your life, running after papooses, and cooking over an open fire for that Indian buck."

A shudder worked its way through her, and she

hit him away. "Better an Indian's woman than…than your whore."

"Tut tut tut. Ain't no call to speak like that."

"Just keep your distance."

With a chuckle he bowed deeply. "Yes 'am." He strode away to help Tuttle with the animals.

Christina stood paralyzed. William started bawling. What could she do? Nowhere to go. If it were only her life at stake, she would risk anything, but she couldn't risk William.

Dark and stale met her senses as she stepped into the snug shack. Fading sunlight through the door showed a large stone fireplace protruding from one wall with two narrow cots hugging another. On each lay a large, matted buffalo hide and woolen blankets.

With the few options available, Christina moved to the single chair and several stumps which probably served the same purpose. Grabbing the back of the chair, she hauled it to the wall near the fireplace, and then grabbed the long, iron fire poker, leaning it nearby. She hurried to unbundle William and get him fed before the vulture entered.

Tuttle came first and closed the door behind him. "I'll get that fire started and some grub on. I'm sure you are as starved as yer young'un." He stacked wood, and used flint to get a flame glowing but seemed to sense something was missing. His gaze fell on the fire poker at her side. "What do you want that for?"

"I'm not really safe here, am I?"

His face remained unreadable. "What would make you think that?"

The mules. The lies. "The way that man looks at me…as though he hasn't seen food in weeks."

"Months probably." Tuttle shrugged. "It's a hard

and lonely life up here for a man, but especially a young man like Ryder."

"Does that somehow make it right? He lied to me to get me up here. You both lied."

He shook his head and tossed more kindling on the fire. "Nope. I just kept my trap shut. I don't want anything to do with this, but I figured I owed him that much."

"Why?"

"He funded this venture." Tuttle set his hat aside on one of the stumps and raked fingers through the few strands of hair left on top his head. "The summer didn't treat me well, and I didn't even have enough for a grubstake."

"So the mules, the money, everything, Mr. Ryder provided?"

"That's right."

Christina cuddled William closer as he hushed. "How long ago?"

"'Bout five weeks—a little less." With the fire growing large, he took a pot from a peg and opened a can of beans. "I wouldn't fret too much. Ryder seems a reasonable man. I'm sure he won't force you."

Reasonable? A liar, and a possible thief and murderer.

The door burst open with a chilly gust. And Edwin. Judging from the white piled on his shoulders and hat, the gentle fall of snow was quickly becoming a blizzard. How many more months before spring?

Oh, Lord, please help me!

11

Towan nudged the snow with his toe, in no hurry to return to the wickiup and every reminder of Christina and little William's absence. Night spread over the valley and exhaustion gnawed at him, but it wasn't as though sleep would come even if he lay down. Not when he couldn't be sure she was safe. And that baby. What had possessed her to take her son away from shelter and protection?

Doubts and worry bit at him like a hill of ants. Why had Tuttle kept eyeing him? Had they met before? Not that Towan remembered. Ryder was the one who seemed vaguely familiar. And what of his reaction to the monogramed saddlebags? Had he recognized them? Or just the initials? Christina had said her husband had taken them with him on his mule. Had Ryder been the one to leave them behind at the wagon? He probably worried someone would link the bags to their dead owner.

Towan rolled his palm over the hilt of his knife. What ate him the most was how Edwin Ryder looked at Christina—like a hawk spotting its next meal. That and the fact she rode away with him without a second thought.

Fool woman.

He circled to the east side of the village, seeking the tracks of the horses and mules. He followed them a few yards then crouched and ran his fingers over one of the perfect indentions in the snow. *What's wrong with me?*

Towan rocked onto his knees. He clasped his hands and let his head tip forward. "Father..." He blew out his breath. Though he read the Bible most every day, prayer was something he hadn't yet breached. For some reason whenever he started, the title of father drew his mind far from thoughts of a kind God.

Maybe that was the problem. Father. Not his favorite word.

"God..." Much better. Now only the storm of thoughts and feelings muddied the waters. He clamped his eyes closed, focusing on the blackness. "God, You know all things and see all things. Everything I do not. Please speak to me. Is she safe? Is her child safe?"

Instead of the peace he had hoped for, the storm in his mind and heart deepened into a full winter's blizzard. Blinding. He looked back to the trail the four animals had left. Just as real snow began to fall.

"No." In another hour or so the path would be impossible to follow. He'd never find her.

Is that what you want, God?

"Lose something?"

Towan startled, then straightened with a glance behind him at Havne.

"Perhaps a fire-haired woman?" Havne gripped his shoulder. "My brother is also disappointed."

Ah, one good result of her departure.

"Not that the elders would have favored him with her. Our father opposed him as did others. I wondered why you did not claim her for yourself, but you are right not to have. A warrior needs a strong woman who can stand against hardships and bear his children. It is better the fire-haired woman is back with her people."

Towan offered a nod. Now to convince himself to agree.

"Even if a cabin in the woods is all they offer her."

He twisted to Havne who watched him closely. "They promised her Fort Hall. What do you know?"

His friend smirked. "You did not watch them. If they'd headed to the fort, they would have gone over the west pass. Instead, they rode toward the river's head."

North-west.

"That is where the old trapper has his cabin."

Towan's heart thudded against his ribs. "You know his cabin and how to get there?"

Havne's smile grew, and he cocked a brow. "And what reason have you to go after the fire-haired woman?"

What reason? Because he'd never live with himself if anything terrible happened to her or little William. Because of a promise he'd been released from the moment she rode out of sight. Oh, but the nagging of his rebellious heart. Better not to answer the question, even to himself. "We will need horses." But he would go on foot if he had to.

"I have one, and I will speak to my father at dawn about another. This snow falls heavy. We can do nothing tonight."

Towan nodded, though the action took every ounce of his will. To sit and wait for morning would prove exquisite torture. All he could do was pray they did not arrive too late.

~*~

Rocking William and avoiding Edwin's gaze, Christina turned her body to face the old mountain man. "Did you ever have a family, Mr. Tuttle? A wife? Children?"

"Whiles back I did." He set the pot of beans over the fire and stirred. "Married a right pretty girl I knew growing up in Virginia. We had a young'un right away." He glanced down at William who blinked long and slow, fighting sleep. "Lot like yours, 'cept blondest curls you ever did see. Full head of hair right from birth."

"Where are they now?"

"Both dead…a little girl, too."

What a horrific loss. Christina's jaw slackened, an ache rising in her chest. "What happened?"

His hold relaxed and the pot lowered deeper into the flames. His free hand wiped down his beard as he stared into the fire. "I'd built Maryann a little cabin in the back country of Missouri. It meant a new start in a good land. Nice, dark soil we had. A fine farm. Burned down one day while I was away to buy seed. Came home to find our neighbors digging three graves. No one knew what happened. Hadn't had Injun troubles there for years." He shook his head, and then stirred the beans again.

"I'm sorry."

"'Twas a long time ago."

Perhaps…but did a person ever recover from such loss? Her eyes misted at the thought of Anthony lying dead. The ache remained.

"You can sleep here." Edwin's voice jerked her attention across the room to one of the cots. He grasped the edge of a large buffalo hide and shook it. Dust billowed. He dropped the hide to the floor. Fanning the air with one hand, the other brushed off the lower hide which apparently served as the mattress. Not nearly as inviting as the pallet of furs she'd left behind in Towan's village.

Was he relieved to have her gone?

Christina bit the inside of her cheek and pressed her lips together against the urge to cry. Was it possible to miss him? Of course not. She missed the security he'd provided. He'd been so kind. The image of William tucked in his arms swelled within her. If only she'd listened. If only he'd come after her.

If only.

With the cot put back together, Edwin moved to a roughhewn chest. "That old hammock you told me of," he addressed the mountain man, "it's in here?"

"Yep, should be. Haven't had need of it for over a year or so, but should work just fine so long as no rodents got at it."

Edwin withdrew the rope hammock and shook it free of the tangled mess it had become. The ropes looked to be intact and he strung the hammock from two beams. With his back to her, Christina took the opportunity to study him. What sort of man was he? "I don't suppose anything you told me about your family is true. If you had a mother, she would have taught you better."

A growl rose in the back of his throat. "Not if she

died before I could walk."

Christina fought down a pang of sadness for his loss. This man had lied to her. "Then how is it you have four younger brothers?"

"Half-brothers. My father remarried. But I wouldn't refer to that woman as my mother."

Again his story tugged at her to pity him, but she couldn't let herself. She couldn't let down her guard. With William asleep and her appetite completely absent, it seemed pointless to put off the inevitable. Keeping the fire poker concealed behind her, she crossed to the cot and laid one of the woolen blankets over the buffalo hides. The blankets appeared to be both newer and cleaner. Small mercies.

Unable to contain a yawn, her eyes watered as she lay down and pulled the second blanket over her and William. Her body begged for sleep, but she couldn't—not until the men retired, as well. Thankfully, they ate their beans quickly. Edwin stretched out in the hammock, while Tuttle climbed between the hides on the second cot. Soon his rumbling snore resonated within the small cabin.

"Good night, Christina." Edwin winked before closing his eyes.

Lord, keep us safe. Her mind chanted the prayer until sleep took her.

It was impossible to guess how much time passed before something rubbed against her shoulder, dragging her back to consciousness. Her eyes flew opened as every muscle tensed. A bristled face brushed across hers, coarse and painful. She tried to scream out but his mouth smothered her. Her lungs burned. She reached out, her fingers franticly searching the folds of the blankets until they wrapped around the cold iron of the fire poker. She swung it upwards.

Edwin's yelp rang in her ears, and he fell sideways. The live coals in the fireplace cast a glow over the unmoving form on the floor. Dark blood flowed from the side of his head. She grabbed William and one of the blankets.

"What's happened? What?" Tuttle sputtered, his words drawled by weariness.

Instead of answering, Christina yanked the blanket over her shoulders and propelled herself through the doorway. Chilly air met her outside, as did a world of white. Bolting toward the woods, her mind came alive. Where could she go? What of the horses? Could she take one? She glanced back. Their corral peeked from the far side of the cabin.

"Christina?"

Edwin's call gave her feet speed, even as the snow deepened, hiding obstacles strategically placed in her path. She stumbled over a fallen branch, bruising her shin through the leather of her leggings. It did little to slow her.

William's screams tore the night, and she clutched him tighter. What was she doing? They wouldn't survive out here. But going back held just as little promise. As strength failed, her legs crumbled and she slipped to her knees. Christina stared at the falling snow. What other recourse was left to her but prayer?

Her trail was not difficult for the men to follow. She remained in the same spot when they came upon her. Edwin had his head wrapped. He sneered and yanked her to her feet. "You should have known better than to run off like that. It's not safe out here for a lone woman."

"I'll take my chances." She gritted her teeth

against their chattering and braced herself as his open palm slapped across her face. Christina gasped at the sting.

A gun cocked behind him. "It ain't right to hit a woman." Tuttle cleared the gravel from his throat. "I'm sure she did what was her right to do. Let's get her back to the cabin."

Edwin grumbled but did as he was told.

Christina pulled away from his grasp and moved ahead of him. "Don't you dare touch me again."

"Or you'll what? You don't have your fire poker anymore. You should be more careful if you care about that baby."

A chill passed through her, and she pressed her lips to William's head.

Nothing more was said until they pushed back into the log shack.

Edwin rolled into the hammock with a moan while Tuttle tossed more logs on the fire and returned the poker to its place.

Crawling between the blankets, Christina watched the old mountain man until her eyes burned.

He stood without motion for a long time and then turned to her, pulling his pistol from its holster. "Try not to use it unless there be no choice." He slipped the gun between the blanket and the buffalo hide.

12

Christina exhaled. What a relief when Edwin finally left to tend to the horse and mules. She glanced at the lump in her bed. Did she dare leave the pistol behind? Her pulse quickened with the memory of Edwin's mouth pressed against hers. How long would she survive if she let her guard down for any length of time—even with the man absent?

Tuttle pulled his boots on, his back to her. She slipped the gun from its hiding spot, under her short buckskin dress and into the waist of her leggings. The cool steel against her skin did little to calm her nerves.

"I'll bring in more firewood so I can cook up some venison for dinner." He pulled his hat over his balding head and tramped out the door.

Christina surveyed the cabin. Now what? The thought of another night on the dirt-ridden, smelly buffalo coat answered the question quickly enough. She made a nest with the blankets for her sleeping infant and then dragged the huge hide from the cot. So much heavier than she'd imagined, but she managed to pull it out the door and through the snow to a row of tree stumps. Finding a branch, she beat the hide—

the perfect release of pent up anger, frustration, and fear.

Tuttle chuckled on his way back into the cabin, his arms loaded with branches. "Going at it that way, you won't have any strength left to get it back on your bed."

Christina wound up for another strike. She'd take her chances. Her hand froze halfway through the motion as Edwin darted around the side of the cabin.

"Get in the house."

Her hold tightened on the stick. "I'm busy."

With a grunt he stomped through the snow toward her, his arm rising as though to disarm her. She brought the branch up, narrowing her eyes at him.

But he no longer looked at her. He slid to a stop, his gaze darting to the side of the cabin and back. "What about your precious baby? Is he still in there?"

"Don't you go anywhere near him."

"Then get in the cabin. Now."

"Fine." She tossed the branch aside and hurried past him, going straight to where William slept.

Edwin slammed the door, a string of curses spewing from his mouth. He grabbed his rifle and loaded it. "Seems those bloody Injuns decided to give us a visit."

"What?" The fire wood tumbled from Tuttle's arms as he spun. "Which?"

"Probably followed us from the village. Maybe they want the girl back."

"Just don't go shooting anyone before we know what they're really after. Last thing we need is a war party sitting on our front porch…if we had one, that is." Tuttle moved to the tiny, glassless window near the door and pulled back the hide covering. He swore.

"You're right. I see that Shoshone half-breed out there."

Christina's heart skipped a beat. *Towan.*

Edwin pushed the older man out of the way and slipped the barrel of the rifle through the hole. "Reckon he's alone?"

"Hard to say for sure." Tuttle placed a hand on Edwin's shoulder. "Either way, we best be finding out what he wants before we start shooting." Tuttle cracked the door open and hollered out in Shoshone.

Christina gathered up William and set him in the cradleboard. Her fingers fumbled with the ties in her haste. She finished securing him when Edwin snatched the baby and carrier from her arms. "Don't get any ideas. You're not going anywhere."

The pistol under her dress pinched as she jolted to her feet. "Give me back my baby."

The door banged closed and Tuttle motioned to her. "He's after the girl, all right. Says he won't leave 'til he's seen her and knows she stays of her choice."

Edwin smirked. "That's easy enough." He held the cradleboard away from her. "You know what happens if you don't tell him right."

Her lungs seized. "No."

Tuttle shook his head. "No good. He says he needs to see both mother and son. This ain't worth losing a scalp over."

Edwin fingered the bandage across the side of his head and scowled. Then he pushed William back into her arms. "All right, Mrs. Astle, this is how it'll play out. You go out there and tell him to step off a cliff. You tell him you're fine here. If you don't, I'll be waiting to blow a hole in his head and anyone else's that comes within ten yards of you. Understand?"

Christina managed a nod as Tuttle draped the pelt wrap around her shoulder and shoved open the door. She stared, for an instant blinded by the brightness as she stepped out. Then she saw him, his bronze skin a wonderful contrast against the world of white. He slipped from the painted horse and moved toward her.

"Towan." She quickened her steps.

A rifle shot echoed off the nearby slopes and a bullet turned up snow only a foot to his right. He stopped, his hands rising, his gaze remaining on her. "You are well?"

No. Please, please take me from this place. She bit back the words. Edwin would be true to his word, and she couldn't risk Towan's life. "I'm fine." *For now.*

"And you wish to remain here with these men." The muscles in his cheek tightened like a strung bow string.

"Yes." The word squeaked out. "Please, Towan…" Christina glanced behind to the door. Still open. They'd hear anything she said. "You have to go."

Towan's expression relaxed, though he peered at her more intently. Silence stretched itself between them. A tear escaped to Christina's cheek as she mouthed, "I'm sorry."

She needed to return to the cabin, but she couldn't. She couldn't remove her gaze from him, aching to throw herself into his arms, to feel the security he had to offer surround her. Another moment. No one moved. Then Towan gave a nod.

Without a word he turned, his gait stiff as he walked to his horse. Two large leather pouches had been tied together and draped over the animal's withers. He loosened one side and withdrew a book—Anthony's Bible. He held his hand up so they could see the book from the cabin then motioned her to him.

A little farther from the cabin, a little closer to him, to freedom. She started toward Towan, her pulse stampeding.

"Not any farther, Christina," Edwin shouted. "We can't trust him."

He was itching to pull the trigger again, but she couldn't stop. Not when she was so close. "My Bible. I need my Bible."

~*~

Towan glanced from Christina to the barrel of the rifle staring at him from the doorway. Edwin Ryder probably wanted a better shot than the tiny window afforded him. The question was, would he take it? Towan gave a quick hand gesture and Havne emerged from the forest, his bow armed. Hopefully his presence would give reason for pause—long enough to get Christina and her baby out of range. Nothing else mattered.

"I need my Bible." With eyes large and pleading, she reached for the book. "Help me." Her whisper thundered in his head.

Towan stepped toward the horse's flanks. The Bible dropped as he grabbed her wrist and yanked her to him, the same motion turning the animal between them and the cabin. He pushed her head down and pointed to the woods. "Run."

Her gaze lingered on him, and he repeated his command. A shot rang out, spurring her to act. Towan twisted as Havne doubled over and dropped from his perch. His horse sprang away. A pool of blood expanding over the center of his chest answered all questions.

The second bullet dug into a large pine at Towan's right as he pivoted after Christina, little William strapped to her back. She and the baby were almost out of sight. He released the horse, whistling for it to follow as he sprinted over a fallen branch and through the foot deep snow, keeping his head low.

He caught up with her and gripped her elbow, encouraging her faster. Down a slope, through a draw and into a quiet valley. She stumbled after him, his hold on her keeping her moving. Finally, she pulled away. "Wait…I can't breathe."

He faced her, and she crumpled into his arms.

"I'm sorry." Her words came between gasps for air and sobs. "It's all my fault."

Towan held her, bracing her against his chest. He pressed his mouth against her hairline. How could he answer her? It was her fault. If only she had listened to him, Havne… He blew out his breath and held tighter.

Soon both horses followed them into the valley and Towan led her to Havne's, his chest hurting at the thought of his friend. How would they tell his family? Towan swallowed hard and reached for the cradleboard. "I'll take Will."

One of the horses whinnied, throwing its head as the other lurched sideways. Thunder echoed through the valley. Towan's lungs seemed to burst as he slammed against the ground, a cloud of white embracing him. Agony ripped into his head. He rolled and tried to find his feet. He had to get Christina somewhere safe. He couldn't let them take her again. His arms gave way under him and he fell. Dark splotches filled his vision, stealing away the brilliant scarlet spreading over crystals of white.

~*~

A scream scratched Christina's throat, and she dropped to her knees at Towan's side. Clutching his shoulders, she turned him onto his back. Blood ran from the wide gash above his left ear and soaked into the snow. "Towan?"

He pushed her hand away as he again rolled onto his side, pulling his knees up and pushing to stand. His eyes rolled, and his balance wavered. He staggered to his knees. Blood flowed down his face and onto his clothes. Crawling to him, Christina braced his head against her shoulder, one hand laid directly over the wound. She had to stop the bleeding.

"I failed." His breath warmed her neck. Then he slipped away, his body falling sideways.

"Towan, no!"

"Christina, get away from him."

She glanced to Edwin who moved toward them, his revolver trained on Towan's head. "Please. You can't do this."

Edwin's nostrils flared as he glared down at her. "You brought this on him yourself. I warned you. Now get away."

"No." She leapt to her feet, placing herself between the two men. The pistol under her buckskin dress shifted against her skin.

Edwin laughed and shoved her aside. "Do you think he was here to save you? He's a savage, Christina. A red skinned savage who would sooner scalp you than look at you." He grabbed Towan's knife, yanking it from the sheath as he pulled Towan's limp body onto his knee and pressed the blade against his hairline. "How 'bout I scalp him for you as a present. Isn't that what you always wanted—a genuine Injun scalp? They sell for hundreds back east. It'll make us even for the favor you paid me last night."

Christina twisted away and wrestled the pistol free. As she spun back, she laid her finger over the trigger. "Leave him alone."

Edwin released Towan, and he slumped back to the earth. Blood still poured from his wound.

"You've already killed him."

"No." Edwin stabbed the knife into the ground and stood. His hand dangled near his revolver. "You killed him. And if you're not careful, you'll be the death of that boy of yours, too."

She stared down the barrel of the pistol, centering the sight on his chest. Anthony had shown her how to shoot, teaching her the importance of deep breaths and a steady hand. All she had to do was squeeze easy on the trigger. It wouldn't be murder. Self-preservation. Protecting her child. Avenging Towan. So many reasons to finish this now.

"You'll not pull that trigger."

"What makes you so certain?"

"Because you've never killed a man, and I promise you it will haunt you your entire life, a scar that never heals. Trust me, I know. You're a good Christian woman. Your Bible sits up by the cabin, but I'm sure its words are ingrained in everything you are."

"You're wrong. I've hardly read it." Christina squared her shoulders and tried to put his warning from her mind. "The Bible was my husband's and he was murdered. Most likely by the same man who made off with our mules. Tell me, did you buy those mules, or did you find them a short ways off of the Oregon Trail in a grove with a wagon? Did you kill my husband?"

Edwin's lip twitched, but he shook his head. "I don't know what you're talking about, Madam. I traded for those mules at Fort Bridger. Some Indians brought them in."

Her hands trembled. "I don't believe you."

A moan pulled her gaze to where Towan lay, his head still bleeding profusely. He was alive. How long would that last if she didn't help him?

"Lower the pistol, ma'am." Tuttle stepped from the ridge and made his way down through the speckling of trees. "Let's get this boy back to the cabin and see to that wound of his. Ryder will behave himself." He gave the other man a pointed glare. "Won't you?"

Edwin raised his hands, palms out. "Of course. No one else needs to die today."

13

Christina didn't look up from where she knelt on the dirt floor of the cabin as Edwin plunked his boots down by the fireplace and took the only chair. "Keeping him alive is a mistake. Bury the bodies and make sure no one finds him or his friend. Then lead the horses away from here before releasing them. Nobody will know they came this far."

"We'd be asking for trouble." Tuttle shook his head as he handed Christina a pot of fresh water. "Their kin are too close for comfort."

She rinsed the blood soaked cloth and reapplied it to the side of Towan's head. They had brought him back to the cabin, but he only flirted with consciousness. "Can you find me some bandaging?"

Edwin called after Tuttle as he moved to the wooden chest. "Which kin are you more worried about? Those Indians in the valley or O'Connell?"

The older man's hands hesitated over the lid.

"I'm right, aren't I? This half-breed is O'Connell's."

Christina looked from one man to the other. "Who's O'Connell?"

Edwin snorted. "An old drunken mountaineer who had an eye for dark-haired maidens."

Towan's father?

Tuttle shoved a threadbare shirt into her hand. "Here, use this."

"Thank you." She eyed the homespun cloth. Not much to look at, but it seemed to be relatively clean. She tore the shirt into strips and wrapped Towan's head. Her stomach knotted at his ashen complexion. If not for the blackness of his hair and the feathers still tangled in a small braid, it would be easy to forget his full lineage. Not that it bothered her anymore. His mother and everything she had given him was simply a part of him—and not horrible in the least.

Christina tied off the bandages, her gaze wandering to Towan's mouth. How good it had felt to be held by his strong arms, the warmth of his lips on her forehead. To feel protected and safe…and loved?

What a ridiculous thought. She shook her head and withdrew. Christina could not say why he would come after her, or risk his life to help her leave, but it was not because he felt anything so deep or profound. Duty? Perhaps. He *had* promised to keep her safe. Maybe he only felt sorry for her. All the same, she was grateful and indebted to him—yet again.

"So is it true," Edwin said from his seat, "that O'Connell struck it rich in California back in Forty-nine, at the beginning of the rush? I hear tell everybody knew he had the gold, but never saw him spend more than a pittance of it." He leaned forward. "Do you reckon he still has it hidden somewhere?"

Tuttle's laugh came out as a snort. "If he did, you'll never get your hands on it. That was a full decade ago. I spent the winter of Fifty-one with him on a trap line with not enough of a grubstake to last us 'til spring. We would have starved if not for the meat we brought in from the traps. No, if he had gold as they say he did, it was long gone before that."

Settling back into his chair, Edwin stuck a cigar in his mouth but never lit it. Tuttle took up pacing near the door, one hand attempting to rub the beard off his chin.

Edwin shot him a glare. "Would you sit down already?"

"You don't know Bill O'Connell like I do. He's got an Irish temper if I've ever seen one, and he's not slow with that Colt of his." He adjusted the hat on his head. "And don't even get me started on what he thinks of his boy."

"You worry too much."

"Do I? Where was I planning to trade our furs next spring? Fort Bridger's been O'Connell's home for almost two years now. He has a say in some of what goes on there. Never mind, I wouldn't put it past him to shoot a man in the back if given cause."

The baby cried from the cot where he lay, still fastened in the cradleboard. With nothing else she could do for Towan until he awoke, Christina stood, stepped over Edwin's feet then brushed past Tuttle. This shack was much too small for five occupants.

Edwin rested his elbows on his knees and addressed the older man. "What do you propose?"

"You could let us go," Christina said as she pulled William from the cradleboard and cuddled him to her shoulder. She motioned to Towan. The blood had already begun to soak through the cloth binding his wound, but at least the flow had slowed. "Let me take him back to his people. Please."

Edwin leaned back, his hand brushing over his coat momentarily as though checking for something in his breast pocket. His lips thinned. "I'm not certain that's the wisest course of action, Mrs. Astle."

~*~

Their conversation buzzed in his head, but Towan tried not to care what was said. What did it matter, anyway? He could do little about it with the pain pulsating through his skull and far beyond the reach of the actual wound—unless someone had shot him through the temples when he'd lost consciousness for those few minutes. At least, it seemed like a few minutes. He'd still been lying in the snow, Christina standing near as Tuttle talked her into giving up her gun. How she had come by the weapon in the first place remained a mystery.

He'd lost consciousness a couple of times more when they had loaded him onto the back of the horse like a set of mule packs and hauled him up to the cabin, but he'd still seen Havne lying where they'd left him at the edge of the clearing. And Christina as she'd picked up the Bible from the horse's tracks. Mostly Towan kept his eyes closed, the light only increasing the agony, and Edwin Ryder and his companion's complacency his one remaining weapon.

A toe nudged his ribs and he released a groan, nausea on the verge of making him retch. Ryder gave a grunt of his own. "I think he's waking up. Pass me those ropes, John. I want to make sure he stays where he is until we finish deciding what we'll do with him."

The cords dug into Towan's wrists as they were fastened together, followed by his feet. So much for complacency. He cracked open an eye to gauge his surroundings. Ryder worked with his bonds, Tuttle walked the floor, and Christina tended to little William on a cot. One door. No real windows. Fireplace. Ax leaned near the door. Knife on a stump beside a pot. Forks. Plates. A pair of calf-high boots. A piece of flint. A sharpening stone. A bucket with moisture darkening its lip.

"What did I tell you? Looks like our Shoshone warrior is done with his beauty sleep." Ryder stood, sneer in place.

Towan pushed against the wall to prop himself up a little. He swallowed back the bile burning its way upward. Between his unsettled stomach and the intense headache, the bonds had little to do with him remaining in one place.

"So you decided to stick around, did you? Shame." Edwin settled into the chair.

Christina came to her feet and took a step toward them.

"Stay away from him unless you want me to put my next bullet in a more permanent location."

Her gaze remained on Towan, but he only met it briefly. "Can I at least give him something to drink?"

Ryder ignored her. He withdrew a revolver and began to fiddle with it. "I think I met your father once, half-breed. Good man. Good Indian killer. He told me all about his red-skinned son. Said he'd just as soon kill him along with the others. I said if I ever run across him, I'd surely do the job." He released the cylinder and slipped shells into the empty chambers.

Towan refused a reaction though the mention of his father seared his chest.

"Let me see if I can remember. William, wasn't

that what you were called? A white man's name on a red Injun. William O'Connell Junior. Can't say I blame your father much. Them girls down in your village are right tempting."

Towan let his eyes close momentarily. It was all he could do to keep his jaw from tensing, but that would only reward Ryder for his efforts.

Leaving her baby on the cot, Christina crossed to the fire, shoving Ryder's feet off the stump as she passed. She dipped a tin cup in the pail of water before Ryder lunged and caught her arm.

"He doesn't need anything from you."

Christina jerked away, water sloshing. "Would you prefer I give it to you in your ugly face?" She held his gaze as though challenging him to test her threat.

He raised his hands, revolver dangling from his thumb, stepped back and sank into his chair. "Fine, but if I see you even eyeing those ropes…"

She nodded and knelt at Towan's side. He allowed her to give him a sip, but only a sip. Towan's insides still churned, probably his body adjusting to the loss of blood or the blow to his head. Hopefully it would soon pass. He let himself sag against the wall and caught a glimpse of Ryder fussing with his coat pocket. As though the man fought an impulse. His gaze was trained on Christina.

Towan closed his eyes, pondering the behavior and working his mind through all possible means of escape.

God, give me success.

~*~

Huddled under the woolen blanket with her

infant, Christina tried to let sleep take her. Of course, it would help if she could stop her vigil over Towan. The flickering of low flames lit the angles of his face. Edwin's taunts tumbled through her mind. William O'Connell? Was there any truth to his words? Towan hadn't reacted to them, but then she wouldn't expect him to. Not if he'd prepared himself.

"You named him William?" He hadn't been so collected when he'd learned the name of her son. No wonder. And if he'd been called after his father—by the sounds of it not the most worthy of souls—understandably, he preferred his Shoshone name.

Towan.

She didn't know what the word meant, but it fit him all the same. She continued to watch him, but her eyelids grew heavy. *Why did you come for me?*

Christina jerked awake to a gust of cold air from the door. Moonlight illuminated the snow-laden ground and the black wall of the forest beyond.

Edwin cursed, darting out the door. The silhouette of the rifle flashed across the lighted opening.

She glanced at Towan. Gone. She clasped her hands and squeezed her eyes closed. "Lord, please let him get away. Protect him, Lord. Please."

A shot shattered the silence. Then another. And a third.

She waited. What a familiar sensation. So much like that long night alone in her wagon, Anthony already dead on the side of the trail, yet to be found.

Edwin hardly glanced at her as he tromped back into the cabin and plunged them into darkness with the closing of the door. He leaned his gun against the wall and stoked the fire. "Well, John, I suggest you stay clear of Fort Bridger in the spring." He looked to

Christina. "And as for you, Mrs. Astle. Maybe you'll sit tight now. I haven't quite decided what to do with you."

Christina sank into the buffalo hide and pressed her palm over her eyes. Two images etched themselves into her mind—one of Anthony, her beloved husband, the other of Towan, her blue-eyed warrior. Both dead.

14

Towan clung to the thick mane and planted his head beside the horse's withers. He relaxed his body into the movements and let the animal choose their course, his only focus not falling off until they reached the village. Maybe he could convince others to come back for Christina with him. As Havne had?

He forced himself to think past the pain in his head. Bringing others with him would only endanger more lives. What would a war party do? Storm the cabin and hope not to catch Christina or little William in the crossfire? Not worth the risk.

Humph. A war party. More likely the elders would blame him for his friend's death and allow him neither horse nor warriors.

With a groan, Towan slipped his hand to the base of the horse's neck, applying pressure until its pace slowed and then stopped. There hadn't been time to halter or bridle the animal. He slid to the ground, not even attempting to stay on his feet. Rolling onto his back, he looked up at the sky speckled with tiny lights. The horse hovered over him.

"You are there, aren't you, God?"

He closed his eyes and relaxed into the snow as the cold gradually seeped through his buckskin clothes. At least they held out the moisture better than cotton. Wool, on the other hand…

If God was there, what sort of game was this? Ever since Towan picked up that Bible, his life spiraled out of control. He'd tried to put behind him everything to do with white men and their world. But now look at him. First Christina, then little William—both found their way past his resolve not to care. Those feelings had cost Havne his life.

Towan linked his fingers over his forehead and pressed his thumbs into his temples. As much as a part of him wanted to forget her and ride away, could he leave Christina or that baby to the mercy of a man like Edwin Ryder? Still, he was hardly in the condition to ride back and steal them away.

Towan reached into his shirt and found the gold watch he'd taken from Ryder's coat pocket. The man had not pulled it out even once, though his hand had reached for it often enough. What was it about this gold watch? Towan peered at it in the abundance of light the snow reflected from the full moon. The watch appeared to be gold, an elaborate design etched into the front, a short length of chain…he flipped open the cover and ran his finger over the inscription then tipped it to catch the light.

To my dearest, Anthony M. Astle.

Christina

Towan stared, nausea returning at the memory of the young widow standing over her husband's body. No wonder he recognized Ryder. The man had been painted to look like a warrior, but he had been there, terrorizing the wagon train, killing two men, and making off with everything of value they could get their hands on, including this watch. Christina's husband and the older man had probably come upon Ryder and his fellow marauders by accident when returning for her.

Pushing the timepiece back under his shirt, Towan dragged himself to his feet and took hold of the horse's mane. He had to get back on the animal—had to go back for Christina and little William. Now.

Pain stabbed through his head and his vision clouded. "God, help me. There must have been a reason you brought her into my life." He pressed his forehead into the horse's warm coat. "I only want to protect her."

Only? It was one thing to lie to himself, but to lie to God?

Better to not even contemplate what he really wanted. God would have to forgive the discrepancy. The important thing was to keep her safe. Take her back to the village. Ignore his feelings until he could return her to her people in the spring.

A simple enough plan…if he could somehow get on this horse again.

~*~

Edwin's curse jerked Christina's head off her elbow, the best she had for a pillow. He shoved his coat on the chair, turning to eye her. She settled her head back down and cinched William closer. Best to avoid Edwin's hard gaze.

"Did you take it?"

"I have no idea of what you are speaking. But I assure you I have no desire to come near anything of yours with a ten foot pole." *Including your person.*

Instead of being pacified, he swore all the louder. "That half-breed." The chair toppled over with the assistance of his boot. "His knife's gone as well. I should have put a bullet through his head when I had the chance."

Christina sat up and brought William to her shoulder. A weight lifted from her heart. "Then you did miss. Towan's alive."

The morning sun accompanied Tuttle into the cabin. He carried a load of firewood.

Edwin looked from the old trapper back to her. "All right. He got away with one of the horses, but don't be too hopeful he survived. I got off several good shots before he disappeared. Besides, that head wound did more than slow him up."

The split logs tumbled from Tuttle's arms to the floor, piling against the wall. He shook his head and tossed a couple into the fire. Steam rose from snow on the logs as it melted and dissolved.

Towan was alive. He had to be. Christina's hand stole to the weathered Bible, still not completely dry from its spill in the wet snow. Straightening her spine, she laid William down and walked to the fireplace. She set the book near enough to garner some heat without being affected adversely by the flame.

With a curious glance, Tuttle took up the pot and moved to his stash of canned beans.

Christina snatched the pot from his hand. "Why don't you find me the fixings for a stew?" For some reason, knowing that Towan got away spilled hope into her. She would make the most of this situation until she could follow his lead. "I saw you had some of those tubers the Shoshone use."

"Camas?"

"I suppose." She had no idea what they were called.

He dug her some out of a mule pack and they looked right. Christina washed them and chopped them as her mind continued to plot an escape.

Camas, venison, and some dried onion and carrot made for the best meal she'd had in a long time. To think she'd not even known how to cook before she'd left home. She'd baked pies and cakes with her older sisters, but cooking? It had never been a requirement, until she'd had nothing but a campfire to learn on. Thankfully, Anthony had known how to prepare several dishes, and the other women on the wagon train showed her more of the basics. Including how to improvise. She pictured the grand kitchen at her home in Cincinnati. What sort of luxury must a real stove be? Maybe when she returned…if she returned.

First she had to survive.

Christina used every drop of water washing the dishes, taking her time until both men left the cabin. Then quickly set them aside.

The roughhewn wood chest was almost empty, with nothing but a pair of pants and a shaving kit. Strange, she couldn't imagine Tuttle without his generous beard. What had the whiskered man looked like in his younger days?

Christina wrapped the shaving kit in its leather cover and set it back into the chest. Her hand hesitated over it. Then slid the blade from its sheath. With Tuttle reclaiming his pistol, and the fire poker under constant watch, it was time to get a little more creative. As much as the thought of cutting someone turned her stomach, she would not let Edwin hurt her child. Or herself. She needed a weapon. With the edge of the razor covered, she fastened it under her buckskin dress.

Closing the chest, she moved next to Tuttle's cot. She wrinkled her nose at the filth and carefully employed two fingers to lift the edge of the buffalo hide. Beneath lay more large mule packs. Foodstuffs, beans, gunpowder, and empty cartridges. Even some fierce looking traps. As she slid them back under the bed, a smaller canvas satchel caught her attention. She reached for it, her fingers finding something warm and soft. Furry? It moved.

She yelped, snatched her hand back and peered into the shadows as a fuzzy-tailed rat scampered behind the larger packs. A shiver tickled her spine. She made a face at the rodent and pushed up. Enough snooping. She had a weapon. Now to venture a little farther.

William fussed before she made it to the door.

"Hush, little one." Christina sat on the edge of her cot and fixed her dress so he could nurse. Then she covered herself in case one of the men returned. Anxious, but fixed in one position, she tapped the toe of her moccasins on the dirt floor and stared across the room at Anthony's Bible. She hadn't been able to find it in Towan's hut. Had he kept it with him this whole time? The memory of him reading it in the dim light of the fire he'd built in the cave pulled at the corner of her mouth. A smile. She missed smiling. Missed not being afraid.

When William returned to sleep, Christina tucked him in a blanket and laid him on the cot. She snatched up the wooden bucket and headed outdoors. The sun glared off the snow, instantly blinding her. She squinted against the brilliance and fought the need to close her eyes completely. Who would have thought light could invoke such pain?

Doing her best to ignore the discomfort, she moved away from the cabin. No sign of either of the men. *Perfect*. She crouched and pushed the moist snow into her pail until it was filled. The task gave her enough time to scope the area. The place Towan had stood as he beckoned her to him. The red still marked where his friend had fallen. The young Indian had died because of her.

With the pail heaped with snow, Christina circled around the cabin to where the corral stretched across the small clearing. One of the mules was gone, but an extra horse took its place. The painted mare Towan had ridden—a horse from the Indian village. Perhaps the animal knew its way home, even if she did not.

"What are you doing out here?"

She steeled her hope before rotating to Edwin. He stood with the missing mule, an assortment of traps slung over the animal's back. Genevieve. Christina had made certain each of the mules had a name before they left Missouri. Genevieve, in honor of her sister's European travels—and not being able to say goodbye. But Edwin wouldn't know that, and he didn't need to know what she planned. Christina scowled at him, the most natural expression with her eyes already as narrow as they were. "I need more water for washing soiled napkins." That should keep him away for a while.

He grunted. "I don't want you coming out without asking first."

"Pardon me?" She raised her brows at him and would have placed her hands on her hips if they weren't already full. "And what, pray tell, am I supposed to do when neither you nor your hairy friend are present to grant me permission? My sense of propriety restricts me from elaborating further."

"Fine, come and go as you please, but remember, there's nowhere you can run. You'll never find your way off this mountain, and if you try, it'll be the death of both you and that baby of yours." He led the mule toward the corral.

The pail hung heavier as she hauled it into the cabin and lowered it beside the fireplace. She set three more sticks over the flame. Even with the extra heat, the snow would take a while to melt. William still slept. What was she supposed to do but sit here and second-guess her scheme to escape this place? Christina glanced to the Bible. She could always read…only…it was gone. She scoured the area. It had been right there when she'd left the cabin. How could it have vanished?

A thorough search still didn't turn up the book, but by then the water had thawed enough to begin washing.

Hours passed before Tuttle and Edwin tramped into the cabin, knocking snow from their boots. The younger man stopped in his tracks, his face ghastly red. "Why are those…*things* hanging off my hammock?" A stream of curses both preceded and followed the words.

Though the profanities warmed her face, Christina had the strange urge to smirk. She gathered the diapers, folding as she removed them from the improvised laundry-line, the coy expression held at bay for the time being. Thankfully the thick layers of cloth—made from every scrap that remained of her only gown—had dried quickly.

She slipped the diapers into the saddlebags she'd brought with her. Not only was it a clean place to store them, but would allow her to leave in a hurry if the need arose. Not today. Probably not even tomorrow. But soon, she'd take her leave. She'd wait for the right opportunity…and the courage.

Christina sighed. What if Edwin was right? What if she killed herself and William with her foolishness? If it were only herself to worry over, she'd leave tonight. But her precious son…the deepest source of her fears rested with him.

After a supper of roast rabbit supplied by Tuttle, she cuddled up under the scratchy blanket with her baby and tried to close her eyes. An arduous task. They kept glancing to the last place she'd seen her Bible. Had Edwin come into the cabin before finding her at the corrals? If so, what had he done with the book? Surely he wouldn't have burned it, but she'd already searched everywhere.

Nothing made sense. Even if Towan had come back and sneaked into the cabin, why would he take the Bible and not her? Maybe he decided it was worth the trouble and she wasn't. He probably missed those holy words more than he missed her.

Was it possible to be jealous of a book?

15

In the light of the full moon, Towan's breath billowed before his face. The snow squeaked under his feet as he crept along the wall of the cabin. Every one of his senses was on high alert. Hopefully everyone slept.

Towan laid his ear to the wood and listened. A deep rumble like an angry bear drowned out any other sounds. At least one of the men was asleep. But which? If Tuttle caught him, the man would probably keep his mouth closed. Ryder would shoot first. With his hand on the latch, Towan pushed the door open slowly enough to keep the hinges silent. An inch…then two. Three. He paused, waiting, every muscle primed for action at the slightest provocation.

Nothing.

Live coals gave just enough light to make out the sleeping forms and any obstacles between him and Christina. Closing the door behind him to cut off the draft, Towan stole across the short distance, staying low. He crouched beside her cot but forced one more glance at Ryder in his hammock before he allowed his gaze to settle on her. Even asleep, a crease formed between her eyes, marking unpleasant dreams. Still, with the soft tones of shadows laid across her face…such beauty. Why was it every time he saw her that beauty increased? And little William, his head resting peacefully on her arm. The ache in Towan's chest rivaled the one in his skull. If only he could sit here and watch them until morning came. A strand of hair rested on her cheek, begging to be brushed behind her delicate ear.

Ropes groaned and Towan hit the ground.

Ryder shifted on the hammock. The man began to sit up.

Towan rolled under the cot, a tighter squeeze than anticipated. His shoulder scraped against the old buffalo hide. He controlled his breath, fighting the urge to gag on the heavy mustiness and settling dust, all the while marking Ryder's movements.

The man took the several steps to the fireplace and set a couple more logs over the coals. His gaze lingered on the door. He reached to where his revolver hung in its holster from the head of the hammock. With gun in hand, Ryder walked to the door, opened it, and looked around. After a while he seemed satisfied and returned to the hammock. Stretching himself over it, he set the revolver on his chest.

Towan relaxed against the ground and ran a hand over his face to clean away the grit. Nothing to do but wait until Ryder slept again. Nothing to do but lay there, his mind filled with the woman only inches away and the image of her sleeping. Nothing but time.

He tried to wait at least an hour, not wanting to outrun bullets a third time. When Towan finally pulled himself from under the cot, he resisted the need to awaken Christina and take her with him. Too dangerous. Instead he tucked the Bible under the blanket with her and turned away.

Once back in the cover of the woods, Towan glanced back at the cabin. Dark and solitary. *God, help her understand.*

~*~

Christina covered a yawn. Her eyes watered, not wanting to be open. With a sigh she released William to the cot and rolled onto her back. Something hard dug into her spine. She sat up and twisted toward the offending object. Her Bible?

Edwin was still in his hammock.

Tuttle was pulling his boots on.

Christina stared at the book. Had she moved it without remembering? Wouldn't she have found it when she laid down last night? Of course. After seeing the rat, she had shaken her blankets out and checked under her cot before retiring. The Bible hadn't been here.

But then…where had it come from?

Her sudden movements woke the baby, and he began to fuss. Christina lay back down and pulled the blanket over her shoulder so she could nurse him without drawing Edwin's attention. The way he looked at her was still unnerving. She ran a finger over the cover of the Bible and let her eyes close. *Dear Lord, please keep us safe until we can leave this place. Help me find my way back to the village. I'm trying to believe in You. If You exist, please don't let my prayers be in vain.*

Edwin gazed at her. With a shiver, she tugged the blanket higher around her neck. His leer distorted what might have been considered a smile. It faded as the door swung wide and Tuttle reappeared.

"Grab your coat and get out here, Edwin. Are you sure you fastened the gate after you put the mule away yesterday?"

The younger man shot to his feet. "Of course."

"Well, it's swinging wide now and all the animals are gone. They left a visible enough trail, but who's to guess how many miles they wandered."

"You think they got out on their own?" Edwin pushed his arms into his coat and grabbed his boots. "They couldn't have untied those knots by themselves." He gave Christina a pointed look. "Don't you leave this cabin, you hear?"

She flashed him a thin smile. "I believe we have already had this conversation."

Edwin grumbled something and pushed past Tuttle, who followed. Christina stared at the door. So much for letting the Indian horse carry her back to safety. What other choice was left to her? None, unless Towan…she glanced at the Bible. What if Towan had come back for her a second time? Careful not to disturb her suckling infant, Christina opened the heavy book, flipping through the pages. Why would Towan have taken the Bible just to return it hours later? A dangerous game. Especially since Edwin always wore his gun.

Abruptly she stopped. And flipped back several pages. Her pulse accelerated. A long delicate feather lay in the crease of the twentieth chapter of First Samuel. She looked the feather over, recognizing it as one Towan had worn in his hair. Then she studied the page. Was he trying to send her a message?

As soon as Christina found the dirtied finger print smudged under verse nineteen, she wondered how she hadn't seen it immediately. She lifted the Bible closer and read.

And when thou hast stayed three days, then thou shalt go down quickly and come to the place where thou didst hide thyself when the business was in hand, and shalt remain by the stone Ezel.

Christina stared at the words. Could it really be so simple? She counted. Three days. This was the third day since her arrival here. He wanted her to meet him today. And she knew exactly where he would be waiting.

"Oh, Lord, thank You!"

It was painful to lie any longer and let William finish his meal. Her muscles twitched with expectancy, but trying to escape with a hungry baby would be less than wise. And so she waited, aching to hurry, praying the horses had indeed wandered far.

No sooner had William released her breast than Christina sprang to her feet and tucked him into the cradleboard, strapping him to her back. She grabbed up the saddlebags, the Bible, and bundled the blanket under her arm. Opening the door, she looked out over packed snow, trails leading in every direction. No sign of either of the men. No sound but a large black bird's caws.

Now or never.

Pulse muting the rest of the world, Christina darted across the distance between the cabin and the woods. She followed the path she'd taken with Towan when he had first come for her. Breath hitched in her throat as her legs propelled her forward through the snow, over fallen logs, under branches, long pine needles grabbing at her clothes and head.

Lord, help me. Lord, help me. Her prayer continued

until she emerged from the draw into the small valley. A horse pawed, nibbling at what forage it could uncover. A man pushed off the ground.

Towan. She hastened to him, fighting the sudden urge to throw herself into his embrace, to feel safe once again. Instead, Christina pulled to a halt not two feet from him. "You came back."

The corner of his mouth pulled slightly. "I never left." He took the blanket and Bible from her and set them aside so he could remove the cradleboard from her back. She craned her neck to see what took him so long. Emotion pinched his brow as he stroked the baby's cheek. His voice low, he mumbled something in Shoshone.

Towan released a breath as he pulled the cradleboard onto his own back and moved to boost Christina onto the horse. The straight razor pinched her waist and she paused to remove it. She wouldn't need the weapon so long as she had Towan. She dropped the blade to the ground.

"Planning to give someone a shave?"

"Only if Mr. Ryder had asked for one."

Towan stepped behind her once more, and his hands warmed her waist. "I'm sure it was only a matter of time." He hefted her onto the back of the horse.

Straddling the animal without a saddle gave little security. Christina grabbed the mane and shifted her position.

Towan's hand covered her knee. "Are you all right?"

She nodded despite herself. She'd be fine as long as they went slow.

After bundling the Bible in the blanket, Towan set

it in front of her. "Hold this." Next he handed her the single rope fastened into a halter around the horses head. "Keep him still while I get on behind."

Behind? Christina scooted forward, trying to give him as much room as she could without landing herself on the sharp withers. "You opened the gate, didn't you?"

His "yes" came as a grunt as he heaved himself onto the animal's back. He slid his body against hers and encircled her with his arms. "I wanted to give you opportunity to slip away."

"Um…"

His fingers brushed hers as he took the rope from her hand and something fluttered inside her.

"Why—why didn't you take your other horse while you had the chance?"

His breath was warm on her ear as he reined the horse out of the valley. "I considered it. Especially since neither of these horses are mine. But the other horses and the mules wanted to follow. I didn't know how long it would take you to understand my message—could I risk them finding me before you did?"

"I suppose not." Christina tried to relax. Her stiff body only made riding the horse uncomfortable for both of them. Her knees hugged the sides of the animal as he started up a short rise. "Do you think they will come after us?"

"Unlikely."

"What makes you so sure?"

The rumble of a laugh rose from Towan's chest. "They'll track their horses. A woman isn't worth losing your life for. In these mountains, that's what a horse can mean for a man."

Christina tried not to give in to the urge to squirm. That was not the most flattering sentiment, no matter how much she appreciated the reality of it in this situation. She would have liked to think she was worth a risk. Maybe not to a man like Edwin—it was a good thing he preferred the horses—but Anthony would have given his life to keep her safe, wouldn't he?

Heat filled her cheeks, contrasting the chill in the air, at the thought of the bandage binding Towan's head dyed deep crimson. He had risked his life. Twice. Three times? For her? Why would he do that for her when according to him, most men wouldn't?

~*~

Even as Towan had said the words, his own actions screamed against him. He believed his statement to be true for men such as Edwin Ryder and *Bill* O'Connell, but he'd decided long ago not to be that kind of a man.

"How is your head?" Christina asked.

Perhaps he needed to clarify his statement about what sort of man risked his life for a woman. But how to word it? *A man would do anything for a woman he cares for.* It was probably better to move the conversation forward. "I've survived worse."

"I imagine it's still quite painful."

Yes. Yes it is. "It's fine."

"I am sorry. About your head. About the horse." She sighed. "I'm especially sorry about your friend."

The mention of Havne hit like a blow to his gut. Strength stole from his body, and his shoulders sagged. His first real friend. Five years his junior, Havne had been like a younger brother. A lot like little Matthew might have been if he'd lived longer. Towan clamped his eyes closed against the emotion rising in his chest. Even after all these years, the wound refused to heal. But how could it? He'd been sent away shortly after his brother's death, when he should have been home to comfort his mother. O'Connell hadn't stayed around long enough to help her grieve.

Towan struggled to turn his thoughts away from both the past and his friend's death. Though Christina faced away from him, she'd know if he started sobbing like a child.

Tightening his grip on the rope, Towan focused forward. Snow-laden branches, the dark texture of bark against a backdrop of white. The feel of Christina's body against his, her hair brushing his cheek. He turned his face slightly and breathed her in. Smoke and hints of earth mingled with a scent distinctly hers. He glanced to her ear, mere inches away, tempting him to brush his lips over the delicate ridges and valleys. Or to press his mouth to her temple. To whisper to her how grateful he was that she was safe now.

I am grateful, God, but…I shouldn't feel this way.

Her voice interrupted his plea. "Will we make it back to the village before evening?"

He sighed. "I reckon so."

Christina twisted to look at him. "You said *I reckon* as though you were from the south. I gather you've read a lot," she gave up mimicking the drawl, "but you can't tell me you got that out of a novel."

He lifted his shoulder with a shrug but couldn't meet her gaze. Mrs. Anderson had tried to break him of using that word when he'd first been sent to boarding school in St. Louis. He had tried to appease her, one more way to distance himself from his father, but it still slipped out now and again. "Lots of trappers and explorers who come through here are from the south."

"Like your father?"

A bolt of lightning coursed through him. He should have expected her to ask about O'Connell after everything Ryder had said back at the cabin, but Towan wasn't sure how much he wanted to tell her. "Let's leave my father out of this. The truth is I was raised in Missouri. Near Independence."

"Independence, Missouri. I honestly think you speak better than most of the men I met when we passed through that town."

"I was educated."

"Educated?" She sounded much too surprised.

"Yes. Who would have thought they'd let a savage into one of their schools, but they did." Towan couldn't keep deep rooted bitterness from drenching each word.

She glanced forward again, her body inclined away from him. "I only meant, I didn't think Independence had much by the way of schools. I wasn't suggesting—"

"I spent five years in a private boarding school in St. Louis. I know it was probably not as prestigious as ones in the east, but it was far from a log-house schoolroom." He didn't know why, but he had a strong desire to crush every assumption she'd made about him.

Christina was only silenced for a moment. "Why do you live out here then? Living like this? Dressed like a…"

"Like my people? The people I share blood with? The only people who've willingly accepted me even though I might not be exactly as they are? They welcomed me with open arms when *your* people made me feel inferior and shunned."

Towan encouraged the horse to pick up its gait, and Christina settled back against him. Not the effect he'd been trying for.

"You're right," she said after a while. "*My* people can often be both quite arrogant and ignorant. But they are your people, too, aren't they? Because of your father."

"I don't have a father. No more than little William does." He'd give anything to trade places with the child. It would have been better to never have known the man who'd contributed to his existence.

16

Towan tightened his hold on the rope, slowing the horse's gait as they approached the village. Everything in him begged to rein the animal in the opposite direction, to not bear both the news and responsibility of Havne's death. A man already waited for them, white hair mingled with black far past his shoulders. Towan swung from the horse and led the way, head tipped forward. It was easier to stare at the ground than into the face of an expectant father.

"What happened?" the man asked in Shoshone. He motioned to Towan's bandaged head.

"A graze. There was trouble."

His face tensed. "Havne follows?"

Towan glanced at his dark eyes. "No. Havne was killed."

The man's nostrils flared with emotion, the wrinkles on his face deepening.

"I—I..." What could he say? Towan looked at Christina still perched on Havne's horse. The last three days had worn her thin, and the baby was beginning to fuss. "I will return soon and tell you all."

As he moved away, Christina leaned down. "Who

was that?"

"My mother's brother. Havne's father."

"Your uncle?" She slumped over the horses withers. "Then Havne was your cousin?"

Towan's feet paused. "You never understood that, did you? They are all my family. The only family I have known beyond my mother."

"I'm sorry."

"Sorry for what? For not understanding, or for the death of my uncle's youngest son? For my aunt, who will cry herself to sleep tonight and for many more nights?"

Wide-eyed, Christina straightened on the horse. She swung her leg over and slipped to the ground. Her mouth opened as if to speak. Nothing came. Without a word she turned and started into the grouping of wickiups but didn't make it far before looking back. "I know my words mean little, but I am sorry. I know he wouldn't have died if I hadn't been foolish enough to go with those men. I should have listened to you and…what can I say…but that I am sorry."

Towan stood silent for a moment, soaking up the earnestness in her large eyes as they glistened in twilight. Even knowing everything he knew now, he couldn't say he'd not go after her if given the chance to rewrite the past. Even though it had cost Havne his life. Though, perhaps, if he were given that chance, he would convince Havne to show him the cabin and then stay back out of harm's way. Guilt twisted his gut. He forced his jaw to relax. "You look like you're waiting to say something more."

A broken laugh spilled from her throat, and a tear trickled down her cheek as she waved at the wickiups. "I still don't recognize which hut is yours. And I need

Will. Sounds like he's getting hungry again, and he's probably wet."

Towan pressed a smile and led the way with a motion for her to follow. He held the door-hide out of the way while she ducked in, met by his mother's gasp.

"He find you. He find you." She embraced Christina like a daughter, before looking to him. Her grin faded to sternness, and she switched to her native tongue. "What do you there, with that baby in the cold? Bring him in. Bring him in."

Instead of answering, Towan handed the cradleboard over the threshold. "I must first see to the horse. Then I will return."

As soon as the thick hide hid him from Christina's stare, he wiped a hand over his face. What he wouldn't give to lie down and rest both his body and head. Perhaps sleep would ease the torture between his temples and at the site of his wound, but first he had a duty to Havne's parents.

~*~

Oh, the comfort of the blanket of furs laid over her weary body and soul. It seemed a month since she'd lain here, her heartbeat steady. No fear. Christina pressed a kiss to the silky softness of William's hair and then laid her own head down. Instead of closing her eyes, she studied Quaritz, who watched the door for the return of her son. The torment these past three days must have been hard for Towan's mother, with her son gone and no knowledge of whether or not he was safe.

Christina nestled her baby under her chin, grateful her own son had a few years before he would put her through similar torture. It felt so good to hold him and keep him close.

The flames danced wildly as a breeze announced Towan's arrival. His mother all but pounced on him with questions. He answered in Shoshone, which was fine.

Christina didn't need the events of the last few days to be recounted.

Towan winced and drew back as his mother reached for his bandages. He waved her away. She would have none of it. She ordered him onto his back and gingerly unwrapped the old fabric caked with dried blood. Quaritz shook her head at the wound above his ear. She gathered clean water and cloths as well as an herb that she applied to the open flesh before bandaging it.

With a hand pressed across his forehead, Towan remained laying down, declining Quaritz's offer of food. He glanced at Christina once before rolling over to face the wall. He didn't move again for the rest of the night.

As morning light filtered through the walls of the hut, Christina blinked awake.

Towan still lay in place. His arms crossed over his chest, he stared up.

"How are they?" She regretted speaking as soon as the words left her mouth.

Towan did not turn his head, but hopefully that was to avoid his wound. "Who?"

"Havne's family."

Shadows flickered across his cheek. "Naturally, they are upset."

"I imagine so."

"I do not know if it will be safe here for you much

longer."

Christina pushed up to face him fully. "What do you mean?"

He continued staring at the thatched slope of the hut. "Havne has an older brother. Tucwatse. He has always had an eye for you, and now that his brother has died rescuing you, he feels that should give him a right to you."

"A right to me?"

"He wants to take you as his wife."

Christina's jaw slackened as a thousand thoughts bombarded her mind, overwhelming her. Silence resounded off the walls of the hut as she formulated a stuttered response. "He expects me to marry him?"

She didn't give Towan a chance to answer. "I won't. I'm sorry that his brother was killed, but he has no right to me. I won't. I can't. I'm going home in the spring. I want to leave this place. I refuse to marry anyone."

"You might not have that option."

The cold finality of his voice settled over her with a sense of doom. "Towan. Why bother saving me from Edwin Ryder only to hand me over to someone else? Why didn't you leave me there? At least..." Christina bit her tongue. Pointing out that at least Edwin was white and spoke the same language would not aid her in convincing Towan to help her. She needed a way to reach him personally. She glanced to Quaritz's neat roll of furs. She had probably started her day hours ago. "Was your mother married to William O'Connell?"

Towan covered his face with both hands before giving a nod.

"Was it her choice? Was she happy? All those years in Missouri, away from her people?"

"It wouldn't be the same." His voice cracked. "Tucwatse would be kind to you and your children."

Children? The reality of what he was saying clutched her. "I won't bear his children. I won't marry him. I'll leave if I have to. I won't stay here. They can't make me." She glared at Towan and his reclined position, not moving, simply laying there as though none of this were his concern. "You promised me I'd be safe here. You promised me you would take me to Fort Bridger in the spring. You swore it to me."

"Yes. I did." He still didn't move.

She lifted her chin. "Then you'll help me. You'll protect me from your cousin."

Towan massaged his temples before sitting up. "After the time of mourning is past, I will speak once more with Tucwatse and his father, but if they are decided, as I believe they are, there is only one thing left to do."

Dare she ask? Christina forced herself to swallow. "What would that be?"

His clouded blue gaze flicked to hers before dropping. "To take you as my wife."

"You?" How did becoming his wife fix anything? "I don't want to marry you any more than I want to marry your cousin."

His expression hardened, but his eyes betrayed hurt. "It's the only way I can protect you. Do you think I want this anymore than you? Maybe I should have ridden away when I first saw you that day on the Oregon Trail. I lost my horse, I dragged you over a mountain, I've been shot, my closest friend has been killed, and now I stand to lose my freedom, and still all you can think about is yourself. Yes, I was foolish enough to swear to protect you, but you've already walked away from that. I owe you nothing." Towan disappeared from the hut with a flash of morning sun.

Christina sank back down beside her baby. His eyes were wide, staring at her with interest, though he could not understand the sting of Towan's rebuttal. The innocent child had no idea how dreadful his mother had behaved to the man who had already risked everything for her. And still Towan offered more.

But to marry him?

~*~

Towan grabbed a short length of branch while lowering himself to the boulder. He pressed the blade of his knife through the soft flesh of the wood, skinning away layer after layer, whittling it into nothingness. Of course Christina didn't want to marry him. He hadn't expected her to be overjoyed at the possibility, but her words scratched open old wounds. Rejected once again. Never good enough. Not because of who he was—but what he was.

The knife slowed, and he tipped the blade until he could make out his hazed reflection. The bronze of his skin after a summer in the sun. The dark outline of his hair, hanging long past his shoulders. He hadn't cut it in eight years. In boarding school they'd kept his hair short, and he'd spent most of his days indoors reading the books Mrs. Anderson had given him, making his complexion almost white. New students hadn't been able to guess his ancestry. Not until the older boys had made it known.

Christina didn't need to be told anything. And she would never change her view of him.

A chunk of the branch flew several feet at the flick of his blade. What if he had stayed in that world and found a trade after finishing school? What if he had met Christina before her beloved Anthony? Dressed in a suit and with a proper hat, whatever the fashion in Ohio, would she see him differently?

Probably not.

The knife dug deep in the wood, becoming wedged. Instead of withdrawing, Towan powered it through. The branch snapped in two. He tossed both pieces aside, stood, and started walking again.

He didn't care what she thought of him. Christina was the same as all the people he grew up with.

"Towan."

His feet stopped, but he didn't turn. He didn't want to look into her beautiful face and feel her rejection anew.

"Towan, I'm sorry." Her fingers caught his sleeve. "Will you please listen to me?"

He folded his arms across his chest. Couldn't she leave him alone? He was tired of this wild horse ride. Tired of being bucked off and trodden over.

"I thought about what you said. If I agree to marry you, will you honor your word and take me to Fort Bridger so I can return home in the spring?"

Agree to marry him? As though she were doing him a favor. He should keep walking and let Tucwatse have her.

"And it can be a marriage in name only. You wouldn't expect…anything…more."

Expect anything from her? That would be foolish of him.

Christina circled, squaring off to him. "Are we in agreement?"

He gritted his teeth. Keep her safe, supply her with all her needs, marry her so no other man could have claim on her, and then deliver her back to her people, and in return—the pleasure of her company, evidently. Not that he wanted anything from her, but still the arrangement was quite one-sided. He nodded. *Be my strength, God.*

Christina stepped back before turning. She immediately halted. "Who is that?"

Towan followed her gaze to the warrior standing near the river. Broad shoulders and an inch or two taller than Towan, Havne's older brother scowled at them together. Towan nodded and Tucwatse returned it, with a motion to the knife strapped to his leg.

"That may very well be your groom, depending what happens in the few days." Towan glanced at Christina.

"What do you mean? You just agreed—"

"To fight him for you." He gave her a thin smile. "He warned me last night he would challenge me if I tried to stand in his way. Either way, you're stuck with a Shoshone husband. Though, if he kills me, he might expect you to carry more than just his name."

17

A full two days of the village wailing over Havne's death left Christina's nerves frayed. Add three more days of waiting. Christina kept her gaze on her hands, forcing herself to chew the meat though everything about it turned her stomach. Any food would probably have the same effect with Towan seated across from her, Bible propped between his knees as he ate. How could he appear so calm when he would fight Tucwatse this very morning? Her entire future depended on his success.

Not to mention, his life.

"Shouldn't you sharpen your knife?" Even as she spoke, her stomach threatened to expel her breakfast.

Towan didn't grace her question with a reply. She could hardly blame him, but how could he bury himself in that book with so much at stake? Was he hoping for a miracle? Trying to strengthen his trust in God's help? Christina doubted that He was even there. Just when it seemed He took notice of her and stepped in to help, the situation only worsened. Off the spit and into the fire.

She set aside the last of her food and lay down with a hand over her stomach. If Towan wanted to ignore her, she'd return the favor. At least, she could pretend to ignore him.

He closed the Bible, and then his eyes. He tipped his head forward, clasping his hands over the book.

Listen to him, Lord...if You can.

Towan stood and their gazes met. Briefly. Before he fastened his knife to his thigh.

Christina pressed her lips together. She should say something to him, but everything that came to mind seemed quite pathetic.

Then he was gone.

Quaritz followed in his wake. Naturally she'd be unable to sit here while her son risked his life. She'd been cold to Christina ever since Towan had told her of Tucwatse's challenge, rightfully blaming Christina for putting her son in danger once again.

Ears attuned to every noise outside the hut, Christina rolled onto her back and hugged herself. She glanced to her sleeping baby. Which was worse? Lying here wondering, or watching every slash of their knives. Towan's mock fight with Havne had been awful enough. She couldn't stand the thought of the real thing.

And so she waited. And waited.

Men called out, cheering perhaps. A dog barked. Someone yelled. Others hollered.

Every sound strung her nerves tighter. How much longer could she bear not knowing? Guilt pricked. Was she more concerned for Towan...or herself?

A bloodcurdling scream jolted Christina to her feet. She couldn't tell if it was the cry of a woman or a man. Surely not Towan?

The brilliant sun met her as she hurried from the hut. The immediate area was abandoned, and she looked to the commotion just east of the village where it appeared every man, woman, and child stood in large circle, blocking Towan and his opponent from her view. Her legs carried her to the edge as she tried to see past. Someone stepped out of her way.

The two men grappled close, a single knife in Tucwatse's hand being held at bay by Towan. They used their free arms and even legs to try to break the hold. A blow to Towan's knee buckled him, and the blade skimmed beside his head.

Christina didn't realize her gasp was audible until Towan glanced over, his gaze catching hers.

In that brief second his focus was lost, and Tucwatse brought his foot to the center of Towan's stomach and dropped back. Towan flew through the air over him, skidding to a stop. The other man had already come to meet him, and the knife slashed toward his chest. Towan rolled out of the way but could not escape completely. The blade slid across his arm, drawing blood.

Christina clamped a hand over her mouth, but she couldn't look away.

Knife raised, Tucwatse lunged again.

Towan swung his leg and kicked the attacking arm off course. He followed the momentum, pushing his body off the ground and into the Tucwatse's side. Towan's arm wrapped the man's torso as the other hand reached for the weapon. He gripped the wrist, twisted his body, and lifted his knee into Tucwatse's stomach.

Christina held in a cheer, but her celebration was short lived.

The man barely grunted. Instead, he hooked Towan around the neck and pulled him over. Again they tumbled to the ground.

Christina forced herself to step back until they were obstructed from her sight. How could anyone stand to watch?

Abruptly everyone moved, some hurrying forward, others pulling away as their voices rose with unintelligible chatter. Glimpses of someone lying motionless on the packed snow. Blood. But whose? Three men lifted the body. A trickle of blood left a trail. His hand moved, and he released a groan. He was alive!

They moved past with him, and she caught sight of the face. Not Towan's.

On his knees, his head lowered, Towan remained in place as the area cleared.

Christina hugged herself, her arms cold. She'd forgotten her wrap. Searing glares grazed her as Tucwatse's family moved past. She wiped at her eyes with her hands, needing to see Towan. The familiar feather hung from his long hair. The crimson staining his left arm. The knife on the ground. A tremble passed through Christina, and she stepped toward him. "Towan?"

He didn't budge. Didn't look at her.

"I'm sorry."

Still nothing but the emotions that distorted his face. So many mingled together it was impossible to discern what he felt…and yet she felt it all with him.

Oh, Towan.

She had thoroughly turned this man's life upside-down and backwards. It would have been better for him to never have become involved with her. To have left her and her baby to die in the wilderness. Unfortunately there was no way to remove herself from his life until spring. Which left only one thing to do.

A boy she recognized hurried to Towan and crouched beside him to tell him something in Shoshone. Towan's chest expanded, and he nodded. Relief eased across his face.

"What did he say?"

Finally, he glanced to her. "They believe Tucwatse will recover."

She was glad for his sake. "What now?"

"It is best done tomorrow." He stood and slapped the packed snow and dirt from his leggings.

"Tomorrow?" Christina echoed. He had to be speaking of their wedding. What a frightful thought. "If you think that best."

Towan nodded. "And in the spring I will take you as far as Fort Bridger where you can find a wagon train headed east." He studied her.

"That's all I ask."

"And you will forget this nightmare."

Aptly stated. She doubted, however, that the memories of this nightmare would ever fade.

~*~

Towan held himself stoic as his soon-to-be bride approached. Despite this marriage being hardly more than a charade, his mother had not forgone any of the traditional displays. The dress she had given Christina hung past her calves with an elaborate fringe and thousands of tiny blue beads. The sleeves and neckline were equally decorated. Beads, fringes, feathers. Even her hair had not been overlooked. Two long braids hung over her shoulders like rays of sun, feathers and beaded leather weaved throughout. Not that she required any ornamentation. Whether from the winter breeze or the anxiety she undoubtedly felt, her cheeks wore a blush. And her eyes, large and dark, drew him in.

He looked away.

The community closed around the couple, forming a complete circle. His mother's uncle, the senior elder and spiritual leader of their family, came before them.

Towan could hardly focus on the words spoken as a strip of leather bound Christina's wrist to his. He wrapped his fingers around hers as the elder spoke of becoming one. Of love. Of devotion. Then Towan was told to speak his promises. He glanced to Christina who stared straight ahead. She would not understand his words in Shoshone, why not recite the poem that his mother had often shared—the words that had been rehearsing in his brain for the better part of the day?

"'Fair is the white star of twilight, and the sky clearer at the day's end, but she is fairer, and she is dearer. She, my heart's friend. Fair is the white star of twilight, and the moon roving to the sky's end, but she is fairer, better worth loving. She, my heart's friend.'"

Only words, and not even his. How could they mean anything to him? His tongue could not be stopped from forming his own verse of devotion.

"A promise to care for and protect, to cherish and to love, like the white star of twilight she is always before me, my heart's desire, if only…my friend. My life I give to her, my hopes and my desires…I sacrifice for her. And pray my heart will never mend."

Towan looked to their arms bound together, a

symbol of what marriage should be.

His mother's eyes glistened as she stepped to Christina's side, giving her the words to say, words Christina neither understood nor felt. She merely repeated them as best she could, her tone level and emotionless.

The old elder took a strand of hair from each of their heads and tied them together. Another symbol of their unity. The hairs were handed to Towan's mother who secured them in a tiny pouch for safe keeping. As long as those hairs remained joined, nothing could separate this marriage.

If only.

Drums and singing accompanied the couple to the wickiup. His mother came forward and kissed them both before stepping inside to lay the baby on the bed of furs and withdrawing. She would spend the first few weeks with her sister's family. It would be expected.

Towan held the hide out of the way for Christina and then followed, letting it plunge them into solitude.

"Can we untie this yet?" She untangled her fingers from his.

He nodded, not trusting himself to speak. The leather binding fell away, and she stepped back. Towan moved to stoke the fire while Christina stood near the door as though she'd never been there before…or had never been alone with him before.

He smiled when his back was to her. Was she concerned he'd changed his mind about allowing her a purely platonic marriage? When she did lower herself onto her bed beside little William, Towan allowed himself an admiring look. Her attention was on her braids, loosening them, combing out the adornments.

Waves cascaded across her shoulders. He never knew a more beautiful woman—a woman who warmed him from the inside. What would it feel like to take her in his arms, to entangle his fingers in those glorious tresses, to cover her mouth with his own…to truly be her husband?

Heat surged through him, and his chest expanded. Why shouldn't he have her? She was rightfully his wife. And it wasn't as though he didn't deserve her, or that she didn't owe him. He'd risked everything—given everything. How many times had he saved her life and the life of her child? He'd given enough. He deserved something in return.

Crouching before her, Towan smoothed the tips of his fingers across her cheek, tracing her jaw and sinking them into her silky hair. She tried to pull away, but he held her in place. His other hand braced her shoulder as he leaned in. And brushed his lips over hers. He paused with their mouths barely touching before deepening the kiss, baring his soul to her and plying for acknowledgment.

For a brief moment she softened, her hesitancy giving way. But only briefly. Her withdrawal broke through his fantasy as did the slap of her palm across his face.

She gasped. "You promised."

Shame scorched him and he pulled away. Perspiration poured from his body. He dove out of the wickiup, not able to remove himself quickly enough. Avoiding being seen, Towan hurried into the shield of trees, not stopping until he was concealed.

"What was I thinking?" He braced his hands against a wide trunk of a pine. The bark bit his palms. With his eyes clamped closed, he relived that moment, her hair between his fingers, his mouth against hers. Again, her rejection sliced deep and festered the wounds his father had inflicted. Why would Christina want him any more than anyone had? Towan sank to the snowy ground, scooped a handful, and laid it to the back of his neck. His skin tingled under the searing cold. Chill droplets ran down his spine. What had he been thinking?

He wiped the remaining handful of slush across his forehead and then down his face. It wasn't as if he was a real groom and this was his wedding night.

~*~

Christina stared at the entrance, not sure what to feel. Sorry—that she couldn't offer Towan more than the sharpness of her hand after all he had done for her. Confused at the familiar emotions his kiss had evoked in her. Angry. He had promised. Did he feel he had a right to her now?

Had he tricked her into marrying him?

Not Towan. He wouldn't have. He wasn't that kind of man…was he?

"No." Her body shivered with an inhale. He had walked out instead of insisting on the consummation of this marriage. But what now? She lay down but couldn't find a way to shoo the thoughts of Towan or his kiss from her mind. She needed a distraction before she lost her sanity.

Leaving the baby on the furs, Christina crawled across the hut to where Towan left the Bible on top of the saddlebags. She ran her finger over the monogram. How she missed a good man at her side she could trust. As she had trusted Towan. Now she didn't know what to think.

A glint of gold caught her eye and she peered at the small circular object that peeked from between the folds of Towan's shirt—his mother had given him a fancier one to wear for the ceremony. Hand trembling, Christina withdrew the timepiece. Though she already knew what she would find within, she flipped it open.

Her mind raced. None of this made sense. Why would Towan have Anthony's watch? Had he stolen it from Anthony's body? Why would he do that? Her thoughts wondered another direction without permission. What if Edwin had spoken the truth about buying the mules from some Indians at Fort Bridger? What if Towan hadn't been alone in those mountains? Havne. Tucwatse. Any one of his family could have been with him. After they raided the wagon train and killed Anthony and Cal, what if Towan's friends had taken the mules to Fort Bridger to sell while he'd gone after her? On horses, the others could have easily made it to the fort and back.

Impossible. She couldn't believe that of Towan. He was too kind. He'd sacrificed so much for her.

But…what if…this *marriage* had always been Towan's plan? Why else would he have risked his life going against Edwin if not because he expected something from her in return?

It couldn't be true. She knew him better. She'd seen how gentle he was with William. He loved her baby. And for some reason, he kept coming back for her.

What if…

Christina clasped a hand over her mouth. She forced herself back to some form of rational. Most likely there was some explanation. Edwin had to be the killer. She could believe it of him so much easier. Still, she'd been too trusting in the past, and she wouldn't make that mistake again. Settling the Bible back in its place, she reached instead for Towan's knife. Christina withdrew the long blade from its sheath. She would do what she needed to protect herself…even from Towan.

18

Christina tensed when Towan returned to the hut hours later. She kept her eyes closed, feigning sleep. Under the furs, her fingers skimmed over the hilt of his knife, though she remained uncertain if she'd be able to use it against him even if she had to. Maybe to threaten...but could she bring herself to ki—*hurt* him? Definitely not until she knew the truth.

Towan kept his distance and crossed to the opposite side of the hut to roll out the several hides that made up his bed. Instead of lying down, he seated himself on them and gazed across the hut at her. She watched him in return through a shield of lashes.

"You have nothing to fear from me."

His words held earnest apology, but how talented an actor was he? Eyes now wide, Christina lifted the hand closed around Anthony's watch and let it slip from her fingers, only maintaining a grip on the short chain. She let it dangle between them.

His gaze danced between her face and the timepiece. "I cannot guess your thoughts. Perhaps you should speak them."

"Do you know who killed Anthony?"

"Yes, I do."

"*Was* it you?"

Deep creases cut into his brow as the corners of his mouth curled downward. Disgust? Pain? "You believe I killed your husband." He shook his head. "After everything I've done for you, this is what you—"

Christina's mouth opened with an apology, but she'd spent too long tumbling this around in her mind. "How do I know this isn't some sort of game to you?"

He lay down and folded his arms.

"You won't answer me? You said you knew who killed him."

"And obviously you do, too."

She gaped at him and his confession. "Then you did kill him?"

Towan pushed himself up and rotated to her. "I did not say that."

Flinching at the sudden movement, Christina gripped the knife but kept it concealed. "Yes you did."

"I only meant you seem awfully convinced already. Why should I try to argue with you? One look at me and you knew exactly what I was capable of. One look at Edwin Ryder and you follow him anywhere. Who am I to disagree with your remarkable abilities to discern a man's character?"

Christina lowered the watch, Towan's words like a slap across the face. Enough riddles. "You had both Anthony's saddlebags and watch. Tell me what you know."

His gaze smoldered. "The saddlebags were on the ground near your wagon. I assume whoever dropped them there feared the monogram would identify them. Your charming Edwin Ryder had the watch. Just as he had your mules. How did you not recognize them?

And why do you think he fought so hard to keep you? He probably suspected you knew what he'd done." Towan half laughed. "Seems he gave you too much credit."

"I did recognize the mules." Her voice barely rose to a whisper.

He cocked a brow and then dropped back onto his bed. "Then what are you asking me?"

She hardly knew anymore. Christina wrapped her husband's timepiece in one hand while her other released the knife.

My husband?

Anthony was gone and today she had taken upon herself another man's name. Towan…O'Connell? She'd only gone through with the marriage to remain under his protection, and she was not the first woman to do so. Who did that make her? Christina O'Connell? Mrs. Towan O'Connell? Or was it Mrs. William O'Connell?

Her mind continued forward on the same route, pushing Towan's question aside with any suspicion she'd had about him. What sort of marriage was this? How binding? Would she be able to leave Towan in the spring and go back to her life in Cincinnati but as a young widow? Or would she have to forgo future callers due to her marital status? So much she hadn't considered. It happened too quickly and had been too vital. Now that survival was secured, their marriage loomed over her just as Towan had, his eyes filled with desire.

Towan's eyes were closed now and his breathing even, but he hadn't yet succumbed to sleep. He probably pondered the same questions, though from a different angle. Perhaps he wondered how he'd survive a woman who believed him to be a murderer.

Or what he, a young, attractive man had been thinking in securing a wife who would never be a wife when he could have had his pick of any maiden in this valley? Any maiden west of the Great Plains probably.

Rolling over, Christina tried to empty her mind—or at least turn it to pleasanter thoughts—but Towan and the passion with which he had said his vows refused to be set aside. She couldn't hope to understand the words, but she didn't doubt that he meant them. She couldn't doubt that he…loved her? Is that why he had come after her, risking his life to save her from Edwin, and fighting his cousin to keep her from a life that would have crushed her?

And she could give him nothing in return. No devotion. No marriage. No love.

"I'm sorry." Her voice sounded strange drifting across the distance between them, perforating the silence of night. "I was just so surprised to find my husban—Anthony's watch. What now?"

"I will keep my promise." Towan's tone was low and tired. "Until you leave."

Strange that nothing had really changed in his promise to her since she'd arrived. He would protect her and return her to her people in the spring. Yet now, leaving him seemed more like betrayal.

~*~

Tension radiated up his spine, neck, and through his head which throbbed. Towan massaged his temples, tempted to sleep for the rest of the day. No one in the village expected to see him. The mewling of an infant dragged him onto his elbows. Christina still slept, turned away, but William looked quite ready to greet the morning.

Keeping his movements hushed, Towan scooped the baby and returned to his side of the wickiup. He couldn't help but smile at the small face staring back at him with large blue eyes and o-shaped mouth. "Shall we let your mother rest a little longer?" Christina probably hadn't gotten any more sleep than he.

At the rumble of his voice, William's mouth stretched into an open-mouthed smile. Warmth expanded through Towan and his own smile grew. "Look at you." He touched his finger to the tip of the baby's nose. A squeak sounded from William.

"Is that so? Do tell me more."

Christina sighed as she rolled onto her back, waking.

Towan ignored her but switched to his mother's language. "You are growing fast, little warrior."

William cooed as though to agree. Again a smile flickered across his face.

"Is he smiling at you?" Christina said with marked surprise, despite the weariness lacing her voice.

Towan kept his focus on the child. "He seems to be a good judge of character."

"He hasn't smiled for me yet." Her tone belied her disappointment.

The urge to comment perched on the tip of Towan's tongue. He'd hold it but no more catering to her every need. For the next few months this was his family, and he was the man. "Come get him."

He tried not to take too much pleasure in the extended moan as she pushed herself up. Red lines on her cheek showed the texture of the sleeve she'd rested her head over. Otherwise her face was almost ashen white, and she appeared half dead from lack of sleep.

She collected William and dragged herself back to her bed, flopping down.

Towan reached for his sheath. "I'll be back in shortly with some venison for you to cook for…where is my knife?"

Another feminine groan extended itself across the wickiup. "Here it is." Christina withdrew it from under her covers and let it dangle between two fingers.

He opened his mouth to question but thought better of it. Easy enough to guess her intentions.

With the knife again fastened to his thigh, Towan wandered toward the grove where he had hung his deer almost a week earlier. Thankfully the temperature had stayed cold, and he'd taken the hide off before he'd gone after Christina or the meat might have spoiled. As it was, the time spent hanging would only make the flesh more tender.

Towan untied the cord and lowered the deer within reach. Already much of the venison had been cut away by others of his family, but another deer already hung nearby ready for use once the first was used.

Keeping his face passive, Towan returned to the wickiup with a chunk of meat on the tip of his knife. He slapped it down on the stone his mother used for preparing food, before glancing to Christina where she discreetly nursed William. "I'm hungry."

She narrowed her eyes at him. "What?"

He seated himself across from her and folded his arms over his chest. "I am hungry."

Christina looked from him to the slab of meat. "Why don't you cook it, then?"

"I hunt it, you cook it…wife."

Her eyes grew round. As did her mouth. She

clamped it shut and offered a coy smile—if it could be called a smile. "Of course."

Not budging from his place or pose, Towan watched as she finished feeding William and laid him down. The babe kicked his legs and waved his arms happily as though anticipating what was about to take place. Kneeling at the fire, Christina glanced around for what was available to her. She chose his mother's cherry-wood spit, braced the raw meat with the tip of one finger, and speared it through. She set it over the fire and sent him a triumphant glance, but it was all he could do not to grimace as the flames lapped all too close to the cold meat.

Though she disguised it well, her triumph gradually transformed to frustration. She yanked the meat from the reach of the fire and thrust it toward him still on the spit. With a carefully cocked eyebrow, Towan accepted her offering and his knife, which he had since cleaned. He sliced into the venison—through the charred crust to the juicy center, red and bleeding. He bit into the meat, gnawing it down, before extended a piece to her.

Christina wrinkled her nose at him. "I'm not hungry," she mumbled in her retreat.

"You're sure? Its flavor is most unique. Something I don't taste often."

"I can cook," she shot back at him.

He withheld his doubts.

"Just not like this. I need a pan or pot or something besides a stick and a rock. How primitive can a people be?"

"Primitive?" He glared at the back of her head for all the good it would do.

Christina spun to him. "Look around you, Towan,

or William, or whoever you are. Don't tell me you don't miss living in a solid house with four walls and a roof. And a floor made out of something besides dirt. Don't you miss sleeping on a real bed, a stuffed mattress with downy quilts and pillows? What about a table and chairs to sit on? Carriages. Mercantiles with everything you could possibly want waiting for you on a shelf. A different suit of clothes for every day of the week, so you don't have to wear the same one until it wears off of you. How can you not miss any of that?"

Towan jerked forward, pushing the meat off the spit until it fell into the heart of the fire. "I'll tell you what I don't miss. I don't miss being trash to be walked over. I don't miss mercantile proprietors who won't serve me, or the insults spewed against my mother, or the saloons and taverns poisoning men and stealing what should have been used to provide for their families. What good is a house if it is never a home? What use is a chair shattered in a fit of rage against the solid wall you so highly praise?"

Winded, Towan sank back and folded his arms. He wanted nothing more than to escape her studious gaze, but undoubtedly everyone had already heard their raised voices, and seeing him make an escape would only convince them he'd lost the argument. Not the image he wanted as a new husband no matter how torturous remaining proved.

"I'm sorry." Christina's face softened and moisture pooled over her dark brown irises. "I'm sorry you had such a miserable youth, and that your father was not a good man. I can only imagine how cruel some people can be…but not everyone is like that. There are kind people, too." Her shoulders trembled as the first tear formed at the corner of her eye then slid free, a single trail down her cheek. "I still miss my home. I miss everything and everyone."

Of course she did. She was one of them.

Christina reclined onto one elbow facing William, and played with his tiny fingers. Other than random squeaks and grunts from the baby and the external commotion of the village, silence settled into the wickiup.

Towan reached for the Bible and flipped open to the Gospel according to Mark. The feather now marked where he'd read last. Probably the best way to pass the long hours ahead of them. He'd only read half a page before Christina interrupted.

"If you hate everything about your life in Missouri, everything about white men and their society, what is your fascination with that book?"

A laugh tugged at the back of his throat. No, that probably didn't make sense to her. It didn't always make sense to him either, but… "It's true."

"So you believe in the *white man's* God?"

Towan closed the book. "There is only one God. Only understanding of Him differs. Knowledge about Him. Where knowledge lacks, men form opinions, some true, some false. I believe the Bible contains a near personal account of God's works, yes."

Her focus remained on William, his hand gripping her finger, her thumb smoothing over his dimpled knuckles.

"And maybe you're right."

Christina glanced to him and he tried to smile. His success was minimal.

"I do miss one thing."

"Books?" Her eyes twinkled.

He nodded. "I had a teacher—the kindest woman I

have known—who seemed to understand how much I didn't want to be there. So she showed me how to escape." He lifted the Bible. "And Who to take with me." Towan sat silently.

Christina regarded him, her expression studious, as though she still sought to discern what sort of man he was.

He hardly knew himself.

19

Christina swallowed down the last bite of her dinner. Still a little pinker in the center than she liked, but at least the outside wasn't black this time…too black, that is.

Towan finished off his as well and nodded.

She would take the gesture as praise. Loading the flat stone with the knife she had used, a wooden spoon and the spit, Christina motioned to William's sleeping form. "Can you watch him while I clean these in the snow?"

Towan reached for the Bible and nodded again.

"Thank you."

A fresh blanket of white lay over the dirtied snow that had all but melted away. That made it easier to find a clean place to do her scrubbing. She filled her lungs. What a lovely day. Taking her time, she meandered toward the river and the thicker evergreen foliage. A little freedom. A little seclusion. Only a week since the wedding, she still garnered looks from everyone she passed. Especially the younger women. Undoubtedly, they hadn't liked their two most eligible bachelors fighting over her.

Kneeling under the broad expanse of branches, Christina dropped her load to the ground and pressed handfuls of snow over the smooth surfaces. Not too different from washing dishes in the streams passed on the Oregon Trail. Only the dishes had changed.

A twig snapped nearby, and Christina scanned the area, her hand frozen around a ball of melting ice crystals. Her palm tingled from the cold, but she could see nothing, the village mostly blocked from view by a scattering of evergreens. Snow crunched. Footsteps. Someone was headed in her direction. Droplets of water ran down her arm.

Towan stepped through the branches and tried to dodge a ball of ice. It smacked his shoulder before Christina realized the ball had left her hand.

"What did I do to deserve that?"

She held her hands up to him. "I am so sorry."

He raised an eyebrow. "Are you?"

A chuckle could not be held in. "Maybe not. You left Will alone?"

"My mother came after you left." Towan glanced around casually as he spoke. "She's sitting with him." His arm brushed over the expanse of a low-hanging fir branch, powdering her with snow.

Christina yelped and spun away. With the motion, she crouched and grabbed another handful to hurdle at him. He anticipated the move. His snowball caught her chest as she turned back. Hers barely skimmed his head, still wearing the thin bandage—she should probably aim better to avoid his injuries.

He reached for more.

Scuttling under a branch, she tried to run but didn't make it four feet before two strong arms swept her off the ground. They spun as they fell, his motion positioning him under her as they thudded against the ground. Before she had a chance to move, he rolled, dragging her under him.

"No!" Christina grabbed at the cold white crystals beside her, but his hand was already full. He abandoned his attack to catch her arms and force them back down. The snow he dropped fell across her neck with its icy chill. She squealed and tried to wrestle free. Her own laughter did nothing to help.

Towan held her in place with a thinly masked grin. "Are you finished?"

"Yes. Just let me back to my feet."

He stood and pulled her up after him but didn't release her wrists. "You're sure?"

Frigid droplets trickled down her collar. She shivered more from the tickling sensation than the cold. Or maybe it was the intensity hidden within his gaze. "Yes." She pulled free.

Chuckling, Towan brushed his fingertips across her throat, removing the flakes that hadn't yet melted. She feigned a glare.

"I only defended myself."

Christina folded her arms across her abdomen. "It seems to me you enjoyed your defense all too much."

The corners of his mouth curled up. "I am unable to deny that." As the smile lit his eyes, something fluttered in her stomach.

Ignoring the sensation, Christina scowled one last time and turned away. There was only so long she could hold her own smile at bay. "I should finish up and get back to Will."

Towan followed.

"I take it this wasn't your first snowball fight. You probably got plenty of practice growing up with the other boys your age."

A grunt signified she'd trespassed unwanted memories. "Let's just say, I learned to defend myself."

Christina glanced at his stone expression. When she'd asked the question, she'd pictured him tussling in the snow with other young children, like Havne or even Tucwatse. But that hadn't been his life. "Your childhood wasn't very pleasant at all, was it?"

His mouth twitched downward. "Not one I'd wish on anyone."

A lonesome smile tugged at her own lips. "I wish you could have had one like mine. It's strange to look back, but a year ago I'd been so certain growing up had been simply awful. I was so focused on everything that didn't go the way I'd wanted. How protective and…smothering my parents had been. How jealous I was of my sisters." She raised one shoulder. "And now, all I can think is how blessed I was to be so loved and shielded."

One glance at the cloud in Towan's eyes and Christina regretted her words. "I don't mean to sound as though I'm better or more deserving than you. I am just so much more aware now of how grateful I should be. That is the life I want William to have. In Ohio with my parents. He'll grow up embraced by society and educated to be a fine gentleman. Though…" *Though, I would be a very proud mother if my boy grew up to be half as good a man as you.* The words climbed to the tip of her tongue, wanting to be said. Towan deserved to hear them.

"I have some things I need to take care of." He stepped back. "I'll return before dark."

"Towan…"

He turned and walked away.

~*~

Towan's mother had left by the time he returned to the wickiup, and Christina had his supper waiting. Camas and venison or rabbit stew—one of her staples. She said nothing as he lowered the short fir tree, about the length of his arm and with all its branches attached. He wasn't done yet. When he'd first left her, he'd been upset. Her words had cut; though it was understandable that she wanted her son to be everything he wasn't and have everything he hadn't. *Embraced by society.* His name sake would have no difficulty with that. Both his parents were white.

But Towan couldn't take his hurt out on the baby or Christina. He thought about everything she wanted for her son and couldn't blame her in the least. And then he started calculating.

Against his will, he'd put some thought into this.

Near the wall, but far enough out that there would be room to stand up the miniature tree, Towan took his knife and carved a small hole in the packed earth. He planted the trunk, and then sat back to eat Christina's offering. She eyed his gift, but she'd have to wait a little longer.

After setting his dish aside, Towan extended his arms toward little William. "Can I see him?"

A toothless smile greeted Towan as Christina passed him the baby. She shook her head. "He's always so happy to see you. I must admit to being jealous."

Towan fought to keep his mouth a straight line. "You wish you were happier to see me?"

"Precisely." She chuckled.

"You'll have to strive a little harder." He turned

his attention to the bundle in his hands. "But in the meanwhile, winter is a time for the telling and retelling of stories to pass the hours and teach children the legends of our people."

"Don't you think he's a mite young?"

"The story I have to tell carries great importance."

Christina settled back, raised brows suggesting curiosity.

Little William stared with his usual wide eyes. Towan's chest tightened. Christina was right. This boy deserved more than he could ever offer.

He cleared his throat. "Many years past, a maiden, pure and fair, was visited by a messenger from the heavens. The messenger praised her virtue and told her of the great plans God had for her. Though a maiden, she would bare a son, even the Son of—"

"The story of Christ's birth?" Christina glanced between him and the pitiable fir. "Is this supposed to be Christmas?" Panic lit her eyes. "Is it Christmastime?"

"Give or take a few days." But as near as he could estimate. "I didn't think you'd want Will to miss his first Christmas."

She blinked rapidly as her gaze turned steady on the tree. "Christmas?"

"Is something wrong?"

"Everything. I'm not ready for it to be Christmas." She continued to stare at the tree.

"What's there to be ready for?" He'd already provided as much as he'd ever had.

Maybe that was the problem. How much grander her Christmas celebrations must have been. Fancy decorations. Parties. Feasts…gifts.

Tucking little William in the crook of his arm,

Towan grabbed the tree out of the ground and moved to the doorway.

"What are you doing?"

"Getting rid of it."

"Don't do that." She took the small fir from him, plopped it back in its hole and packed the earth around to support it. "I'm sorry if I appear ungrateful. You caught me by surprise. It probably sounds strange, but my favorite part of Christmas has always been anticipating its arrival."

It did seem strange, but maybe only because he'd given up anticipation a long time ago. Anticipation only brought disappointment.

"I can't help but think of what my family is doing right now," she continued. "This is the first Christmas I've been away from them. And then to realize that it has almost come and gone without my knowledge..." She shrugged as they settled back down across from each other. "Lillian, my sister, is supposed to be home from Europe by now. And my brother will probably be there as well. Laughter. Sweets. Carolers." A sigh escaped. "This is not how I pictured Christmas. Anthony and I were supposed to have a little house or cabin in Oregon. We'd sit near the fireplace and sing carols." She smoothed the tips of her fingers under her eyes, catching the tears before they fell. "He had a wonderful voice. He'd sometimes sing while driving the wagon." Sadness lingered on her face.

Towan attempted to keep his own from deepening his frown. Holding his expression neutral did nothing to decrease the sourness sitting heavy in the pit of his stomach. How pathetic could he be? He was jealous of his wife's affection for a dead man.

She's not your wife. He had to stop thinking of her

in that regard.

"Do you know any carols?"

Towan sat little William on his knee, bracing his body upright. "No." Though he'd been taught Christmas songs in school, he doubted he could remember the words if he tried.

"That's all right. I'm not much in the mood for singing." She laid her head down but kept looking at the tree.

No longer in the mood for telling stories, Towan pulled out the Bible. He'd read it, instead—to himself. The baby wouldn't get anything out of it yet, and Christina…looked content to be left to herself. He opened to Luke. Might as well start at the beginning with the angel Gabriel coming to Mary.

"Why are you so good to me?" Christina's tone held both questioning and weariness. "How many times have you saved my life? You've supplied for my every need. And still more." She waved toward the tree. "You didn't have to do this. So why did you? What do you get out of it?"

Lowering the book in one hand, Towan brought little William closer with the other. There was something about the little fellow. Maybe because he'd been the first one to hold the baby. Maybe it was watching him grow, and giving everything to keep him safe. Towan couldn't imagine loving his own child any deeper. Christina's question taunted him. There were too many answers. But one stood out among the rest. The deep-down, honest motivation for everything he did. "I don't want to be my father."

"Your father? William O'Connell?"

Towan nodded but kept his focus on the baby propped against him. "He took my mother to Missouri shortly after I was born. Built us a small cabin on the outskirts of Independence. He'd stay for a while and then be gone for months, sometimes years. When he was around…he spent a lot of time at the saloons. And he had a short temper."

More than ever before, Towan couldn't understand his father's frequent anger against him. He stared down at the dark fuzz crowning little William's small head. How could a man bring himself to hurt his own child? Purposefully. Cruelly. Unless that man absolutely despised the creature he had created.

Of course, it had been different after Matthew was born. For a short while. "I don't want to be the sort of man who would walk away from a woman and child."

"You needn't worry," Christina whispered. "I don't know your father, but you are nothing like the man I've heard him to be. You are the kindest, noblest…you are one of the best men I've ever known."

Towan gritted his teeth. He didn't want her to see how much her praise affected him or meant to him. He'd already opened up enough to her. Already given too much of himself. He already felt no hope of walking away from her in the spring unscarred.

20

"My son good husband."

Christina tucked William's small foot in her hand and slipped the damp cloth between his toes. Guilt spiked through her. She had no doubt that Towan would be—was—a good husband. But she was hardly the wife a mother would wish upon her son. Though Quaritz hadn't spoken a word last night, her eyes had demanded why Towan moved to his separate bed. She no doubt wondered why they remained apart after three weeks of marriage, maybe realizing that he had forfeited his rights as a husband. Christina's face heated. "Yes. He is."

"You care for my son?"

As a protector? A friend? "Yes." But that changed nothing. She didn't love him. And she wasn't about to stay out here in these mountains.

Christina sat William up, bracing him with one hand while the other wiped the cloth under his chin. Chins. With his head constantly tipped to his chest, it was hard to tell that his neck even existed. A throaty giggle sounded as he scrunched his shoulders to his ears. The new laugh so infectious, Christina smiled and wiped his chin again. Same reaction, his mouth wide. Dimples showed. She chuckled, for a moment pushing thoughts of marriage and mothers-in-law aside.

Then Towan entered. He set an armful of sticks next to the fire pit.

Christina waved him over. "You may have gotten his first smile, but listen…" She stroked the baby's neck, but he only squirmed.

Towan nodded.

"Last time he laughed."

"Oh?" He traced the tip of his finger under William's chin and then down his bare chest to his belly. An airy laugh erupted from the baby. "Like that?"

Christina elbowed him out of the way and picked up William. "You can go back to what you were doing."

Towan chuckled as he withdrew. "It's warmer today. When you get him settled, you should go out. The sun will do you good. And you must strengthen your legs. You will become weak sitting here as much as you do."

Christina ignored him, swaddling William. Thankfully, Towan left as quickly as he'd come.

Quaritz stayed but worked silently.

As soon as William drifted asleep, Christina pulled on her moccasins. "Towan's right. I should stretch my legs…if you are all right keeping an eye on Will."

Quaritz waved her away. "You go."

"Thank you." Christina made a quick getaway. Now that they again shared the small hut with Towan's mother, she'd probably spend a lot more time out of…doors? Outside. Hadn't Towan informed his mother of their arrangement—that theirs wasn't a real marriage? How long did he plan to keep it from her?

Despite the chill of the January day, rays of noonday sun heated Christina's head and back as she tromped toward the river. For some reason she always found herself drawn toward its frozen banks. Maybe because it reminded her of the Ohio River. A little. This river was quite a lot smaller and not snugged up against a bustling city.

Pausing at the river's edge, Christina looked out over the ice's sheen. The warmth of the last few days had melted the layer of snow, but should have had no effect on the thickness of the ice. It would probably be safe enough.

Christina stepped onto the river and her foot slid from under her. She yelped. The smooth sole of her moccasins gave little friction against the sheer ice. Her arms shot out, but she maintained her balance. She wet her lips and pushed away from the bank. She glided along the edge of the river, sometimes almost falling, but smiling the whole while. It had been too long since she'd gone skating with her siblings, a favorite winter activity before everyone else had become too busy with their own lives. Courting, marriage, politics, society…one by one her brother and then sisters had filed off to live their dreams, leaving her.

Until Anthony stepped in and shared his dream and his desire for adventure.

Now he was gone, taking all that with him.

She just wanted to go home. She'd figure out her life from there.

Boyish laughter assailed her from the ridge.

Christina whirled around. Towan stood half concealed by a leafless brush with two young boys, the ones she'd watched him wrestle. In the instant of taking her mind off her feet, they continued on without her. She dropped. Her right hip and palm took the brunt of the impact.

"Umph." Her whole body jarred.

She'd clambered to her feet and was brushing off her backside by the time Towan reached her. He braced her elbow. "Are you hurt?"

"No, I'm fine." Her hip throbbed, but there was nothing he could do about that. Her palm, however, stung from its icy excursion. Christina laid it across his neck, smiling as he flinched away.

"You're freezing."

"Just my hand."

He cupped it between his hands and breathed into the cocoon he'd formed. The warmth seemed to extend through her whole body, and she turned her attention to the boys as they chased each other onto the ice. Towan called to them in Shoshone and then looked back to her. "It's safe enough here, but the water underneath is always flowing so it's hard to judge the depth of the ice farther out."

"I imagine so. The Ohio River never really freezes over where I grew up. I've been told it has, but I've never seen it." She glanced to her hand still in his embrace and slowly withdrew it. "I should probably start back."

He released her and stepped away.

Christina moved past, half slipping as she maneuvered around a protruding rock. He again gripped her arm, and her face flamed. "Thank you. It's because the ice is slippery, not because my legs are weak."

Towan steadied her and walked with her up the slope. She didn't need him, but appreciated the gesture.

Behind them the boys shouted at each other. The younger had fallen on his back and scrambled to get out of the way as the larger boy assailed him with a shower of snow.

"What is *Tackavit*?" If she was stuck here, maybe it was time she started learning their language.

"*Tuckavit*," he corrected. "It is snow."

She repeated it a few times as they continued walking.

Towan relaxed his hold as the terrain flattened, and they moved under a canopy of naked branches.

"Willow?"

"*Sheherbit*."

Christina recognized that one. "Like the girl's name?"

He nodded. "Havne and Tucwatse's sister."

"All your names mean something?"

"Of course." Towan chuckled. "As I understand it, most names in most languages have meaning."

Christina held back from the urge to nudge him with her shoulder as she would her brother. She'd like him a lot better if he wasn't so well-read and didn't know everything. No. She liked him just the way he was. A most peculiar mix of the Rocky Mountains and civilization. As refined as any gentlemen, yet as wild as nature itself. He was a living, breathing, walking paradox.

"What does your name mean?" she asked as he followed her into the hut.

"*Towan* is fox."

"Dark," his mother added from where she knelt grinding pine nuts to powder. "Black fox. His father was hunter of black fox when I find him. Fox bring us blessing and happiness. When son born we call two name. Towan and—"

A quick word from Towan, and Quaritz gave an understanding nod. Christina looked between the two. Strange how Quaritz could talk of William O'Connell with none of the animosity Towan apparently felt. Why hide from her what she already knew? "You named him Towan William O'Connell?"

Quaritz appeared surprised. "William after his father." She seemed to sigh as she looked to her son who sat and reached for his Bible.

Christina recognized it as his way of detaching himself, pretending not to care. She had stopped thinking of the book as Anthony's. It was now Towan's. She would leave it with him in the spring.

~*~

Towan could feel the intensity of his mother's gaze from the instant Christina stepped out of the wickiup to refill the clay pot with water. He tried to keep reading, but the black marks on the page refused to form words. He blew the remaining air from his lungs and looked at her.

His mother shook her head at him.

"Should I have let Tucwatse have her? Or left her to those white men?"

"Your marriage to her does not make me unhappy."

But she was unhappy. Why then?

Little William grunted, announcing his wakefulness, and Towan set the book aside. Small arms flailed, already free of the blanket. Taking his little hands in his, Towan guided him upward. His neck held up his head and his legs straightened, supporting the weight of his body. Towan felt the smile stretch across his face. He was a strong little man, his tiny namesake. Towan could no longer hate that name as he once had—only the man who had given it to him.

"Come on." Towan picked up little William. He nestled the baby into his chest as he sat back down. William gurgled and tried to wedge his fists in his mouth, which was fine as soon as Towan removed his hair from one of the tight fists. He looked up to see his mother still watching. This time sorrow puckered her brow.

"She is not a weak woman," his mother said. "Only young. She would make you a good wife."

"I have to take her back to her people in the spring." Towan had to find a way to make his mother understand that their union was only temporary.

"Perhaps you return with her."

His jaw stiffened, making it difficult to reply. "I do not belong among them."

"She is your wife."

"She is not my wife!" He sat back and pressed his fingers over his temples and the pressure building between them. "She's not my wife."

"But you love her…and the boy. And she cares for you."

He could only shake his head. Christina had no room in her heart for him. She loved her dead husband and the life she'd left behind in Ohio.

His mother reached into her neckline and withdrew a small leather pouch—the one that held two hairs bound together.

"I'm not what she needs, Moqone," he moaned. Or

what she wanted.

His mother returned to grinding, now dried berries between her stones. Towan pressed his mouth to the top of little William's head. His chest felt as if someone chiseled away at it, hollowing it out. The winter was half over. Only a few more months.

The scraping of rock on rock paused. "I do not believe your father sought to bring you pain."

"And what about you? Did he not mean to hurt you or abandon you?" Towan tried to swallow the burning in the back of his throat, but the sourness remained. "Of course he meant it. He drank on purpose, he hurt us on purpose, and he left on purpose. And he never returned because he didn't want to. Six years, Moqone. We waited six years." And they would still be waiting if he hadn't convinced her to give up and return to her family.

It was probably for the best Matthew hadn't lived. How long before their father tired of his second son, too?

~*~

Christina lingered outside the hut until the voices quieted. Though the words were foreign, the emotions spoke clearly. A mother concerned for her son, and a man…

Towan's feelings were harder to recognize. A lot of anger. Hate. But mostly he sounded weary. The kind of weariness that even sleeping a month of Sundays wouldn't cure.

And she was probably the cause of it all.

Christina lowered the water pot to the ground and started back toward the river. She couldn't hear

William, so she wouldn't be needed. Of course, that baby was the only one who needed her. She was a thorn in the side of everyone else.

Looking out over the frozen waters and the forests rising up from the opposite slope, Christina stiffened her spine. Most likely about the middle of January. In another three or four months, she could leave. She'd return home, and Towan could go back to living his own life. Until then she'd try to stay out of his way, try not to need anything from him. She'd keep her distance. As much distance as could be maintained in a small hut.

21

William's pudgy hands grabbed at his legs, pulling his bare toes to his mouth. Christina slipped a clean napkin under him then fought against the child's desire to play with his feet so she could fasten the diaper. He'd grown so much in the last two months and was now so different from the tiny infant Towan had handed her that first day in the cave. Five months? Some days it felt much shorter than that, while at other times meeting Towan and giving birth to William seemed an eternity ago.

Christina swaddled the child and tied him into the new cradleboard. He'd completely outgrown the one Towan had made. The not-fully-cured hide had grown brittle and William was no longer a light load. Not in the slightest. All the more reason for today's excursion. In another month they would start for Fort Bridger, and there was no way she'd be able to tote her child through the mountains if she didn't strengthen both her legs and back.

With William loaded, she headed toward where Quaritz stood speaking with a group of other women. Christina remained outside the circle, close enough that she would be seen, far enough back not to intrude. She didn't understand very much of their conversation anyway. Just bits and pieces, words and phrases she'd learned. While she waited, Christina glanced around for Towan. She hadn't seen him since first thing that morning, and he hadn't said where he was going. He was gone a lot now that the weather turned warmer and food grew scarcer…and she kind of missed him.

Christina forced her gaze off the distant slopes and repositioned one of the straps over her shoulders. The truth be admitted, she missed him more than she intended. She missed the long winter days and the stories he told—both from the legends of his people and the novels he'd read. She missed the sound of his voice as he read aloud from the Bible, upon her request. She missed his overall presence. And that's why his absence was for the best. She'd grown too dependent on him for too much. The time had come to stand on her own feet.

The chatter never ceasing, the women started toward the river. Two carried babies, while several others propped toddlers on their hips. Older children ran on ahead, their laughter leading the way. A couple of women granted Christina welcoming smiles, and one grandmother gently touched her elbow as they moved past. She followed. If only she could be more like these women. They worked hard to feed their families and raise their children in this wilderness. Everything they had, from the garments they wore, the shoes on their feet, the dishes they used, to the huts sheltering their heads were the genius of their hands. A tight-knit family and community who strived together for the benefit of all.

Each woman carried leather sacks or woven

baskets. They walked along the river until they came to an especially narrow section where two pines extended between the two banks. The first log was still attached to the stump from which it had broken, while the second was smaller and appeared to have been dragged there to form a more secure bridge. The branches along the top side had been hacked off so to not impede passage.

Christina looked down at the ice below them, shining with moisture as the sun worked to melt it away. It still seemed solid enough, but no doubt very slippery. Soon the ice would break up and the river would run. Already the warmth of approaching spring had stolen the snow from everywhere the sun's rays could reach. Only the shadows and higher slopes clung to winter.

On the far side of the river, the women fanned out, already busy scrounging for dried berries and pinecones. The cones they either dropped into their baskets or pounded on rocks to loosen the seeds. These they dusted into pouches. Christina stooped and picked up a pinecone only to drop it back to the ground. A rodent had already beaten her to the nuts. She really wouldn't be much help to Quaritz and might as well keep out of the way.

Staying close to the river so she wouldn't get lost, Christina picked her way upstream. Her legs burned from the extra weight on her back. Either her muscles had lost all the strength she'd gained crossing the plains last summer, or William was simply getting too heavy. Judging from the ache extended across both shoulders, she could place the blame easily on her child's hearty appetite.

The visiting and laughter faded, and Christina

slowed her pace. The scent of mildewing leaves and grasses wafted on a light breeze with hints of pine sap. She was beginning to love the smell of pine. Maybe that's why she always welcomed Towan's presence. Being near him was like a summer's walk through a forest. She closed her eyes and deepened her breath. Towan's face filled her mind.

With a huff, Christina forced her eyelids open and thoughts from Towan. She needed to start thinking about going home to Cincinnati, seeing her parents again. And her siblings. Maybe after she was settled, she'd take a trip to Tennessee and visit her nieces and nephews. It had been far too long since—

Branches rustled and a twig snapped. The huffing of heavy breath rose between thick evergreen foliage.

Christina's feet shuffled to a stop as she pivoted and peered into the shadows.

A dark form moved. The breathing deepened into a grunt. Large eyes glowed from the shadows.

She stepped back, her legs faltering as they struggled to heed her head's commands.

Run.

Instead she stared. Bears weren't supposed to be awake during the winter.

The lumbering animal, its coat tawny with shades of ground cinnamon, bore the fact that spring had indeed arrived. His nose wiggled as he raised his head to look at her. His skin hung loosely, testifying to the fact he'd only just awakened from long months of fasting.

Christina couldn't make herself look away. Or turn, putting William between them. She would do anything to keep her baby safe.

Another step back as the bear circled to her right,

blocking her from her path of retreat. Was that the animal's plan? Maybe he'd patiently waited there for someone to cross into his trap.

She would have expected her heart to race, but instead it sat quiet in her chest as did her breath. The river lay behind her, but the ice was still firm. Surely it would hold her.

One step after another, Christina backed away over the shimmering surface, her hands outstretched in case she should slip. The bear stood on the shore, watching her withdrawal. He didn't follow.

A groan stretched itself across the ice, and Christina's gaze dropped. No cracks. She'd be fine. The ice was thick enough. It had to be.

Two more steps. Then a third. A light popping announced hairline cracks. Her lungs refused more air as she crouched. She would crawl if she had to. Christina's hands hadn't yet touched the ice when her feet plunged into the river below.

Her stomach plowed into the edge of the ice, knocking any remaining breath from her. Pain burned through her center. She clawed at the slick surface, the only thing keeping her and William from being sucked under by the swift current. The water's frigid arms wrapped around her, dragging her downwards.

"Help!" The cry clung to her throat. Her screams seemed to dissipate on the breeze with nothing to propel them farther. Millions of icy needles prickled her legs. The surface under her torso began to sag, sinking her body into the river.

William's wails rang in her ears.

"Oh, God, help me!"

There had to be a way to get him off—to keep him safe. She reached for the leather that bound him and slipped farther. She gasped for breath as the water crawled up her body. Her vision blurred. She couldn't save her baby any more than she could save herself.

Please, Lord.

A shadow waved across the ice, and Christina raised her gaze. Quaritz scrambled toward her. The ice moaned like an old man, and something within Christina shouted at her to warn the older woman back, but she couldn't. Quaritz was their only hope. She couldn't let William die. Not her baby.

Quaritz flattened herself to the ice and half crawled, half slid the last few feet to Christina's outstretched arms. Their fingers brushed and then clutched.

It sounded as though pebbles danced against hollow wood.

"Your feet," Quaritz shouted at her.

My feet? Christina kicked, surprised she could still command them. Her legs felt stiff and slow, but they pushed her forward as Quaritz dragged her out of the rushing water.

The ice creaked.

"There. Go." Quaritz motioned to the far side of the river.

Christina looked up to where Towan raced down the bank and onto the ice. It seemed strange that both shores were now equally close. Had she really come out so far? She crawled toward him, wanting to join her baby in his bawling. They were safe. Everything would be all right. If only that infernal popping would stop. But for some reason it only deepened.

Towan slid to a stop.

Why?

Christina looked down at the ice under her red

hands. Cracks. Everywhere, cracks. Again her instincts screamed at her to stand and run, but that would only make the ice break apart faster. She lowered her body against the sleek surface and looked to Towan, who already reversed his course.

"Keep coming." He nodded at her, though the panic in his eyes did little to comfort.

Christina kept her eyes on him even as more men gathered behind him. All she had to do was make it to him, and she'd be safe.

A cry pierced through William's bawling and the rush of the river behind her.

Towan jerked forward. But the cry hadn't come from him.

She glanced back as Quaritz vanished.

~*~

No! Towan watched helpless as the ice holding his mother crumbled into the growing gap of swirling water. For a second she dropped out of sight, but her head quickly reappeared just before she would have been swept under the ice and down river. Her arms flailed until they found the solid ice, but that side of the hole showed cracks as well.

They had to find a way to get her out before she lost strength or the ice gave way, but not until Christina and William were out of danger. They only put more stress on the ice.

"Don't stop," he yelled at her, and then spun to the other men with him. Only a couple stared at the two women on the river. Most were busy scrounging for long branches or anything that could help them reach his mother without risking the ice and more lives. One man raced down to Towan with a coiled cord. Tucwatse. He had a loop tied before he reached Towan. As Towan took it there was only time for a brief nod to express his gratitude.

As soon as someone had Christina, Towan started out. He slipped the loop around his neck and shoulder then made a similar one with the other end. Lowering to his knees, he crawled to the edge of the secure ice where the cracks began to show.

Tucwatse paused a short distance behind.

"Moqone."

She met his gaze.

"Grab this." He tossed the loop and it landed only inches from the tips of her fingers. Her hands slid toward it. And the ice began to give way. Her arms shot out, seeking something solid to hold.

Tucwatse grabbed the rope.

Towan glanced at him as he scrambled to bring the rope in so they could throw it again, but it was too late. He looked back in time to see more ice break away. There was nothing left for her to hold. She was going under.

The rope tightened around his shoulder as he sprinted across the shattering ice and dove in after her. The water hit him like a boulder. Or a slab of ice. His lungs attempted to expand with a gasp, but he couldn't let them. Not until he reached the surface. Not until he had his mother.

22

Christina's heart froze as Towan plunged into the water, sending a spray into the air and over the ice.

Tucwatse flew off his feet onto his stomach as the rope went taut. The loop he held dragged him toward the ever growing hole, now several yards wide and just as long. Other men grabbed hold of Tucwatse. They laid themselves across the frozen surface as a human chain. Together they pulled, oh so slow, and drew the rope back.

With her hand clamped over her mouth, Christina held her breath and counted each second Towan remained submerged. The rope bit into the ice, cutting through it from the pressure dragging it down river. The current was too strong. Towan would be too heavy.

What if the jagged ice cut the rope?

He would die. A cold, suffocating death.

Christina stared at the scene and the world seemed to slow, suspending itself upon the realization that both Quaritz and Towan likely wouldn't survive this. Only God could save them. He'd answered her before, hadn't He?

"Lord, please bring Towan back. Keep that rope strong. Keep that rope strong. Keep that rope strong." *Don't take Towan from me, too.*

Everyone paused. Then the ice bent. The pressure of Towan's shoulder heaved it upward. Christina gasped for air as his head rose above the surface. He grabbed hold of the ice and heaved the upper half of Quaritz's body over the edge. Kicking his legs, he aligned his body so the rope would tow him out of the water, but as soon as his weight met the ice, it threatened to break apart.

Glancing around, Towan seemed to contemplate how to get his mother to safety if the ice wouldn't hold both of them. Quaritz didn't move from where he'd pushed her. Perhaps she was unconscious. Braced against the ice, Towan reached for the rope securing him.

Don't!

He pulled the loop off and hooked it under Quaritz's arms then nodded to Tucwatse. Towan clung to the ice as they pulled his mother to the shore. Again Christina held her breath, her mind chanting for them to hurry and throw the rope back to Towan before he was washed away forever.

As soon as the loop landed over his head and he wrapped his arm through it, Christina couldn't watch any more. Her whole body trembling, she fought to pull William from the cradleboard. She'd hardly been aware of his crying or the fact it hadn't ceased since she'd first fallen into the water. The poor child was frantic. But he was alive. And Towan was alive.

Thank you, Lord.

Tears blurred her vision and a sob escaped. She glanced back at Towan as they dragged him the last few feet to shore. His charcoal hair was plastered to his face, and his chest heaved as he gulped in air. Momentarily his gaze flickered to her. And then he rolled over and crawled to where his mother lay motionless, her face white, lips blue. They rolled Quaritz onto her stomach and water gushed from her mouth and nose.

Hands pulled Christina to her feet and she looked into the faces of women she knew. One took William from her arms and they led her slowly back to the village. To the hut. They lit a fire, and someone brought a dry dress that fit a little smaller than hers. Her wet clothing was removed and taken outside, probably to be hung. One of the older women tucked Christina into her bed, and then stayed to mind William and the fire while she rested and warmed.

Christina struggled to lay still. She continued to shiver a little, but the cold was not responsible for that. She jerked up as soon as Towan stumbled into the hut.

"Here." Christina led him to the furs and let him collapse. The older woman said something as she stepped out, taking William with her. A moment of panic at her baby being taken away was quickly replaced with common sense. William would be safe and watched over until he needed to be fed. They knew where to find her. Having him gone would free her to care for Towan whose body spasmed with shivers.

"I need to get you dry." She tugged on the ties binding his shirt to his wet skin. In the end it was easiest to pull it up over his head. Her gaze followed the contours of his chest and abdomen to his loincloth and leggings. Better to leave them be and get the covers over him. He helped her pull them across his trembling body. She brushed wet strands of hair from his face. "I'm so sorry. Is your mother…?"

"Sh—she is with—with my unc—le." He fought to control his shivering but without much success. "They will—ll try to help her—er."

Christina allowed her palm to linger on his cheek. "I didn't mean for this to happen. When I saw that bear… I was just trying to get away. I thought the ice would be stronger. I didn't think…" Again she'd only caused him pain. Quaritz might die because of her. He had almost lost his own life…yet again. "I'm sorry." What inadequate words.

Towan shook his head, and then gave into the tremors working their way through his body. She set more kindling on the fire. She needed to warm him quicker, without burning down the hut. The flames leapt high and a bead of sweat formed on her brow. Though her legs, now bare halfway up the thigh, still felt stiff, they weren't cold any longer, and the rest of her body was overheating. Especially her face. She had never been so undressed in the presence of anyone but her husband…but then, Towan was theoretically her husband now. And she could help him.

Heartbeat rapid, Christina stole under the deer hide covering him and moved close. Her hand, warm on his chilled skin, slid up his arm, and then hesitated as he looked at her.

"What are you doing?"

Pushing away the initial sensation of embarrassment, Christina encircled his body with her arms and pulled herself against his chest. "You're so cold." She nestled her head under his chin. That way she wouldn't have to see his face and try to read what he thought. She wanted to hear his heartbeat sounding out loud and clear. He was alive. That very fact was a gift from God.

Just as Towan was.

~*~

Towan could control his breathing, but there was no way to rein in the thundering in his chest over which Christina's ear rested. So long as she thought the pounding was because of the excursion of swimming upstream in icy water and not the feel of her body against his, her warmth seeping past the chill. He stared at the top of her head. His own seemed to spin. What was she doing? Other than twisting his insides inside out?

It couldn't last. Soon she would withdraw and take a part of him with her, but he was too tired to fight his need for her or her warmth. Towan let his arms encircle her in return. He closed his eyes. And prayed. Thanking God for getting her and little William safely off the ice. And for helping him save his mother.

He pled that she would recover.

Gradually the shivers subsided and the fire in the center of the wickiup died down, but Christina gave no indication of pulling away. In fact, it appeared she'd fallen sleep. Withdrawing her arms from behind him, Towan settled onto his back. Christina's head remained on his chest. He stroked her hair away from her flushed cheeks.

A familiar cry announced visitors, and Towan untangled himself from her and moved to the doorway just in time to take little William from his aunt's arms.

"He is hungry."

"How is my mother?"

"We wait." She frowned and shook her head, before turning away.

William squirmed in his arms but quieted as he ducked back into the wickiup. Christina hid a yawn and pushed herself up. "I'll take him. You lie back down."

"I'm fine." He handed her the baby and reached for his shirt she had laid out not far from the fire. Still damp, but warm. Towan pulled it over his head. "I need to be with my mother."

He walked to his uncle's wickiup, fatigue dragging his steps. The *bohogant* stepped out as he approached. Towan took hold of the medicine man's arm. He would know better than anyone how his mother fared and if there was anything more to be done. The man put his other arm around Towan's shoulders and directed him inside. "Sit with her."

Draped in furs, his mother lay motionless, her face still without color, her lips a pale shade of blue, her eyes closed. Others moved out of his way and he kneeled at her side. Her hand was no longer icy, but not warm, either. "Moqone?"

Nothing.

Not releasing her hand, Towan bowed his head. *Do not take her, God. Do not take her.*

Hours stretched out, wearing the day thin. Sometime in the night Towan released her lifeless hand back to her silent chest. No more breath. At first his legs refused to move, but he forced himself past the numbness and pain, removing himself from the wickiup and returning to his own. Christina slept, little William at her side. He stepped to the far side and lay down but could not close his eyes, could not push aside the ache expanding through him.

His mother was dead. The only real family he had. Towan sat back up and reached for his knife. The blade glinted in the low light as he drew his hair together into a fistful. The razor-like edge severed the black locks from his head. He would mourn as her people did. Though now he was alone. Completely. Utterly.

~*~

Christina's eyes burned every time she looked at Towan sitting cross-legged, staring into the fire. His hair, now chopped just above his shoulders, hung across his face. No expression. No movement except the regular blink of his eyelids and the rise and fall of each shallow breath. Her heart hurt for him, and for Quaritz, who'd welcomed her without judgment and had been kind.

"Are you sure you don't want to try and eat something?"

Towan didn't so much as look at her. He'd been this way for almost a full day, ever since his kin had ended their formal mourning, two days of soulful drums and wailing voices. Of course he was hurting. She only wished there were some way she could comfort him. Let him know that he didn't have to mourn alone. "Is there nothing I can do for you?"

No response.

Christina knelt beside him, facing him. She laid her hand against his arm.

A flicker of emotion touched his face.

"Towan?"

A muscle tightened in his cheek and he tipped his head away, as though wanting to hide the pain.

"Towan." Emotion snagged her voice as she repeated his name. Black fox. How foreign the word had once sounded to her. Now it was almost as familiar to her as her own name. Christina couldn't leave him to suffer alone. Her hand slid across his chest and hooked around his neck. She leaned her forehead against his temple.

Towan's shoulders trembled.

"I wish there were something I could do," she whispered into his ear.

He looked at her. His blue eyes glistened.

Christina's heart throbbed and she pulled him to her. Slowly, Towan's arms slid around her torso. She combed her fingers through his hair, over the long healed scar left from Edwin's bullet. She touched her lips to it. She'd never be able to repay Towan for everything he'd done for her, but she could hold him…help him mourn. Let him know he wasn't the only one to grieve.

Wasn't that the duty of a wife?

Christina's grip on him slackened at the thought, but his only grew stronger. He needed her just as dearly as she had once needed him, lost in the mountains, afraid and alone.

23

Towan couldn't seem to let go. The more he considered the inevitability the tighter he held her. The closeness, warmth, and the gentle caress of her fingers over his ear—everything he craved.

And then William began to fuss.

Christina lingered another moment before pulling away. "He's probably tired and hungry."

Towan withdrew his arms and sat back. He heaved a cleansing breath. He tried to focus on the fire again, but unwittingly his gaze wandered to where Christina covered herself and nestled the baby to her. William immediately quieted in his mother's embrace. Comfort. Acceptance. Unreserved love. That was the blessing of a mother.

And now his was gone.

William was asleep by the time Christina laid him back down. She slipped him under covers and turned to Towan. "Do you want me to read to you?" She fetched the Bible from where it had sat untouched for most of a week. Towan didn't really feel like having scripture spouted at him, telling him he should be stronger and trust, but the sound of her voice would help distract his thoughts. He nodded.

Christina sat beside him, her arm against his as she flipped open the cover. "Where would you like me to start?"

"Doesn't matter."

She turned to where he'd left the feather and started reading a chapter he'd already read. Towan didn't listen to the words, but they still laid themselves over him, the melody of her voice soothing. He wiped his hand over his face and covered a yawn. He hadn't slept much in the last three days, and his weariness only added to the overwhelming ache.

Christina paused her reading to rub his arm. "Why don't you lie down? You look exhausted."

Probably because he was. There was no use in fighting it, even if he didn't think he'd sleep. Towan stretched out on the thick hide, and Christina pulled a second one over him as though she were tucking in a child. But he was no longer a little boy, and the memory of her in his arms was too powerful to ignore. He wrapped his fingers around her wrist and led her down.

She didn't resist him but settled her head over his shoulder, her arm across his chest. Towan combed his fingers through her hair, bringing it away from her face. "Thank you," he mumbled against the top of her head.

Christina's hold tightened. "Just sleep."

Though sleep threatened to be the farthest from his mind, he compelled himself to relax and simply hold her. She only attempted to comfort him. Nothing more. She didn't love him. She didn't want this marriage. And in a few weeks they would leave for Fort Bridger. She would find passage back to *civilization*. If he were wise, he would push her away now and not let himself drown in her embrace.

But tonight he was weak and wisdom was fleeting.

~*~

Christina's pulse continued to race even after Towan drifted to sleep. What was she thinking, laying here with him as though he were her husband? Of course, legitimately he was her husband and she wasn't doing anything wrong, but…

She drew her hand back across the breadth of his buckskin clad chest and looked to his face, still darker than hers, but surprisingly pale after a winter away from the sun's touch. Pushing herself up on one elbow, she allowed her hand to linger over his heart. She'd never forget the feeling that had passed through her as she'd watched him vanish from sight into that icy water, knowing he wouldn't survive it. She couldn't bear the thought of letting him out of her sight again, of not knowing he was safe.

She couldn't even stand to see him hurting like he was. She ached for him.

She loved him.

The realization sat her upright. Was it possible to wake up one day and realize you loved someone? When she'd met Anthony, she'd been attracted to him from the start and, when he promised her adventure, she'd quickly decided to give him her heart. With Towan the order had been reversed. Christina had feared him and everything about him. He'd been so wild and foreign. She hadn't even considered love. But how could she have possibly avoided it?

She looked at his face, finally at peace, and felt a

smile on her lips. How could she have ignored how very handsome he was? Or how striking his smile? How gentle his touch. How good his heart. Would it be wrong to love him? To be his wife?

Christina withdrew to the far side of the hut. She lay next to William and looked at the thatched ceiling overhead. As much as she wanted Towan, could she imagine remaining in this wilderness for the rest of her life? When she couldn't speak their language? Especially now with Quaritz gone, the isolation sometimes threatened to strangle her. And what of William? She wanted him to have an education and to know of the world, not just one corner of it. No, she had to go back to Ohio, but maybe she could convince Towan to return with her.

Hopelessness threatened to overturn even an attempt. Towan hated her world. But she had to try.

When she awoke with William in the morning, Towan was gone. He returned in the early afternoon with a rabbit already skinned. What had once disgusted her had become a part of everyday life. She gave him her sweetest smile as she took it from him. He didn't smile back, but his eyes seemed brighter in the light of day. A dark grey ring circled sky-blue orbs. It was all she could do to look away.

~*~

Why did she smile at him like that? The shy smile had become a frequent ornament on Christina's already beautiful face during the past four days, and Towan wasn't sure what to make of it. But it gave him hope. He'd feared that after holding her so tightly in his arms that night, she would want to keep her distance, but that did not seem to be the case. Instead she went out of her way to be near him, often letting their arms touch as they walked together. Even now, she sat at his side, Bible in hand. She passed it to him.

"Do you mind reading tonight." Again, that smile. She leaned back on her hands and looked at him as if she knew something he didn't.

Moistening his lips, Towan opened the book to where they'd left off. This was becoming their evening ritual, sitting together, reading from the New Testament. More and more the words brought him peace and acceptance. He wasn't alone. He had a Savior, a Father, and a woman with tresses like a mountain sunset.

As he read, Towan became aware of Christina's fingers at the nape of his neck, toying with the uneven ends of his hair. He tried to concentrate, but the meaning of the words faded, his focus no longer on the book. As the apostle Paul continued with his lecture, Christina ran the back of her hand down the length of Towan's arm. He glanced at her.

She smiled.

"You still want me to read?"

"I do." Yet her fingers dawdled at his elbow.

Towan read one more verse then set the book aside.

"You don't want to read more?" Christina looked surprised.

"It'll hold." His hand moved with a will of its own to trace the slope of her jaw. He paused at her chin, his thumb marking the hint of a cleft. His gaze, following the route his fingers had taken, ended its journey on her lips. A slight curve added to their fullness. He leaned forward and found them with his own.

Towan half expected the sharp slap of her hand to mirror their wedding night, but this time her mouth softened against his and her hand stole to the back of his head, combing against his scalp, awaking a fire within him. Towan maneuvered to his knees and pulled Christina to hers as his lips continued to bare his soul. And she replied. Slow and gentle, as though a breeze through a mountain pass. Telling him to set his hurt aside.

When he released her, her lips traveled up his jaw to his ear. Her arms encircled him and smoothed across his back.

William whimpered from where she'd laid him. Towan held his breath. The child seemed to have a sixth sense Towan wasn't sure he cared for. *Not now. Not this time. Please go back to sleep.*

Christina paused as well, perhaps thinking the same—hopefully thinking the same.

Unfortunately William did not quiet. His tone and pitch increased until his mother unraveled herself from Towan. She sent him an apologetic glance before turning to her baby.

Deep breath. Towan sat back down and picked up the Bible, not because he intended to read it more tonight, but because he needed to do something to curb the energy surging through him. Flipping pages would have to suffice. For now.

Christina had her back to him as she leaned over William and patted his back, hushing him. But even after he quieted, she remained in place. Doubts churned in Towan's stomach. "Did you want me to read any more?" he whispered, not wanting to wake William again.

Christina looked at him but shook her head. Her

gaze left his face momentarily to comb over his hair.

"You could fix it."

"Your hair?"

He reached for his knife.

"I'd probably make it worse," she said moving to his side. She ran her fingers through his mane, curving over his ear.

"Unlikely."

Christina grasped the knife. She worked slowly and he closed his eyes, losing himself in the sensation of her nearness, so much more pleasant than thinking of how often they'd cut his hair in school. This time was different—a tradition of his people for mourning the loss of a loved one. The sorrow of loss would fade with time, and his hair would grow back.

Finally Christina set the knife aside. "Not much better, but a little more even." Kneeling in front of him, she brushed his hair back with her hands. "You look so different." She no longer smiled. "Towan."

Something in her tone held him in place. He waited.

"William." Her voice was little more than a whisper.

Strange the name no longer grated him as it once did—now that it attached itself to the next generation instead of the previous.

"O'Connell."

His gaze dropped and his muscles tensed. "That is not who I am."

"I'm sorry, Towan." She squeezed his arm. "I'm still trying to understand who you are...and who I am."

He looked at her.

"If I am your wife."

His Adam's apple clogged his throat. "What are you saying?"

Instead of answering right away, Christina fingered the mended cut in his shirt that resided over the scar Tucwatse's knife had given him. "I do, Towan. I didn't. But…I do." She leaned into him with a kiss.

Towan dragged her into his arms. Just to hold her, to know that she was and always would be his. He swept her toward the furs laid out for his bed.

"I love you, Towan," she breathed into his ear as she fell beside him. "Come back with me." Her mouth pressed against his lobe "Or on to Oregon. We can build a house and raise a—."

Silky waves of hair slipped between his fingers as he moved his hand to the back of her head then turned his face to hers and cut off her words with a kiss. Towan finished her sentence in his mind. To raise a family. Children. His kiss deepened. She wanted to bear his children. He cinched her against him, overcome by her warmth and the feel of her in his arms. He would be little William's father, the father of all her children. Towan broke off the kiss.

She wanted him to return with her.

Your childhood wasn't very pleasant at all, was it?

Not one I'd wish on anyone.

Not even his own children—especially not his own children.

He pulled away from her. What had he been thinking? Christina couldn't stay here. He'd always known that. Just as he'd known he could never go back.

The spring air outside the wickiup cooled his skin, but what he needed was another icy swim.

~*~

Christina didn't move as Towan pushed into the hut and gathered his weapons. The quiver he slung over his shoulders, followed by the bow. Then his knife and pouches with food. She hadn't seen him since he'd abandoned her last night, and it appeared he didn't plan on staying any longer than necessary.

"Where are you going?"

He didn't look at her. "Hunting. I'll be back in a week or so."

"A week?" Had she somehow misunderstood him last night? She'd been so sure he wanted her as much as she'd wanted him, but why then would he have left so abruptly, leaving her to lay awake through the night? Alone. What had she done wrong?

"We have to travel farther to find larger game."

"You told me we still had plenty of food."

He momentarily faltered, before resuming his preparations. "There are others who need it." He glanced at her. "I have to go."

"You mean you want to go." The hurt was too keen for anger, but it would come. It showed in his eyes, his manner—he wanted to leave her. Christina could only nod, her jaw set. She wouldn't cry. Not yet.

"I asked some of the other women to look in on you, make sure you have everything you need."

The anger arrived much quicker than expected. He was all too noble. "You don't have to do me anymore favors, Mr. O'Connell. I can take care of myself now. Why don't you just point the way to Fort Bridger."

Towan flinched but barely. "Not all the passes have thawed. I'll take you there as I promised when I return. Stay put until then."

He hurried away without another word.

Christina flung one of the wooden dishes across the hut, but it bounced off the wall and landed on the ground without even a scratch. What she wouldn't give for a tall stack of fine china!

The anger fled almost as quickly as Towan. He had his reasons for distancing himself from her, even if she didn't know them. Regret burned her chest. He'd already been hurt enough. She didn't want to be the one to inflict any more wounds. As much as it hurt, perhaps it was better that he be the one to walk away.

Flopping onto his bed of furs, last night tumbled through her mind. The feel of Towan's arms around her, the passion in his kisses. He loved her. She knew it as surely as she knew she loved him.

Christina clamped her eyes closed but couldn't shut out the murmurs of the village as they said goodbye to the hunting party. Did the wives kiss their husbands? Did the husbands promise to be safe and return soon? The scent of dried grasses in warm sun and hides as they gave up what moisture they held from the last rain saturated her breath. The rich soil under her. The smoke that had touched every inch of this hut.

She wanted four walls and a hard floor. A real bed. And a conversation in English.

But she wanted Towan, too.

Christina pushed off the ground and snatched the Bible from where it lay. No more sulking. No more fighting the inevitable.

They didn't belong together.

24

A warm wind washed the valley with the aroma of pine and recent showers. Instead of white, green coated the low slopes, speckled with yellow and purple as the earliest flowers showed their colors. Spring. And all Towan could think was how much he wished it'd wait to arrive. An eternal winter had never appealed to him until now.

The other men hurried to the village to greet their families, but Towan remained at a walk. His legs itched to run. He wanted nothing more than to sprint to Christina, sweep her into his arms, and kiss her with all the passion that raged through him at the thought of her. Then he'd take little William and see if he could invoke a smile or a giggle. Now that his mother was gone, they were his only family.

He held himself at bay, because he loved them too much. The past ten days had solidified his decision to take Christina to Fort Bridger and find her a way back to her home and her parents. Where she belonged and he didn't.

Despite his resolve to keep his distance, Towan couldn't manage to slow his pulse as he approached the wickiup. The hide already hooked up out of the way, he ducked inside. Then straightened. His head slammed into the branch arched above him. Christina wasn't there. He glanced around the immediate area. No sign of her or William. His heart took on a new rhythm but just as fast. He hurried to the closest woman and started questioning. No one had seen her since that morning. Hours.

Towan clamped his jaw shut to keep from yelling at them, demanding why they hadn't kept a closer eye on her. What if she'd wandered too far and gotten lost? It wouldn't be the first time. Or maybe she was in danger. She'd already met a bear and fallen in the river. He should have never left her.

Towan jogged toward the river, her usual direction. Fears compiled. She hadn't taken anything with her, so it was unlikely she sought to find her own way to Fort Bridger, but what if Ryder and his companion had decided to detour on their way out of the mountains?

But no one had seen anything.

Oh, God, "don't let anything happen to her." He glanced to the heavens. *Please.*

"You're back."

Towan spun toward the soft voice. Christina stood on a boulder along the shore, William strapped to her back. The river rushed in his ears, still carrying chunks of ice. "You shouldn't wander off."

The anticipation on her face faded to irritation. Her eyebrows peaked. "This is hardly *wandering off.*" She waved her hand. "Your village is right there. And why should you even ca…" Christina appeared to catch herself and puffed out her breath while averting her gaze. "I'm sorry."

He allowed a moment for the pumping of his blood to slow. William's squawks compelled him toward them. She followed his gaze to the cradleboard and turned so he could see the baby. Full cheeks raised and blue eyes twinkled. And then William began to babble almost as though he were attempting to tell Towan everything that had happened while he'd been away. Towan wiped his thumb over the child's chin, wet with drool.

"I missed you, little warrior," he said in Shoshone. "I missed you and your mother." Only he could never say the same to her. Towan switched to English and addressed Christina. "Are you well?"

"We've been fine." Terseness and sorrow fought over her words.

"Is there anything you need?"

She shook her head. "As I said, we're fine."

Of course she was. Towan moved past and motioned for her to follow. He could no longer stand there motionless without the risk of wrapping her in his arms. Maybe if they walked… "I think it is time you return to your people. It will be difficult because of full rivers, but perhaps—"

"Perhaps it's time. You said as much before you left." Christina kept pace with him, her arm only inches from his, and yet so far away as they followed the river. She sighed. "I want to go home."

"I know." He stole a glance at her but her gaze followed the rapids that had taken so much from him. His heart still grieved his mother. How could he bear this loss as well?

"When will we leave?"

"As soon as everything is prepared—a few days." Unless he asked her to stay. Maybe she'd agree. She cared for him, and she was his wife.

Towan pushed the thought away as quickly as it came. He'd already watched his mother suffer a life among a people who weren't her own. He couldn't do the same to Christina, even if she were foolish enough to agree to it.

He stopped and she turned to him, a soft smile touching her lips. Her gaze brushed his mouth.

"I should start gathering the supplies we'll need." Towan stepped back.

She nodded. "I'm going to *wander* a little farther. I'll be careful."

He watched her move away then dragged himself to the wickiup. If he was to survive this, he needed to end this marriage even if only in his mind. After his mother's body had been prepared for burial, her sister had brought him the pouch containing the two hairs symbolizing Christina and his unity. He would unravel the hairs and burn them.

If he could find them.

He had put the pouch in a larger satchel with the few other possessions he had kept of his mother's, but it was nowhere to be found. He expanded his search to the whole wickiup. Still nothing.

Christina slipped in and pulled the cradleboard from her back. "Did you lose something?"

"No." He dropped her empty saddlebags to the ground. "Nothing."

~*~

Christina remained nestled under her furs even after she woke. She'd already fed William and he'd fallen back asleep. Towan left before the sun crept past the horizon, but that came as no surprise. He avoided close quarters with her at all costs, not entering the hut until after she was asleep, and escaping as soon as he opened his eyes in the morning.

How would either of them survive the journey out of these mountains together when they could no longer keep much distance between them?

Breathing a sigh, Christina took in the now familiar surroundings. To think she had spent a full winter here sheltered by grass and animal hides. Even stranger, the realization that she would miss it. A little. Mostly she would miss Towan sleeping across from her, or watching him read his Bible, the smooth baritone of his voice, the laughter. Watching him play with William. His arms surrounding her. His kisses drowning her.

Christina pressed the heels of her palms into her eyes to dam the moisture springing in them. She pushed herself up and gathered her saddlebags. Time to stop thinking and finish packing. Towan told her he wanted an early start. He would probably return soon for one last meal.

The first thing Christina packed was Anthony's watch. Solid gold, she'd paid a pretty penny for it, but would it bring enough to pay for passage home? Not likely. Probably wouldn't even trade for the food she'd need to sustain her across the plains, never mind induce someone to take along an extra woman and babe. Still, it was all she had unless Anthony's stash of gold coins hadn't been stolen from its hiding place. She could only pray Edwin and his friends hadn't found it when rummaging through her wagon.

The next hour or so breezed by, constant activity keeping more than her hands busy. After breakfast,

Towan packed away the last of the food needed for their journey then loaded the pouches and his weapons onto his shoulders and across his back. Then waited silently just outside the door as Christina finished wrapping William into the cradleboard.

"I'm ready," she announced, joining Towan. She glanced back at what had been her home for the past six months. What if she asked to stay? Would Towan want her to? She shook the thought from her head. Of course, Towan wanted her to. He loved her. But this wasn't the life for her or her little boy. She wasn't strong like the women of his people.

Christina feigned a smile for the ones who came to say goodbye but only caught snippets of what they said. Swift travels. Safety. And a return. Tucwatse and his father approached, leading Havne's horse. Towan had already told her they would have to walk because he no longer had a mount of his own, and having already lost one of his uncle's mares while attempting to rescue her, he would not ask for the use of another. The elder placed the rope in Towan's hand. A gift, he said, and much more Christina couldn't understand.

Towan merely nodded as he accepted the horse, but emotion etched itself into his face. His uncle gripped his shoulder and concluded his speech.

Outside the village, Towan paused to help Christina onto the animal, but she shook her head. "Can we pause at your mother's grave first? I want to say goodbye." *And thank you.*

He led the way up the slope to a small cave, it's opening a third of the size of the one that had housed them in the fall. Stones and branches blocked the entry.

"She's in there?"

Towan nodded.

Her hand moved over the small pouch Quaritz had once worn, now hidden under the neckline of Christina's buckskin dress. She could hear the woman's voice as though they had talked yesterday.

My son good husband.

Yes. He is.

You care for my son?

Yes, Christina cared for him. She couldn't help but wonder if that is why Quaritz had not hesitated to come after her on the ice. The woman had wanted her son's happiness. If only Christina could be the wife Quaritz wanted for her son. Leaving him was a betrayal to the woman's sacrifice.

She glanced to Towan's somber face. "*Moqone*. You never told me its real meaning."

His lips parted with a sad smile. "Woman. Moqone means woman."

"Woman?" Not what Christina expected. While it made sense that he would refer to her as a woman, why would he use that term for his own mother? "I don't understand."

Towan released a breath, hesitancy showing. "I spent five years in that boarding school separated from my mother when she needed me most." He looked at the horse and rubbed his knuckles up and down the white blaze on its forehead. "I was my mother's first born, but after me she lost many babies, most never born. A girl and a boy only lived hours. Finally, when I was about ten, she had a healthy boy. Matthew." A muscle contracted in his jaw and his nostrils flared with emotion.

"What happened to Matthew?"

"He died just before he turned three. The doctor said it was dysentery, but I researched it at school.

Cholera."

Christina couldn't hold herself back. She stepped to Towan and placed her hand on his arm. "I'm so sorry."

His shoulder rose in a shrug, but he didn't withdraw. "My father sent me away and then left, leaving my mother alone. She needed me. She was left with no family, no sons, no comfort, among a people who tolerated her at best. She barely spoke their language." Towan paused to glance past her at Quaritz's tomb. "In the Bible it tells of Jesus addressing His mother several times, including from the cross. He calls her woman. Mrs. Anderson told me she believed this was because it was the most respectful, loving term He knew. I believed my mother deserved as much respect."

"Moqone." Christina blinked rapidly to keep her vision clear. "Then why would you call me moqone…especially at the beginning?"

He looked at her, his expression soft. "Because you were worthy of respect."

Christina laughed out loud. She found that hard to believe. She'd been too weak. Not like his mother.

"You had just been chased from the side of your murdered husband, become lost in the mountains, and given birth, and yet you never stopped doing what you had to, to protect yourself and that child." His finger brushed over the tiny scar her stone had left on his forehead. "Your strength, your fire…"

Towan's words trailed as he held her gaze, his hand moving to the side of her face to catch a strand of her hair between his fingers. He stepped to her. Faces inches apart, he froze. Noses touched. His breath caressed her lips and cheek.

"You..." Christina's mind couldn't formulate a complete thought—not with him so close. She stared at his mouth, only needing to tip forward and deepen this breath into a kiss. But she remained motionless, as did he. She closed her eyes, soaking in the warmth that seemed to radiate from him.

And then the world grew cold. Towan withdrew. "We need to go." He moved to stand at the side of the horse, ready to boost her onto its back.

Steeling herself, Christina set her palm on his shoulder and her foot in his hand. He heaved her upward, and she swung her leg over. His fingers brushed across her knee as they moved to her hands, placing them over the animal's withers and wrapping them around a length of mane.

"Hold on."

Christina nodded, but she couldn't remove her gaze from where his hand resided over hers. Moments passed.

"We need to go."

"Yes."

He pulled away but didn't swing on behind her as she'd anticipated. Coiling a length of rope around his hand, Towan walked ahead of the horse, leading it forward.

25

Three days brought them to an all too familiar valley, and Towan pulled to a stop. He glanced to the high ridges and then to the sun, higher still. Usually he wouldn't make camp for the night until dusk had settled in around them, but already he sought an appropriate site.

"I think Will's still sleeping," Christina said from the back of the horse. "Shouldn't we keep going while we can?"

That would be the wiser course of action. Heaven knew they had to stop frequently enough to meet the child's many needs. But Towan was no longer in a hurry. Not today. Not here. There was something he needed to do. He tied the horse to an aspen sapling with enough length to allow the animal to graze, and then assisted Christina to the ground.

She looked at him curiously. "How long are we stopping?"

"For the night." Towan walked away to collect wood for a fire.

"But we still have hours of sunlight. And what about those clouds. I thought you said you were concerned about them?"

"They're still high and light." He again glanced heavenward. She was right to question him. The threat of rain was real, and they had no good cover here. If they kept traveling a few more hours, they could take shelter in or under her wagon, depending how it had survived the winter. Towan crouched to pick up a long branch several inches in diameter. He propped it up against a rock and stamped down on it, breaking it in half then in quarters. These he tossed back toward where Christina unloaded the cradleboard from her back.

She settled onto a fallen log and leaned the cradleboard against it. William remained asleep. "Why don't I help you?" Stretching her shoulders and arms, she started to him.

"As you like."

He broke another branch and she gathered the pieces. "Why here?"

Holding the answer to himself, Towan turned to rip a dead limb from the closest tree. He snapped it with his hands and passed it to her.

"Can we build a shelter?"

"It probably won't rain." At least, it hopefully wouldn't.

After he'd filled Christina's arms, he waved her away, collected a few more, and then joined her where the horse waited. While he started the fire, William woke. Out of the corner of his eye, Towan watched Christina with the baby, memories forefront in his thoughts.

Almost nine years ago he had camped with his mother near here, perhaps in this very spot—the last leg of their journey before joining her family.

Seventeen. A man in his own right, yet he'd been afraid. Though Towan had been the one to convince her it was time to return to her people, he was not one of them. He'd spent the last five years in a white man's school, learning to read and write, not hunt and live off the land. He knew their language, but he'd been more confident with English. They were returning for his mother's sake.

Towan fetched the pouches of food from where they hung over the horse's back. He handed them to Christina and made his retreat. "I have something I need to do."

He didn't have far to go, over a rise and through a stand of pines. His steps slowed as he emerged, the flat boulder protruding from the rocky earth.

William T. O'Connell.

He knelt and traced the words with a finger. He'd traded for buckskin garb with a Shoshone woman camped outside Fort Bridger. Donning his new life, Towan had buried his white man's clothes, hat, and boots here, along with that identity and everything else his father had given him.

Towan rocked back. For the first time in all those years he almost longed to resurrect that part of him. He'd find land somewhere and build a cabin—four walls—that he and Christina could share. Far enough away from civilization that little William's younger siblings wouldn't feel the shame of their mixed blood.

Towan pushed himself up and stepped back. He couldn't do it. He'd only be able to protect them for so long before the world closed in on them, choking their spirit, breaking their confidence, making them feel less than dirt. Besides, Christina deserved more than the isolation he had to offer.

Better for William T. O'Connell to stay dead for everyone's sake. It wasn't as though he was ready to share that name with the man who had fathered him. That man would have to be buried deep before Towan would consider it.

A shuffle of feet behind and Towan spun to Christina, little William in her arms. She stared at the boulder bearing his name. "Is that a grave?"

The absurdity of how this must appear to her struck him and he released a tight laugh. "It is."

"But…who…?"

"The only man I've ever killed."

Her brow pucker. "Is that your…?" Her horrified expression finished her sentence.

"My father?"

She nodded.

"No. Last I heard, *that* William O'Connell is alive and well." And possibly waiting at Fort Bridger. "This is his son."

Christina stepped closer, again peering past him. "You?"

Me. Towan followed her gaze to the boulder and the deeply etched words.

"Why is the T tipped? I assume it's a T and not an X."

Except it was both. The hazard of reading too many stories of pirates and buried treasure. A chilly droplet splattered itself on his hand, followed by another on his head.

Behind him, Christina gasped. "I thought you said it wouldn't rain?"

"I said probably. I was being hopeful."

She backed into the cover of the woods and he followed as the heavens opened with spring showers.

Taking her arm, he pulled against the trunk of one of the larger pines, bringing little William between them. Christina cuddled her baby closer. "What happened to William T. O'Connell?"

Towan's voice rumbled past the constriction in his throat. "As I said, I killed him."

Her gaze searched his face. "Are you sure you succeeded?"

He opened his mouth to refute her, but…he wasn't sure anymore. Though he had struggled when he'd first arrived in these mountains with his mother, the last few years he'd grown confident in his new identity. Black Fox, a Shoshone warrior. But during the past six months… "I should fetch our supplies out of the rain."

Towan didn't look back. He pushed aside the turmoil in his mind and focused on the needs at hand. This hadn't worked nearly as well as planned, and he didn't want her to know the real reason for their stop here. Not yet. He'd wait for the right opportunity before he started digging.

~*~

The bark prickled through Christina's clothes as she leaned against the tree and placed a kiss on her baby's head. Towan vanished through the smaller pines and new foliage of the aspen grove. She looked back to the headstone and the name etched across it. The pieces of his life tumbled together into a clearer picture, but Towan was wrong on two accounts. He hadn't killed William T. O'Connell—cruel circumstance and abuse had laid him to rest. And William wasn't dead. Probably never had been. Only hidden, buried deep under the need to escape.

When Towan reappeared, he deposited the packs at the base of the tree. Water ran down his face and he raked his wet hair back. "I'll try to start a new fire."

"Is there anything I can do to help?"

"Yes. Stay dry."

Heeding him for the baby's sake, Christina settled onto the cushion of long needles. She couldn't take her eyes off Towan as he worked, breaking twigs and dead branches from the underside of pines, and then making a miniature teepee with them out of the reach of the downpour. Besides the rain, the setting reminded her of their first night together, except, although his clothes and appearance remained much the same, he seemed a completely different man. More likely, she was a very different woman.

He glanced at her, probably sensing the weight of her gaze, and waved toward the boulder, now dark with moisture. "I was standing there when I heard gunfire so I rode down past the wagon train. Edwin Ryder and his band had moved on but they were still up in arms."

Strange, in all the months together Christina hadn't considered that he might know the fate of the wagon train. "Was anyone hurt?"

He shook his head. "Not that I saw. I didn't want to hang around and risk drawing fire from some nervous muleskinner. I left about the same time your…your husband arrived."

"You saw Anthony before he was killed?"

"No. I wanted to put some distance between them and me. Not that I rode much farther. The terrain is a little difficult when you're avoiding the trail. I spent the night not far from your wagon."

"Did you know I was—"

He shook his head. "I was far enough from the trail I didn't even hear Ryder and his friends except for that one shot that would have killed your husband. They probably set camp farther back, not expecting anyone to ride in on them."

"But Anthony and Cal did." If only there were a way to bring Edwin Ryder and those who rode with him to justice. That seemed unlikely this far from the law and order she was used to.

Christina shifted her position and lowered William onto her lap. Every few seconds a drop or two would find their way through the branches overhead and splatter to the ground. One found her and she huddled the baby into her. If this rain didn't let up, it would be a long, wet night.

"Here." Towan unrolled a deer hide, draped it over her shoulders, and wrapped it forward around William. They chewed jerky and nibbled on pine nuts while Towan kept the fire stoked. As the sun settled behind the mountains, Christina lay down to sleep. Or try to sleep. Despite the heat from the flames, moist air carried a chill that was hard to ward off. Sleep came in waves of exhaustion, trying to keep William warm, and making sure she wasn't smothering him. At one point she woke and Towan was no longer in his place beside the fire. She glanced around. Nothing but blackness.

"Towan?" She whispered it, not wanting to disturb William's sleep. Part of her wanted to scream the name. Where would he have gone? He wouldn't have left her.

The scraping of stones stopped her breath. She struggled to listen. Up the slope next to the mock-headstone something clawed at the ground. Christina peered into the dark, and the crouching form of a man gradually become visible. Questions fought for dominance in her mind, but she settled back to wait. The desire for sleep no longer plagued her as curiosity heightened her senses.

Minutes passed before Towan crawled to where he'd propped their bags against the base of the tree—behind her. She kept her eyes closed. The slap of wet leather and something crunching held her attention. No. *Crunching* wasn't quite right. More like pebbles shifting and falling against each other.

The next morning Christina fought the urge to rummage through each pouch and saddlebag before Towan loaded them onto the horse. The rain continued to drizzle down on them, but he insisted they travel a few hours today. He hefted her onto the sleek back of the animal and took his usual place beside its head—too close to not notice her peeking in the bags. He obviously didn't want her to know about whatever he'd buried there or he wouldn't have skulked around in the night unearthing it.

The way was slow as they maneuvered down a steep gorge, across a stream that they followed for a while, and then up the other side. Towan had her walk when the slope became too steep so she wouldn't slide off the back of the horse, and to make it easier for the animal to scale the rocks. As they broke through thick brush into the open, Towan scanned to the left and right, both ways extending themselves in a wide path. Christina stared at the ground, dirt and stone scarred and ridged with wagon wheels and hoofs.

"Is this the trail?" She hurried to catch up to Towan. "This is the trail, isn't it? The one we were on."

He nodded and kept walking.

Christina followed but slower. She sucked in the damp air and almost laughed. How liberating to finally have a sense of direction, something she'd given up the minute she stepped off the Oregon Trail. She raised her head to the trees lining each side and searched for something recognizable. It didn't help that spring wore a different bonnet than autumn.

Towan paused ahead of her, waiting as she closed the gap that had grown between them.

"Are we very far from my wag—" Her feet lost all momentum as she followed Towan's gaze to a pile of stones. About the length of a man. "Is that…?"

"Yes."

Anthony.

Christina stepped past Towan to her husband's grave. A skiff of dirt and a mound of rock. A sensation of numbness crept over her. Numbness and serenity.

"Here." Towan took the cradleboard from her back. She glanced at him and then to little William Anthony who peeked out with open, but innocent, curiosity. It would be years before he would understand the fate of his real father. Someday she would tell him.

Christina looked back to the grave. "Did you do this—bury him?" A second mound showed a little farther down the trail. "And Cal?"

"I doubted anyone else would come this way before spring. It seemed wrong to leave them." He hitched the cradleboard over one shoulder and moved to stand with the horse.

One more thing for which she was indebted to him. "Thank you." Crouched next to the stones, Christina trembled with a jagged breath. No cross or headstone marked Anthony's final resting place. An unknown grave but to her and Towan. She grasped a thin piece of shale and began to scratch lines into the flat surface of the largest rock. Before the A was formed, the shale flaked apart in her fingers. She searched the ground for more.

"Here, let me." Towan passed William to her and took her place, a piece of flint already in his hand. She stood back. He had more experience with this than she.

"Anthony M. Astle," Christina directed. "Eighteen hundred and…" She quickly calculated, not remembering immediately. "Thirty-two. To eighteen hundred and fifty-nine."

Towan etched the words deep and then moved to the second grave.

"Callum Stewart. I don't know the date of his birth." Only that he was a good man, something impossible to cut into the stone for all to know. Two good men killed for…she didn't even know the reason, only that it had been murder.

With the final letter engraved, Towan stood and massaged his arm.

"Thank you." She touched his elbow. A part of her heart would always rest here with Anthony, but it was surprising how much had already attached itself to the man standing beside her. "For everything you've done." Christina jostled William as she backed away from the graves. "I'm ready to go now."

The rain had lightened into mist. Towan helped her onto the horse and led them away. Only one last glance back.

Goodbye.

For the next mile, memories of Anthony danced across her mind. Happy ones. Ones she could take with her and someday share with William. But now was not the time for memories. She searched the trail for something she recognized. Then she saw it.

"The tracks. I think this is where Anthony left the wagon." She grabbed the horse's neck, slid to the ground, and hurried into the young foliage before Towan could say anything.

Excitement slammed against reality as the wagon became visible—along with the ground surrounding it and everything strewn about. Her palm found its way to her mouth. Towan had told her Edwin and his friends had found her wagon, but she hadn't imagined this. "All my gowns. The food."

She stepped over a shattered wooden crate, around the scattering of rodent droppings surrounding a torn flour sack, and then climbed over the wagon's tailgate. The small barrel of coffee beans had been spilled, as well. Anthony's coin purse was gone. "No," Christina moaned. "They found my money." She dropped to her knees and wiped the water from her burning face. "I don't have anything left. Nothing." She yanked a quilt from the neat mound beside her. "Nothing but a pile of books."

Towan climbed in after her.

Wait. Why were the books…? She looked back to the clutter outside. Then to the tidy stacks of novels. "They used to be in that crate." The one smashed behind the wagon. Only one explanation presented itself. She eyed Towan, unable to stop a groan from rolling between her lips. "You couldn't have picked up my gowns while you were at it? You did save these books, didn't you?"

He lifted one of his shoulders. "It seemed an awful waste."

"I agree, but..." She waved toward her scattered wardrobe. "My clothes would have been nice not to waste as well."

"So you could make more diapers?" Though he said it without an ounce of humor, his mouth hinted to the contrary. He reached for a book, and she slapped his arm.

"The way you love these books, I'm surprised you didn't pack them back to your village instead of me."

He sat back and opened to the first chapter of *The Hunchback of Notre-Dame.* "They probably would have been a lot less trouble."

"Probably." A laugh bubbled up. She pulled William off and started unbinding him. Towan's chuckle met her halfway. The most absurd time and situation for laughter, but there it was, making her efforts half as effective. With the baby finally in her arms, she slumped down next to Towan and released a long, halting sigh. "I have been quite the handful for you, haven't I?"

"And yet no book, fiction or other, could compare to you."

She attempted to laugh, but this time tears sprang to her eyes. She turned her head aside as she passed him the baby. "Can you hold him for me?"

Without waiting for a reply, she pushed up and jumped out of the wagon, hand clasped over her mouth.

~*~

Towan cradled little William, Christina's muffled sobs burning his ears. That was not the response he'd expected. And he couldn't sit here and listen to her crying any longer.

Barricading off a small section at the front of the wagon, Towan sat William up and gave him a book to play with. A little drool wouldn't hurt the pages too badly. Then he followed Christina to where she stood, leaned up against one of the large back wheels. "Are you all right?"

She nodded but turned more away from him. Her shoulders still shuddered.

He laid his hand over one. "Christina."

A sniffle was followed by what sounded like an airy chuckle. "I'm fine. I…I don't know what's wrong with me."

His fingers slid down to her arm, and he turned her to him. Eyes shining, cheeks blotchy…and yet still so beautiful. "Come here." Towan wrapped his arms around her and nestled her into his chest. Her body continued to tremble against him but it was hard to tell if she laughed or cried. Perhaps both.

"I'm sorry," she mumbled against his shirt.

"You have nothing to be sorry for." Except for the bittersweet mingling of pain and ecstasy pulsating through him as he held her. Every time they touched—whether he were hoisting her onto the horse, or taking little William from her arms—it became more and more difficult to withdraw. Thankfully that wasn't required of him quite yet. It felt far too good to have her in his embrace.

In a couple more days he would let her go forever.

"We should get you out of the rain." Though it wasn't possible to get any wetter.

"Where's Will?" Her cheek remained against his chest.

"I fixed him a place to play. He's fine." Probably

the most fine of any of them.

Neither said anything more. There wasn't anything left to say. All too soon they would have to return to reality, but not right now. A few more minutes of fiction couldn't make the future any more painful, but it would be something to remember when she was gone.

26

The walls of Fort Bridger appeared as though a division between the past six months and a future Towan dreaded. One without Christina and little William. But he continued toward it all the same. He knew what he needed to do.

A group of teepees stood to the south, and a smaller gathering of army tents had been set up on the east. Otherwise the fort seemed quite abandoned, still too early in the season for much traffic. Uneasiness settled in Towan's gut. There was no guarantee they would be able to find suitable transportation for a woman and child headed east. They might be forced to wait here for weeks. If not longer.

Large gates sat wide open, and he reined the horse through them and toward a large stone building that hadn't been there when he'd come through here almost nine years earlier. The corral and several other stone buildings had replaced most of the wooden structures that had once made the fort. Not much of the old fort remained and what did showed signs of fire damage. Along with the presence of the U. S. Military, the fort seemed completely unfamiliar. He slid to the ground from behind Christina and led the horse to a hitching post, tying it beside a pretty bay gelding.

He was about to suggest Christina wait for him there while he figured out who to talk to, but a few loitering mountaineers and a small group of soldiers gathered near the stables made leaving her alone unwise. He reached up to assist her.

She jumped down without him. "I can take Will," she offered, following his gaze to the mountain men.

He waved her off. "He's fine."

An angry whine from the cradleboard argued.

Christina moved around behind him so she could access her child. "He's probably starving."

The baby's fussing escalated in volume with each passing second. Knowing they were so close to the Fort, Towan had held him off for longer than usual. "Let's find you some privacy then."

William's wails drew everyone's attention as they hurried inside what appeared to serve as both an office and home. A middle-aged gentleman jerked up from the desk and waved them to leave. "Hey, there, you can't..." He looked from Christina to Towan and the baby and then back to Christina. This time his gaze took in the entirety of her, from moccasins to copper hair. "You're not—"

"I apologize for intruding. My name is Christina..." She glanced to Towan, and her tone crumbled. "Christina Astle."

Towan remained silent. He wanted nothing more than to correct her, but the only name he could give her was O'Connell.

This time the gentleman's hand waved at her attire. "But what on earth are you doing with a—"

"I had a bit of a misadventure last autumn, but

before I go into that, my son is quite starved, is there someplace I can go to see to his needs?" Though she spoke with confidence, a blush touched her cheeks.

"Of course, of course." The man rushed forward as she pulled little William from the cradleboard. He took her arm and directed her toward a door at the side of the room. Christina glanced back at Towan before being led from sight. The crying faded behind the closed door.

Forcing a swallow past the tightness in his throat, Towan pivoted on his heel and returned to the horse and the packs. He slung Christina's saddlebags over his shoulder along with another pouch, not about to let that one out of his sight again. He arrived back in the building about the same time the man returned.

"Do you speak English?"

Towan's chest heated as he gave a single nod.

"Well, my wife is seeing to Mrs. Astle, so I doubt you will be needed by her any longer. Are those hers?"

Towan tossed the saddlebags to the man, almost catching him off guard. He fumbled to grab them. The man had a wife out here? The reasons for not bringing Christina to the Fort in the fall dissipated before Towan, but the thought of the last six months without her filled him with an incredible emptiness. He was hardly aware the other man had started speaking again.

"I'll see that she gets them. And that she is taken care of." He eyed Towan. "You are Shoshone? Which tribe? How long has the young woman been with you?"

"First, I should ask who you are." Towan folded his arms across his chest and chose his words with care. "I do not plan on making myself scarce until I know she has everything she needs, including a way to return home."

The man's bearded jaw slacked just a little as his stare deepened. "Carter. They call me Judge Carter now. I'm the appointed sutler of this fort and probate judge for the territory. I'm inferring Mrs. Astle wintered with your tribe. What other interest do you have in her?"

"That is none of your affair. But so we're clear, I can pay for whatever Mrs…." He couldn't say it—couldn't call her by another man's name. His pride had taken enough beating since he'd walked into this building five minutes ago. "Mrs. *O'Connell* needs."

"O'Connell?" Carter's eyes narrowed. "She said her name was Astle."

"It used to be." Towan reached into his pouch and tossed four penny-sized nuggets onto the desk, redirecting the man's attention. "Hold onto those for her, *Judge*. They should more than cover her passage back east. See that she is well taken care of and inform her I'll be back." He stepped to the door. "Tell me, have you seen anything of an Edwin Ryder or John Tuttle. They ran a trap-line this winter."

"Sure. They came in with a load of furs two or three days ago."

Towan measured his breath. "Then they're still in the fort?"

"Probably." Carter fingered the raw gold. "You said her name is O'Connell now? Any relation to Bill O'Connell?"

"None." Towan reached for the door handle. Better to find Ryder before he found Christina. While somehow avoiding his father.

"You know, O'Connell has been working for me

for a couple years now. I hear he has a half-breed son somewhere in those mountains." The sutler chuckled. "You looked familiar. I swear you're almost the spitting-image of old Bill."

~*~

Christina laid William into the cradle and folded the soft quilt over him. To think that this was the first time he had slept in a real bed. She straightened and moved from the room.

Mary Elisabeth Carter stood waiting in the larger living area. "I am glad I had the cradle out already for you to use. I'm sure we can find clothes for him, as well. I kept some from my boy, and I'll have a few months before I'll have to worry about that size again."

"Thank you."

The woman slid her arm through Christina's. "I can't imagine what it must have been like for you this winter." She nodded to her ten year old daughter who knelt playing with two younger children. "Ada will listen for him. I'll have a bath drawn and find something for you to change into."

"You are too kind." Christina took in her surroundings as she followed her hostess. Solid stone walls, furniture, shelves of books that would make Towan's mouth water, rugs, paintings. Not near as lovely as her parents' home in Cincinnati, but a mansion compared to what she would expect in this wilderness. She'd had no idea of what this house contained when they'd passed through the fort in the fall. "How long have you lived here?"

Mary led her through another door and motioned to the four crates stacked across from a masterful bed.

"As you can see, not long. My husband came out three years ago, but he didn't send for us until last spring. While the surroundings are a little more rustic than we're used to, I'm just grateful we're back together as a family."

Family. The word expanded in Christina's center as thoughts of Towan and little William slowed her steps. Mary pulled away and moved across the room. She produced a green gingham gown and laid it across the bed. "Soon we'll have everything we need here. Even a school—so my husband has promised."

Christina stared at the fabric fashioned into a becoming but practical dress. So strange to see this splattering of civilization in the middle of nowhere, like a dollop of paint on a blank canvas. They could create whatever life they desired.

"I think this should fit you well enough. You're a little taller than me, but at least you don't have to worry about fitting a waistline around a protruding middle." Mary smoothed her hands over her stomach.

"Anymore." It had been a while since she'd worn a corset. Was it possible to miss the wretched thing? What would Towan think of her in a gown and with her hair done up in a more womanly fashion? Pins and curls?

Or would it only prove a painful reminder of their differences?

"I should go check with my…" Christina pinched the inside of her cheek with her teeth. What was Towan to her now? If not her husband? "My friend. See what his plans are. Let him know that I'm well. Maybe he's found a way for me to get home." She moved to the door.

"My husband didn't tell you?" Mary followed.

"He's sending his freight wagons back to Missouri for more supplies sometime this week. I know he had loads of furs and such, but I'm sure they can make room for you, if that's what you want. It's by no means a smooth ride."

It couldn't be much worse than a covered wagon, could it? At the moment she didn't care.

"But if you wait, my husband said within the next month we'll start to see wagon trains passing through again."

Wait? Lingering between two points with both pulling her, ripping her? Christina couldn't do it. "I need to go home. I don't care what it takes to get there."

"I understand. And I'm sure you can arrange something with my husband."

But first she had talk to Towan. "I'll be back shortly."

Downstairs Christina retraced her steps to the office. She hastened her pace at the sound of a familiar voice. *Good.* Towan was still there. She burst into the room only to slide to an abrupt halt. She'd been mistaken. "I'm so sorry. I didn't mean to interrupt." Her gaze darted between the judge and the stranger. "I was looking for…"

Towan's eyes stared back at her, only it wasn't his face. The nose, yes. The straight, dark eyebrows. Even the form of his mouth. But not the deep set wrinkles or leathery skin. The man ran his hand over his heavy beard.

Carter perched himself on the corner of his desk. "This is the young woman I was speaking of, Bill."

Christina tried to say something but her jaw failed to respond, remaining disjointed.

Bill turned to face her fully. "Is it true you're married to my son?"

"Towan." Her voice squeaked. "You're William O'Connell."

He gave Towan's typical nod. "So Will did mention me." His eyes seemed to light at the prospect. "And you saw his mother. Quaritz." His brow furrowed. "How is she?"

Christina placed a hand over her mouth lest her expression betray her. "Um…she…passed away not a month ago."

The man's face crumpled, his jaw tightening as he visibly sought to hold his emotions at bay. He sank into the nearest chair. Surely this wasn't Towan's father—the man he hated.

"But my boy." He sniffed as he righted himself. "Tell me about my boy."

"He's…well." Christina cast a glance around the room. She might also be in need of a chair soon. "I don't know what you expect me to say."

His glistening eyes of blue locked on hers. "Is he happy?"

"He's…" *Lost. Hurting. Angry. He hates you.* "I don't know."

"But he has *you* now. Judge Carter said Will inferred that you were man and wife. Is this so?"

Again Christina couldn't speak. Maybe that was for the best. What was the answer? She followed Bill O'Connell's example and sat. Both of them obviously had more questions than could be answered in such an informal interview.

"Our union came out of necessity," Christina began. How much did she want to tell the man? "But yes." *He is my husband.*

Judge Carter stepped behind Towan's father. "And yet, he asked me to make arrangements for you to travel back east? He didn't say anything about himself."

"Towan would never go east." Not even for her.

"So your marriage was never a real one?" Bill O'Connell's question reflected the painful reality.

"I suppose not." Though her heart did not share the sentiment. She redirected the conversation to Towan or *Will* O'Conner. Perhaps if she understood more about his childhood...

Christina listened with rapt attention as Mr. O'Conner slowly unfolded his story. She didn't hear the door open or Mary Carter enter. "I must insist on stealing you away while your bath is warm."

If not so greatly needed, Christina might have refused. She set her hand on her father-in-law's arm. "Thank you. I wish I could speak with you further."

"I'm not going anywhere." He frowned. "Except maybe to track down that boy of mine."

"I wish you luck." Towan could make himself hard to find when he wanted to.

The bath water had already cooled by the time Christina stepped into the small tub, but it was just as well. She no longer had the desire to sit and soak. She washed quickly, donned the gown, and twisted her hair into a bun just in time for her baby to wake and want to be fed again. When he finished, she sat him on the floor to play with a pile of wooden blocks and the Carter toddler and turned to Mary.

"He'll be fine here," the woman said before Christina could open her mouth. "You go find your friend."

With a thank you, Christina needed no more

encouraging. She wasn't sure what she wanted to say to Towan, but she did need to speak with him.

Against the buildings, grass and weeds sprang up with vigor, while the rest of the area bore either ruts from hoof and wheel, or powdered dirt—already broken up from more constant traffic. The horse was nowhere in sight which suggested the stables, corrals, or that Towan had ridden off without telling her—a possibility if he'd seen his father.

She'd start at the corrals.

Only half way across the yard she sighted a man currying a pair of mules. More than the animals were familiar. Edwin Ryder spotted her at the same time and tossed the brush into a wooden pail. He moved toward her. "Well, well, well, it seems you did survive the winter in those mountains after all." His gaze appraised her. "And more becoming than ever."

She backed away. "Don't come near me."

"Oh, come now, Christina." He lunged, seizing her arm. "No reason to be unfriendly."

She struggled to pull away, but he held fast. "If I scream this time, I'll be heard. In fact, I've already made friends with Judge Carter and his wife. Imagine that. A judge way out here. I wonder what they would do to a thief and murderer."

His grip bit her skin. "I don't know what you are talking about, and you'd do well to keep any false accusations to yourself."

"Don't you touch her!" Towan was at a dead run, already half way across the compound. A second later one of his hands ripped Edwin away from her while the other slammed into his face.

Recovering from the initial shock, Edwin brought his hands up to protect his head from Towan's fury. He spared one to set up his own offence. The fist caught Towan near his eye, but he hardly flinched.

Their grappling took them to the ground. Edwin landed on top, but Towan immediately rolled, gaining the advantage. They both jerked as a gun discharged over their heads.

Christina spun to where a mountaineer stood, Winchester now aimed at Towan's chest. "Get off of him."

Towan pushed himself up. "Stay out of this."

"Can't be done. I'm not cotton to an uppity injun beating a friend of mine senseless."

Edwin struggled to his feet and wiped at the blood pouring from his nose. Murder glinted in his eyes and etched itself in every crevasse on his face as he reached for his revolver. His finger closed over the trigger.

27

Towan's hand was only half way to his knife when the thunder of the discharge deafened him.

"I'll drop you where you stand, Ryder."

Towan sucked air as he twisted to the man who had fired the warning shot.

"Tuttle was smart to break company with you as soon as your haul was sold. You and your new pal better make yourselves scarce before I decide on a more permanent solution to you threatening my boy."

Ryder swore under his breath as he holstered his gun and stalked away, the other man right behind him. Towan's heart raced, but he would blame that on the tussle he'd had with Edwin Ryder and coming within a breath of being shot—not the fact that his father stood only five yards away. A year ago he'd convinced himself he wanted to make the man pay for everything he'd done to his family. Kill him, even. But suddenly he realized what he'd really wanted was William O'Connell Senior to acknowledge him.

And he'd done that now.

"Look at you, Will. You've grown a mite since I saw you last."

Towan told himself to turn and leave, but his feet held him in place. He'd been no more than twelve the last time he'd seen his pa. "I should hope so after almost *fifteen* years." The time had changed them both.

O'Connell looked…old. A wide brimmed slouch hat covered his head, but white clung to his chin, and the wrinkles around his eyes were deep.

"I've managed well enough on my own 'til now. I don't need your help, Pa."

"So I should have stood back and watched that rat shoot a hole through that hide of yours?"

"Why not?"

"Because I'm your pa, that's why." The old man deflated. "I only ever wanted what was best for you."

Bitterness rose in the back of Towan's throat. "Then do what you've become so good at and leave me alone."

Towan walked to where he'd dropped his pouch. "And you can have your gold." A shower of glinting flakes and every size of nugget fell to the ground as he shook the bag upside-down. "I only used what it took to bring Mama back to where she belonged and…" He glanced to Christina who stood near, looking like the genteel woman she was—a complete stranger. "And I gave Judge Carter enough to get you home."

"Towan."

He ignored the pleading in her voice and forced his gaze back to his pa, dropping the empty satchel to the pile of gold. "The rest is buried up in the mountains. I'll draw you a map."

"I wanted it for you. That's why I sent it."

Towan turned and started walking. He didn't want to consider Pa's words. They weren't enough. He headed back toward the stables. Since Christina and little William didn't need him anymore, he'd find his horse and leave this wretched mess behind him.

"Towan, wait." Christina's moccasins padded after him. She caught his arm just as he passed behind the stables, out of his father's sight.

He sagged against the wall, for the first time realizing how much his shoulder hurt from hitting the ground. He licked the corner of his lip and tasted blood. Not surprising. The whole left side of his jaw ached from the application of Ryder's fist. "What do you want?"

Her finger brushed over his eyebrow. "Are you all right?"

Physically? This was nothing at all. Emotionally? He wouldn't consider it right now. "I should ask you that." Anger surged at the memory of Ryder grabbing Christina. "Did he hurt you?"

"I'm fine. Only scared." She wet her lips, drawing his attention to them. "I accused him of murder. And I know he did it—I know he killed Anthony and Cal. He was ready to kill you, too. I saw it on his face."

Towan held his arms at his sides, though they ached to hold her. "If Ryder's smart, he'll leave while he has the chance. All the same, you should go back to the Carters. You'll be safe with them until you leave. Word is, the judge plans on sending out his freight wagons tomorrow. His head driver seems a decent man and figures something can be arranged."

Her eyes searched his. "What about you?"

Again he took in the way the gown fit to her womanly curves. The skirt reached to her ankles, and the beaded moccasins his mother had made her peeked from beneath the green and white fabric. Two worlds so fully at odds with each other. "I brought you to the fort as I'd promised, and found you a way home. I think it best I leave now."

"You won't wait to see me off?" Her voice cracked. "Can't you wait?" Christina glanced back to where he had left O'Connell standing. "What about your father?"

Anger again spiked through him, and he pushed himself off the wall, but she set her hand on his chest, hurrying to finish. "I know you're upset and that is completely understandable. Your childhood was miserable and you, in a large part, blame him. He probably is as responsible as you believe him to be, but don't you think you would be happier if you made peace with your father? I spoke with him, Towan. He's sorry about the past. Full of regrets. Shouldn't you at least talk to him?"

"What do you think I just did? I talked to him, and it changes nothing." He slid away from her. "Go back to the Carters. Please. Tell Judge Carter about Edwin Ryder. I'm sure he can help better than anyone."

The trace of hope that had brightened her eyes fled. "Please, be careful, Towan. If anything happened to you...promise me you'll wait until tomorrow to leave."

One more day. He'd already tussled with Ryder and faced his father. All he had to do was lay low and prolong their goodbye for one more day. At least this way he'd be able to see little William one last time. He nodded and turned away before she could see the utter despair fighting to pull him under at the thought of goodbye.

Towan walked past the stables and found himself facing the stone building that appeared to serve as a tavern. Whiskey. Isn't that what cured everything that ailed a man, deadened the mind, muted feeling? It had worked well enough for Pa. Why shouldn't it work for him—make it not hurt to lose his family.

Towan's Adam's apple clogged up his parched throat. He might look a little like the man, but he wasn't his father. And he wouldn't become his father.

Redirecting back to the stables, this time Towan turned inside. The scent of horse met his nostrils, and he wandered to the stalls where a row of bay horses stood. By the looks of them, he guessed them to be Morgans, probably purebreds—unlike him. Towan kicked at a tuft of hay that had been littered on the ground. He leaned into the gate of one of the stalls and scratched the neck of its occupant.

"Hey, you! Get away from there."

He glanced to the three soldiers at the door of the stables. One had his hand resting over his revolver. Towan straightened. He didn't need any more trouble. Not today. He held his expression stoic as he sidestepped them.

"Make sure nothing's missing," one of the soldiers said plenty loud. "Can't trust them Shoshone bucks. Especially around horses."

Towan's moccasins stopped their tread. One more bur under his saddle. The tiny spines dug deep, spurring him to throw off the restraints as he had when he'd seen Ryder with Christina. Only, his knuckles were already bruised, and it would be three armed men against one. What he needed to do was take their taunts to heart. Another reminder why he was no good for Christina. Not because he was Shoshone, but because she was white, and her people wouldn't understand.

~*~

Christina tucked her buckskin clothes into the small trunk Mary had supplied for her use. Not that she had much to fill it. A couple outfits for William, blankets, diapers, and a few keepsakes from her time in Towan's village. Quaritz's pouch remained around her neck. She'd planned to place it in the trunk but couldn't seem to perform that action.

She smoothed her palms over her skirts, the return to a gown a slow adjustment. Her buckskin garb had been so comfortable and liberating. There were many little things she would miss about her time in the mountains. And one big one. The mere thought of leaving Towan and never seeing him was crippling. How could she even consider it?

"If you're finished with the trunk, I'll have it loaded for you." Mary breezed through the room, William on one hip and a toddler tugging at her skirt. The youngster no doubt did not like the thought of being replaced by a younger child and would be glad to see William go—a short-lived victory. Being pregnant had no effect on Mary's exuberance for life, even out here, far from society and civilization.

Maybe a life out here wouldn't be so awful. If they settled near Fort Bridger, William could go to school with the Carters, and she would be able to visit with Mary. Most importantly, she could stay with Towan.

Christina took the baby from Mary and fastened a bonnet under his chin. He laughed as her fingers brushed his cheeks, and all Christina could think about was Towan. A little boy needed a father, and Towan was the only one William knew.

But her trunk was already on its way to the

wagons without her. That was fine. She would talk to Towan, convince him to let her stay when he came to see her off. There would be time to unload her luggage.

Nervous excitement hastened Christina's pace across the compound to the stables where men harnessed teams of mules to the four large Conestoga wagons. A man tossed her trunk into the back of a smaller wagon similar to the one she'd left in the mountains. She needed to hurry.

"I'm sorry we can't offer you more suitable conveyance," Judge Carter said as he approached. "But I've given instructions that you are to be made as comfortable as possible. They are good men. You also have my word that we will investigate your suspicions concerning your husband's murder and do our best to bring the scoundrel to justice."

She should feel grateful for that much, but his lack of response to Havne's death still haunted the victory.

"We'll send word," he finished.

"Thank you, sir." Christina did her best to smile. The anticipation of speaking with Towan left her jittery. "You've been most kind. I'm indebted to you and your wonderful wife." Where was Towan? He should have been there. The mules looked to be almost ready. She was running out of time.

But he always kept his promises.

Warmth spread through her as she caught sight of him striding toward her. "Towan." Hitching William higher on her hip, she started in his direction. The look on his face brought her up short. Bloodshot eyes stared blankly, not really looking at her. She trailed his gaze to his father, standing out of the way, but there none-the-less.

"Towan?"

He refocused and extended his arms to William who gladly offered himself. Christina's eyes watered at the look of torture Towan tried hard to mask. She knew him too well. Every expression. He spoke in Shoshone, but she filled the gaps between the words she recognized. He told his namesake to be strong and good for his mother. To grow into a brave warrior and to learn about God.

Lord, all I ask is that he let me stay.

Christina grasped his arm while sending a glance to the wagon containing her luggage. The driver mounted the seat. She had to be bold or lose Towan. "We need to talk. I want to stay. Here, or anywhere. With you. I want to be your wife. I don't want to leave you."

Instead of sweeping her into his arms as she'd hoped, his eyes closed and jaw tensed.

"Please, Towan. I love you."

A sliver of blue appeared. "And if I didn't love you, maybe I could let you stay."

"But—"

His mouth covered hers, firm and needy as he pulled her against him, William partway between them. Her hands found Towan's face and neck. She answered with silent pleadings. *Don't let me go. Never let me go. I love you!*

But after a moment his arm withdrew. He stepped away and pressed William back into her embrace. "Good bye…*Moqone.*" Towan turned and walked away.

No. Why?

A hand touched her arm but she couldn't remove her gaze from Towan until he slipped from the gates of the fort and vanished…forever. She glanced to Mary's kind face.

"It's time."

"Time?"

"The wagons are ready." The woman took the baby from her arms.

Christina let herself be led past the Conestogas to the smaller wagon. Strong hands braced her upward onto the high seat, and then Mary set William onto her lap. The tears didn't come until the horses lurched forward, jostling the wagon after them, away from Fort Bridger and William Towan O'Connell.

~*~

Towan walked stiffly away from the fort to where he'd left his horse tied. The thud of heavy hooves and creak of the wagons' axles announced their departure and tore him in two. But he wouldn't look back, wouldn't second guess his decision. He didn't slow until he made it into the stand of trees. It would afford him a little privacy. Heat torched his shoulder and he slammed into the ground about the same time his mind processed the crack of a revolver. Sticky warmth poured between his fingers as he clutched his wound. A chuckle brought his head up to where Edwin Ryder stepped from behind a bush. His gun shifted to Towan's head.

"I'm on my way to California, but I thought I'd wrap up a loose end before I go." Ryder's finger hovered over the trigger as he moved closer. "You know the irony? When I killed Astle, I'd only meant to scare him and the older gent. Meanwhile, I've shot at you how many times, and hardly scratched your skull." His upper lip curled. "I may have lousy aim, but I don't think I'll miss this time."

Two shots pierced the air at the same time. Towan glanced to where the bullet had dug into the earth not a foot from his head. Edwin Ryder's brow puckered with both pain and shock. He staggered back several steps and then dropped forward. A shell had ripped through his center, and blood soaked outward from the hole.

A jagged breath shook Towan's body as he pushed to his knees, his brain still trying to comprehend what happened. Footsteps registered in the back of his consciousness. Then curses.

"Will, are you all right?" His father spewed profanities. "Let's get you back to the fort. It looks like his bullet lodged itself. The army has a doctor who—"

Pa tried to help him up, but Towan jerked away. The motion did nothing for the agony throbbing in his shoulder, but he still made it to his feet. "I don't need your help. What are you even doing here?"

"I followed you. Came to tell you you're a fool."

Towan rotated away. "Thanks, Pa." He staggered past Ryder's body. His head spun, but he'd be fine if he could get to his horse.

"Should I have stood back and let you ruin your life?"

"Why not? It's not like it was worth much to begin with." Towan grunted as he leaned into a tree to catch his breath. "You should have let Ryder finish what he started."

Pa stopped. The man looked even older than the day before. He pushed his hat back on his head and ran his palm down his beard. "I don't understand you, son."

"Of course you don't. What I don't get is why

you're even trying. Why pretend to care when deep down you hate me more than any of them do?"

"Hate you?"

Towan's vision swam, but he'd blame that on the pain that grew worse with every passing minute. "I don't even blame you for that anymore. I only wish you hadn't made me in the first place." He slid down the trunk, his gaze going to the crimson stain expanding across his buckskin shirt. Blood trickled down his arm and dripped from his fingers. "I'm nothing. Not white. Not Shoshone…"

"William…" Pa crouched in front of him and wrapped his hand behind Towan's head. "I… Why would I give you my name if I didn't want you? You're my son. I loved you from the moment your mother handed you to me. I know I got mean drunk and I did things that haunt me to this day. I'm a weak man, Will. You and your mama knew that better than any. I tried to stop and for a while I did all right, but when your brother died…" He sniffed and dropped his head forward. "I knew I couldn't keep it up. And I couldn't stand to hurt you anymore."

Towan stared at his father, the words filtering through the pain resonating from his shoulder. "Why did you send me away?"

His lips pressed thin as he swallowed. "So you wouldn't end up like me. So you could make something of yourself. When I struck gold in California that was all I could think about. You could be anything you wanted, do anything, go anywhere. You had education and wealth. I thought I'd done good."

Nausea joined the pain. "Pa, I…"

He stood and pulled Towan up after him. "We can talk later, after we get that bullet out so you don't bleed to death." He hooked Towan's good arm around his neck. "Just one more thing to consider. It doesn't matter to me whether you go back to your mama's people or head east, and I don't care what circumstances made that little woman your wife, but if you love her at all—like I know she loves you—you'll never find happiness running. I can promise you that."

28

Christina planted both feet on the dock. Men and women pushed past her, and heavily loaded wagons rattled along the harbor—Cincinnati, just as she had left it almost two years ago. She hitched William higher on her right hip and tightened her grip on her small trunk in the other hand as she gave in to the flow of the crowd.

"Christina."

A tall man with a rusty beard appeared through the masses, making his way to her. She blinked rapidly but with little effect on her tears. They'd gotten the letter she'd posted from St. Louis. "Father."

His arms enveloped her, drawing her into his broad chest. Safety. Security. Home. Finally home. Instead of saying anything, he just held her. Perhaps he sensed she needed that most. William's complaints pulled her away.

"And who is this strapping fellow?" Her father eyed the little boy, brushing his hand down the child's back. "Not the grandson you mentioned in your letter. You didn't include a name."

"This is Will."

A grin spread across his face. "William?"

"Yes. William Anthony. I named him after you…and his father." Though Anthony's face should have filled her mind, Towan's was the one that settled into her thoughts. William Towan O'Connell had been his father in so many ways. "Where's Mother?"

"She's fussing as usual with the house, making sure your room is ready, planning a dinner, and who knows what else. We should probably head in that direction. I'm sure you and little Will are both exhausted, and she'll be waiting."

Christina nodded.

He hefted her trunk and led her to the buggy—a newer model than the one they'd had when she left. After setting what little luggage she had on the floor, he helped her up and set the baby on her lap. *Baby?* William was almost ten months old now. Strange to think of it now—the disaster that had led her into the valley and brought Towan into her life. Had it really been less than a year since that terrifying Indian had trailed her and then found her a dry cave to birth in? Tears again welled. She had to stop thinking about him.

"Agatha is at home in Tennessee busy with the children, but we wrote to her of your return. Lillian is at the house helping your mother. She wanted to come, but I convinced her to wait. Heaven knows she'll swoop in and I won't get a chance to talk with my baby girl once we get home." He squeezed her shoulder. "James wanted to be here, but he had to leave for Washington yesterday. With the presidential elections soon, he's become quite involved in Mr. Lincoln's campaign."

Christina tried to pay attention as her father

continued about the tensions surrounding the elections but didn't catch half of what was said. What would *her* future bring? She would live with her parents, at least for the foreseeable future, and she would raise her son. He would never know either of his fathers.

The city had changed some, but the closer they came to their street, the less effect time had on the grand houses and great trees stretching over the road, or the women dressed in finery, and gentlemen looking just as they should. Except all this seemed foreign now.

Her father took William again and she climbed from the buggy in front of her childhood home. Anticipation fluttered in her stomach as she moved up the walk and opened the door to her past.

"Christina." Her mother swept into the hallway, skirts swooshing. She embraced her. "My poor child. I knew we should have never let you go. I can't imagine what you've been through. Thank goodness you are home and safe now."

Christina tried to say something, but her mother continued speaking as she withdrew. "I've already told Maggie to draw you a bath, and…" Her brow crinkled as she scanned the threadbare dress, permanently stained in prairie dust. "A gown has been pressed and laid out for you. Though that man you married has been gone for most of a year, I think it best to wear mourning for a short time so everyone can be made aware of your situation without too much fuss."

Mourning? She had just started afresh and saw no end in sight. Christina managed a nod. She reached back to collect William from her father's arms.

"You might as well leave him with us. Go freshen up, and I'll introduce this fellow to his grandmother."

"Very well." Christina planted a kiss on her father's cheek and her son's head, before starting up the grand stairs. She ran her fingers along the smooth finish of the banister. William's cries caught her half way up and she turned. "Maybe I should take him."

"Nonsense." Her mother took William from his grandfather's arms. "He will settle in a moment."

William's fussing followed her to her room. She should rescue him, but it felt too good to have a moment to herself, a minute to relax her arms and simply breathe. Christina sank onto the edge of the bed and laid her hands on her lap as she scanned the walls with their pale pink flowery design. The large chest of drawers. The closet. Everything as she had left it, as though she'd never been away. It seemed only she had changed.

A light knock at the door announced Maggie's arrival, the large metal tub in tow. She smiled and placed it in the middle of the room. "So glad for your safe return, Miss Christina."

"Thank you."

Maggie hadn't made it back to the door when Lillian burst through. "Christina, you poor thing!"

Christina forced a smile though she detested that phrase. After a brief embrace, her sister found a place on the stool near the vanity. "Do tell me everything. Your letter was so vague, but I can only imagine how simply horrifying it has been for you. To go all that way, only to lose Anthony. I did see your little man before I came up. Father is so pleased. I doubt any of Agatha's boys put so much strain on his vest buttons. Imagine, *you*, a mother. Though I suppose that is more acceptable than the thought of you leaving with Anthony like you did and journeying all the way to the

Rocky Mountains in a covered wagon."

Christina ran her hand over the ebony of the gown laid across the bed behind her, not sure what to answer.

"You must be exhausted."

"Yes. Yes, I am." What a beautiful black the fabric was. Only slightly darker than Quaritz's eyes or Towan's hair.

"I don't think you should stay in mourning too long. Mother feels the same. You're young and as beautiful as ever." She brushed a finger across her nose and flashed a smile. "At least you will be after you've cleaned up a little. Men will be lined up again in no time."

Men? Christina's head snapped up and her hand went to Quaritz's pouch. Two hairs bound together. There hadn't been room in her letter to explain it all. "I have no plans for garnering the interests of any men."

"I think it's too late for that. A fine looking gentleman called about a week ago and every day since. Won't say where he met you, but seemed to know about when you'd be arriving."

"That makes no sense. No one I know, other than the family, would be aware of my return. Did he give his name?"

"I think so. I remember Father mentioning it, but I swear can't remember. Nothing unusual." Lillian laughed. "*He* was unusual, though. Tall, handsome, and mysterious. Well spoken, well dressed, but very secretive."

Maggie slipped into the room with two pails of steaming water. She poured them into the tub and left for more.

"Mysterious indeed." Christina stood and started

loosening her buttons. She wanted to sit in the warmth and soak as long as she could. "I should get ready for my bath. Can you tell Mother she can bring Will up here if he gets too upset? He's not used to being away from me or," she waved her hand, "all of this."

The echo of a knock on the front door cut off Lillian's response. A grin of anticipation stretched across her face and she lunged toward the window. "It's early afternoon. I imagine that is your mystery suitor again."

Christina followed slower. Though older, perhaps her sister had a more innocent view of the world than she, but she found nothing romantic or exciting about a secretive man haunting their house, waiting for her return. She couldn't begin to guess who he was. That made her nervous. Lillian pushed the window open, and they both leaned out. Unfortunately the porch both hid the visitor and muffled the voices below. They waited, Maggie emptying another load of water.

Lillian pulled her head back in the window. "Do you know who is at the door?"

A glint of mischievousness in her eyes, Maggie backed out of the room. "Miss Christina's caller. Though, I must say, your father sounded none too pleased with his persistence."

The door below closed sharply, and Christina looked back to the street. A man in a brown suit appeared below, but the top of his hat shielded his identity. Short dark hair. Tanned skin. Frustration showed in his stride. Christina bit her tongue to keep from calling out so she could get a look at the man's face. She was back in society and hollering out her bedroom window was less than ladylike. She'd wait and ask her father what he knew of the stranger. For now all she wanted was to slip into warm water and try to wash the ache from her muscles and soul. And decide what she wanted to tell her family about her stay in the mountains. And her Shoshone groom.

~*~

Towan made it to the end of the block before stopping to glance back at the grand house. Weeks of healing and miles and miles of endless prairie had been good for him, given him time to work through his conversations with his father and sort through everything he had lived his life believing. He convinced himself he could be the husband Christina needed. And then located the address supplied by Judge Carter and his wife.

When Christina had talked about missing four walls, he had pictured four walls like he'd grown up with…not dozens of walls, high ceilings, elegant furniture, and servants seeing to her every want. He again felt like a bear outdoors in the middle of winter—out of place and just as grumpy. She obviously didn't need him anymore. But he needed her. And he loved her.

And he was being lied to.

Towan shoved his hands into his pockets and eyed the mansion. Christina's father continued to insist Christina had not returned, but his gut told him otherwise, as did the whimpers of an upset child. Little William. It had to be him. Which meant Christina was there and may have been there for the full week he'd been asking after her, but for some reason they were keeping her from him. Is that what she wanted, or did she even know he'd come for her?

Towan nudged a peace of broken cobblestone with the toe of his boot and started back to the house. He walked past, paused, and folded his arms across his chest. What was it Mrs. Anderson had told him on occasion? When life closes a door, God opens a window?

Christina's family appeared to enjoy a summer's breeze. Most of their windows sat open.

After taking scope of the street, Towan stole up the steps and skulked to the closest window. Its curtains waved to him, beckoning. He listened. Only the muffle of voices and an upset little boy. He glanced in. Lit with sunlight, the room appeared to be deserted. A desk. Bookshelves. Probably a study or library. He slipped through the opening, instinct crouching him to the floor. What was he thinking, entering their home uninvited? He'd be lucky if they didn't have him arrested. But what other choice did he have—come back tomorrow and let them lie to him again?

He stayed low as he crept to the door, a feat made easier if he'd kept his moccasins.

Again Towan had to question his sanity. He was no longer running wild in the mountains. This was a city and civilized men generally didn't enter another's home without invitation. He would be wiser to have patience. Sooner or later Christina would have to leave the house. He'd already waited over three months, what was another week or two? Besides an eternity.

Footsteps and a fussing baby.

Towan stepped and straightened behind the door as it swung open. Christina's father, Mr. William Hardy, walked in with little William in his arms. Towan's heart leapt. His boy had grown a lot in the last few months. Was he crawling yet? Talking? The child's grandfather strode across the room and began pointing out books, pictures, and a globe. He set his finger somewhere in the middle of the Pacific Ocean and gave the world a spin.

"Really, William," a woman said entering. "You should let me take the baby so he can be bathed and fed." Despite rich brown hair piled on her head and her age, the woman shared many of her finer features with her daughter. Towan remained hidden. Christina's father passed the child to his wife. Probably overtired, Little William continued to whimper.

"Oh. Here you all are." This voice belonged to a younger woman whose energy pranced with her into the room. "Christina's settling in. Any new information on the man who was just here?" She leaned back into the door, shoving it against Towan with surprising force. Not braced for the impact a puff of breath broke from his lungs.

Silence.

Then someone gave the world another spin.

The girl yanked the door away from him and screamed. He was pretty sure Mrs. Hardy screamed too, but his ears rang too much to hear it. She clutched the little boy and stumbled back, giving a clear view of her husband as he threw open a drawer on his desk and yanked free a Colt revolver. "How did you get in my house?"

Escaping the confines of his hiding spot, Towan backed into the hall and raised his hands. With his luck he'd be shot, killed, and carted away without Christina ever knowing he'd been there. "You lied to me that your daughter and her son hadn't returned."

"Summon the authorities!" Mrs. Hardy cried, probably to the servants.

Mr. Hardy kept coming, face scarlet. "I swear I'll shoot you where you stand if you ever come near this house again."

"What does he even want with her?" The younger woman, most likely one of Christina's sisters, threw up her hands. "Who are you?"

Towan bumped into another wall. Far too many in this house. "I'm her husband."

Everyone said something at once to the gist of, "Impossible. He's dead."

"You're not Anthony," the sister added.

The baby wails frayed Towan's nerves, but he fought the need to reach out for him as it would probably get him shot. "Please, just let me speak with her. Let me see my wife."

"Out of the question," Mr. Hardy boomed.

"She's quite indisposed at the moment." The sister afforded him a hint of a smile.

"What's going on here?" Christina's voice drew everyone's gaze to the stairwell where she stood wearing the green dress she'd left Fort Bridger in, a flowery silk robe pulled over it. Her hair hung wildly about her shoulders, the tips wet.

"Christina, go back in your room. I'll handle this." Her father moved to the base of the stairs while not removing his glare or gun from Towan.

"Handle what, exactly?" She stepped forward, revealing bare feet.

"Do you know this man?"

"I…"

Towan removed his hat and tried for a smile. Only half of one was possible. He'd waited too long, come too far, it would be too easy to barrel up those steps and take her in his arms. But again, that would only get him shot, and he was done having lead dug out of him.

Christina stared, wordless.

"Is it true what he says?" her father demanded.

Instead of answering, she released the banister and started down, her gaze locked on Towan. "What are you doing here?"

"I should think that easy enough to guess." He shook his head, feeling a fool. "I was trying so hard not to be the man my father was, that I became him, making his biggest mistake. I let the woman I love and my son out of sight." Towan swallowed past the swell of emotion. "I'm not my father, Christina. I won't abandon my family. Not if I have a choice." He sent a glance to the man blocking his way. "If your father decides to shoot me, however, I won't be held responsible…though, I suppose I asked for it by breaking in here like I did."

"You broke in?"

"Just through the window. I didn't actually break anything."

A smile touched her lips and a laugh slipped between them. She looked him up and down as she stepped past her father. Her fingers combed through Towan's short chopped hair. The sensation of her touch ignited his desire for her. She let her thumb linger along the curve of his ear. "Who are you?"

While he couldn't blame her for the question—he looked nothing like the man she had left in Fort Bridger—it struck him that her timing could have been worse. "Thank you…" He let out a breath and cracked a grin. "For not asking that first. Your Father probably *would* have shot me."

"I'm still not sure I won't." Mr. Hardy glowered

over his daughter's head. "Neither of you have told us who this man is. O'Connell means nothing to me."

Christina's hand slipped away and she pivoted to face her parents. "His name is Towan, or Black Fox. He's the man who saved my life. I wintered with his family in the mountains."

Her sister fell back a step. "He's an Indian?"

Christina nodded and looked back to Towan. "Shoshone. And he's my husband."

~*~

The room exploded with her family talking at once, demanding one thing or another. Mother was the most vocal, her wrath aimed at Towan who stood silently taking it all, his hands relaxed at his sides. Christina's heart seemed to fill her entire chest and beg for more room to grow. She loved this man so very much…and he loved her. She took her unhappy child from her mother and passed him to Towan—probably the surest way to keep her father from shooting him.

"Please!" Christina shouted over the protests. "Enough."

Her father stepped forward to grab her arm. "Go back to your room, Christina. You aren't going anywhere with this man."

"Christina, listen to your father." Her mother grasped her other wrist. "Look what happened last time you didn't listen to us. We're only trying to protect you."

"I don't need your protection. Mother, Father, I'm not a child anymore." Christina pulled away. "I've crossed the Great Plains twice, I've buried a husband, birthed a child in a cave, and spent the winter in a hut in the middle of the Rockies. I've faced murders, bears, frozen rivers, and death itself. I love you, but…" She glanced at Towan and his namesake, nestled comfortably in his arms. Words she had once read in Towan's Bible came easily to mind. "'What therefore God hath joined together, let not man put asunder.'"

The grand house fell silent as she stepped to join her son in her husband's embrace. Her arms encircled him in return and she pressed a kiss to his mouth. Towan deepened it with a promise of what was to come. "I love you, Mrs. O'Connell," he said into her hair. "I'll be whatever you need me to be. And we can go anywhere. I'll take you to Europe if that's what you want. We can see all those places we've only read about."

"If you wish, Towan. All I want is you, Will, and maybe, at some point, a house with four walls."

He glanced down at her and cocked a smile. "Only *four* walls?"

She nestled under his chin, exactly where she belonged. "And a roof."

A Devotional Moment

He gives strength to the weary and increases the power of the weak. ~ Isaiah 40:29

We Christians worry about appearing weak—weak in our own lives, weak when we are with others, weak towards those we love, weak in our faith; and often we attempt to bolster our emotions and feelings on our own. When trials abound and evil is afoot, we hope we can stand strong against it. But with Jesus, we are backed by a strength beyond our imagining. When we rely on our Father, we will be strengthened. By the grace of the Holy Spirit, we can know that when troubles show up, they will soon pass. By holding firm and leaning on the wisdom and might of the Trinity, we can weather any storm that comes our way.

In ***Heart of a Warrior***, the protagonist is confronted with the most difficult decision of her life. Lost and alone, her choices are few. With a baby on the way, she is in a fight for survival… for her child and herself. She can go back to nothing or go forward with hope in a future that is not guaranteed. Fear drives her forward, but when an unexpected turn of events thwarts that plan, she must not grow weary, but lean on the strength of God.

Have you ever been thrust into the unknown? An unexpected circumstance causes you to question your own abilities, the reliability of others, perhaps even the reason for your very existence. It is difficult, but important, to remember in these times, that we aren't meant to handle problems all alone. We have an Advocate who is not only all-powerful, but also all-knowing. He knows who our true enemy is. He knows exactly what we need to do and where we need to be. Leaning on God in the midst of frightening or uncertain times is the first thing you should do. Never go it alone. Why? Because you don't have to!

LORD, WHEN I HAVE A DIFFICULT PATH BEFORE ME, GIVE ME THE STRENGTH TO GO FORWARD WITH YOU BY MY SIDE, AND SHOW ME THAT I CAN LEAN ON YOU AND NEVER FEEL ABANDONED. IN JESUS' NAME I PRAY, AMEN.

Thank you

We appreciate you reading this Prism title. For other Christian fiction and clean-and-wholesome stories, please visit our on-line bookstore at www.prismbookgroup.com.

For questions or more information, contact us at customer@pelicanbookgroup.com.

Prism is an imprint of
Pelican Book Group
www.PelicanBookGroup.com

Connect with Us
www.facebook.com/Pelicanbookgroup
www.twitter.com/pelicanbookgrp

To receive news and specials, subscribe to our bulletin
http://pelink.us/bulletin

May God's glory shine through
this inspirational work of fiction.

AMDG

You Can Help!

At Pelican Book Group it is our mission to entertain readers with fiction that uplifts the Gospel. It is our privilege to spend time with you awhile as you read our stories.

We believe you can help us to bring Christ into the lives of people across the globe. And you don't have to open your wallet or even leave your house!

Here are 3 simple things you can do to help us bring illuminating fiction™ to people everywhere.

1) If you enjoyed this book, write a positive review. Post it at online retailers and websites where readers gather. And share your review with us at reviews@pelicanbookgroup.com (this does give us permission to reprint your review in whole or in part.)

2) If you enjoyed this book, recommend it to a friend in person, at a book club or on social media.

3) If you have suggestions on how we can improve or expand our selection, let us know. We value your opinion. Use the contact form on our web site or e-mail us at customer@pelicanbookgroup.com

God Can Help!

Are you in need? The Almighty can do great things for you. Holy is His Name! He has mercy in every generation. He can lift up the lowly and accomplish all things. Reach out today.

Do not fear: I am with you; do not be anxious: I am your God. I will strengthen you, I will help you, I will uphold you with my victorious right hand.

~Isaiah 41:10 (NAB)

We pray daily, and we especially pray for everyone connected to Pelican Book Group—that includes you! If you have a specific need, we welcome the opportunity to pray for you. Share your needs or praise reports at http://pelink.us/pray4us

Free Book Offer

We're looking for booklovers like you to partner with us! Join our team of influencers today and periodically receive free eBooks and exclusive offers.

For more information
Visit http://pelicanbookgroup.com/booklovers

CPSIA information can be obtained
at www.ICGtesting.com
Printed in the USA
LVHW011729180820
663527LV00007B/941